D0887346

If I Was Your Girlfriend:

An Atlanta Tale

APR - - 2023

If I Was Your Girlfriend:

An Atlanta Tale

Marlon McCaulsky

www.urbanbooks.net

Urban Books, LLC
300 Farmingdale Road, N.Y.-Route 109
Farmingdale, NY 11735

If I Was Your Girlfriend: An Atlanta Tale
Copyright © 2023 Marlon McCaulsky

All rights reserved. No part of this book may be repro-
duced in any form or by any means without prior consent
of the Publisher, except brief quotes used in reviews.

To the extent that the image or images on the cover of this
book depict a person or persons, such person or persons
are merely models, and are not intended to portray any
character or characters featured in the book.

ISBN 13: 978-1-64556-474-4
ISBN 10: 1-64556-474-6

First Trade Paperback Printing April 2023
Printed in the United States of America

10 9 8 7 6 5 4 3 2 1

*This is a work of fiction. Any references or similarities
to actual events, real people, living or dead, or to real
locales are intended to give the novel a sense of reality.
Any similarity in other names, characters, places, and
incidents is entirely coincidental.*

Distributed by Kensington Publishing Corp.
Submit Orders to:
Customer Service
400 Hahn Road
Westminster, MD 21157-4627
Phone: 1-800-733-3000
Fax: 1-800-659-2436

If I Was Your Girlfriend:

An Atlanta Tale

A Romance Novel by

Marlon McCaulsky

Acknowledgments

I wrote this story thirteen years ago. The first version of this was called *Taboo*. In retrospect, the story was a great idea, but the writing was horrible. Years later I dusted it off and reread it. Cringed at some of it and decided to revamp it with more mature viewpoints, and what happened was that this went from a simple erotica type of book to a story of romance and sisterhood between these four unique ladies.

Thank you to my cousin Rashida Malcolm, the real-life owner of Shidas Styles, for inspiring me to create such a wonderful character with Rashida. I'm so proud of you. Thank you, Nyeema Carmichael, the other half of Rashida. When you read the early draft of "IIWYG" and fell in love with it, I knew I had something special. You are the African samurai goddess. Thank you for gracing the cover! And thank you, Carlette Williams. Told you I was gonna get you on the cover! Tai Renee, I had no idea when I was writing Taylor that she was so much like you! Thank you so much! Subria Rivers, this is cover number two for you! You're incredible! You're gonna do great things, and I'm glad to have been able to work with you. Lamont Gant, you did it again! This is probably the best cover I've ever had on a book! You took my concept and added that creative genius touch to it! Fabulous! Thank you, my friend.

Cynthia Marie Jones, my writing is nothing without you. I kinda feel at this point we have a Vulcan mind meld

Acknowledgments

when it comes to writing and editing. I know as soon as I write something what your sarcastic comments will be, and I love it. Thank you for always having my back.

A special thank-you goes to Diane P. Rembert for making this release happen. Thank you for believing in me. Thank you, Robert White, from *Robert Reading Room & Reviews*, for loving this book and putting it in Diane's hands. Thank you, Ebony Evans and EyeCU Reading & Chatting, for all your support!

Sheena McCaulsky, you're the love of my life. Thank you for allowing me to do this. Without you, I simple can't do it. I love you, babe. Thank you, Priscilla V. Sales, always.

A special thank-you goes to everybody who said no to this book. You made me work harder.

Until next time, deuces!

Marlon McCaulsky
5/18/18 - 9:30 a.m.

Originally from Brooklyn, New York, and raised in St. Petersburg, Florida, Marlon McCaulsky is the author of nine novels, including *The Pink Palace, The Pink Palace II, The Pink Palace 3: Malicious, From Vixen 2 Diva, Used to Temporary Happiness, Born Sinners, Returned, Blush, Real Love, A Dangerous Woman, My Current Situation, I Wanna Be Your Lover,* and *Romance For the Streets,* and a contributing cowriter of the screenplays *Returned, Temporary Happiness, No Time For Love,* and *Annulment* for Creative Genius Films. He lives in Atlanta, Georgia.

www.marlonmccaulsky.com

Also by *Marlon McCaulsky*

Novels

The Pink Palace
The Pink Palace II: Money, Power, & Sex
The Pink Palace 3: Malicious
From Vixen 2 Diva
Born Sinners
Used To Temporary Happiness
Returned
A Dangerous Woman
Real Love

Anthologies

Blush
Romance for the Streets
Love & Life
The Freak Files Reloaded
Urban Fantasies 1–4 (eBook)
Bad Girl (eBook)
Returned

Nobody's perfect, but you're perfect for me

Chapter One

Ladies' Night

RASHIDA

"I tell all my hoes, 'Rake it up, break it down, bag it up.' Fuck it up, fuck it up. Back it up, back it up," Taylor rapped at the top of her lungs while two-stepping to the beat.

I once heard someone say that you were defined by who your friends were; and if that was true, I was in good company. Most of the time. Taylor Fenty, Joyce Roland, and Denise Varner were my closest friends. We'd been close since our teen days at Decatur High School, and now as grown twentysomething women, we had the type of bond that made us more like sisters than anything else.

Taylor had decided to go all out for her twenty-sixth birthday, so of course, we had to be there, and by there, I meant at the sexiest strip club in Atlanta. As soon as we stepped through the doors, the aroma of buffalo wings filled our nostrils. Going farther inside, past security, we were greeted by a voluptuous hostess who had more curves than Jessica Rabbit on steroids. She gave us a wide smile, and I gave her the name of the birthday girl.

She escorted us to our reserved section near the stage. As we weaved through the crowded club, the dimly lit pink and blue fluorescent lights illuminated the way. The demographics of folks in here ranged from couples on dates to men who looked like they worked at JPMorgan Chase and everything in between. An assortment of liquors was being served, and half-naked women were onstage, bouncing to a ratchet beat. Hell, I was bopping to the music too. I had heard that a former stripper named Jasmine now ran the club, and she had transformed it from a hole-in-the-wall to an upscale establishment. Looked like the rumors were true.

"What the hell is this?" Joyce groused.

I didn't think Joyce was too happy after we got there. She was more bougie than hood. Not a snob in a bad way, but she carried herself in a way that some might find stuck up. If we got a few drinks in her, however, she would turn up. She was, in my opinion, an around-the-way beauty. She had the kind of body the brothers loved to watch—slim but thick in all the right places. The mustard-colored dress she wore had open shoulders and highlighted her round backside. Before we'd left my place, I'd done her hair in a sexy crinkle style, but the most alluring thing about Joyce was her pretty brown eyes.

"It's the Pink Palace. Don't act like you never been in a strip club before," Taylor replied. She was a natural-born party girl and was determined to have fun tonight. It was in her nature. She was of mixed heritage, half-Trinidadian, thanks to her father, and Irish on her mother's side, which gave her a caramel complexion. She was the shortest of us, at five feet two. Her bubbly personality and the way she seemed to be the center of attention always made people think she was famous. Tonight she was dressed in a tight gold spaghetti-strap dress that showed off her sexy curves. Her ample cleavage made it hard for men to keep their eyes on her beautiful face. Earlier in the week, she had decided to dye her long naturally black hair an auburn shade. We called her the turnup queen, so naturally she had wanted to go to a strip club for her birthday.

Joyce frowned as she stared at the topless women dancing on the main stage. "Yes, I've been to a strip club before," she said sarcastically, "but I thought it was, like, a male revue going on tonight."

"Ah . . . no." Taylor smirked. "What fun would that be?"

Joyce glared at her, then looked at me. "'Shida, you knew too?"

"Yeah. It's not a big deal. Come on, Joyce, lighten up."

"I don't wanna sit here with some ho shaking her stank ass in my face."

Taylor stared at Joyce and shook her head. "Joyce, just relax. I just wanna see how it is in here. We don't have to stay long."

Joyce looked at me again, and I smiled. I looked at Denise, who looked like she was in a state of shock. This wasn't her thing at all. I knew for sure she was uncomfortable. She considered herself a plain-Jane type of girl, even though she could be as sexy as any woman dancing in this club. Denise was slim and beautiful, at an even five feet four, with a body that would make men drool. She had a figure that was built for high fashion and runways, but she was way too modest to show it off in public. Tonight she wore a silver dress, with a black shawl draped over her shoulders. Her long black hair framed her beautiful face.

I stared at her. "Are you okay, Denise?"

"Ah . . . yeah. I'm fine."

I could tell by the look on her face she was anything but.

Joyce was just complaining for the sake of it, but Denise wasn't the party type at all. If it weren't for us,

Denise would have spent her whole college experience in her dorm, with a book in her face.

"If you're not feeling it, we can go," I told her.

Denise looked over my shoulder, and I knew Taylor was behind me, mean muggin' her. Denise forced a smile onto her face. "I'm okay. It's Taylor's b-day. Let's just do what she wants tonight."

Taylor smirked. "Well, if Wallflower can stay, so can you, Joyce."

Joyce exhaled. "All right, but I don't want them hoes touching me."

Denise rolled her eyes. I hated when Taylor threw shade at Denise. I would normally pull Taylor to the side and tell her to chill, but I decided not to scold her, since it was her birthday. That was the role I, an Afrocentric Jamaican girl, usually played in the group—the unofficial surrogate mother of us all.

My mother was from St. Catherine, Jamaica, and my father was born and raised in Birmingham, England. They met while my mother was attending university in England. A few years later they married and moved to Atlanta, Georgia, because my father had taken an executive position at PricewaterhouseCoopers. A few years after that, they had me and my little brother, Raheem. I inherited my mother's sense of style and my father's business sense, two things I cherished about them after their untimely death.

Tonight it was my mother's style I was channeling. I had recently unbraided my coiled locks, and they hung loose past my shoulders. I loved my natural hair. It made me feel free and sexy. It wasn't always easy to maintain, but it was all me, all natural. I wore tan thigh-high boots with a black and orange tribal-print dress. Joyce had said I looked like an African samurai goddess.

As the night progressed and we drank more and more liquor, things got better. We were all having fun, but not as much as Taylor. She got tore up drinking moscato, Bacardi, and Grey Goose. The waitress had arranged a little surprise for her. She came out of the kitchen with a little birthday cake, and instead of everybody singing "Happy Birthday," they gave her a free lap dance as 50 Cent's "In Da Club" played and we all sang the lyrics.

"Go, go, go, go, go, go. Go, shawty. It's your birthday. We gon' party like it yo' birthday!"

All of us were shocked to see how much Taylor was getting into it while she recorded it all on her phone. The alcohol had her open all night. Just like I had thought, Joyce had lightened up and was now enjoying herself, but I could tell Denise was counting the seconds until we left. Me, I was good. I had always loved a good party, and it wasn't my first time in a strip club. But as usual, the turnup queen was doing the most. Taylor was slapping asses and pushing singles between G-strings. Pretty soon she was onstage dancing too.

We ended up staying until the club closed.

Somehow I dragged myself out of bed and went to class the next morning. I was taking a business management course at Clark Atlanta University. I had missed class last week, and no matter how hung over I was, I couldn't afford to miss another day. My economics instructor, Mr. Robert Baker, was putting me to sleep with his lecture. The struggle was definitely real as I tried to keep my eyes open, but I wasn't going to be disrespectful and put my head down on my desk.

Mr. Baker stood up behind his desk. "Okay, ladies and gentlemen, I want you to read chapters four and five this weekend, and we'll review them next Tuesday. Class is dismissed."

Everyone gathered their things and began to leave.

"Miss Haughton, may I speak to you for a moment?" Mr. Baker called as I gathered my things.

I stopped what I was doing and looked at him. "Sure."

He waited for the other students to leave before he spoke. He wore brown khakis with a brown blazer and a burgundy tie. His hair and mustache were neatly trimmed. He was a man who knew how to put himself together.

"I was wondering if you were going to make up the quiz you missed last week?" he said as I got to my feet.

"Oh, I'll be able to do that whenever you want me to."

He walked around his desk and over to where I was standing, As he stood in front of me, he said, "Well, normally, I don't let students make up quizzes, but you're one of my best. Lately, you seem a bit preoccupied, so I'm a little concerned."

"I'm sorry, Mr. Baker. It's been hard balancing all my classes. I think I may have taken on a little more than I can handle this semester."

He gave me a friendly smile. "It's okay. I understand. How about you come an hour before class on Tuesday and you can take the quiz then?"

I smiled. "That would be great. Thank you."

"No problem." He grinned. "You have a good night."

That was the first time we had really spoken to each other one-on-one, and that was the first time I had really paid attention to how attractive he was. He had pretty eyes, a gorgeous smile and, from what I could tell, a well-toned body. Until now, I hadn't even thought about him in a romantic way. I had just gotten out of a long-term relationship a few months ago and was enjoying my freedom. Mr. Baker was an attractive older man, but I was there to get my degree.

***

After class, I went over to Taylor's apartment to see how she was doing. I must have rung her doorbell twenty times before she answered. When the door finally swung open, she glared at me.

"Stop ringing the damn bell."

She looked like death warmed over. She was wearing a pair of boy shorts and a gray hoodie, and her red hair was a mess.

"I guess you're still fucked up?" I said as I stepped inside.

"My head is killing me. I'm never drinking like that again." Taylor shut the door, then stumbled back to her room and crawled back in bed. I followed behind her.

"It looks like you've been in here all day." A faint funk lingered in the air. "Smells like it too."

"Girl, the only place I've been is to the toilet to throw up."

I sat on her bed. "Oh, poor baby. You see why I didn't mix my drinks?"

"It's not fair. I was supposed to get laid last night," she groaned.

"Well, you almost did. The way you were bumping and grinding on them strippers, I'm pretty sure you would have got turned out."

Her eyebrows rose. "I was what?"

I smirked. "You don't remember what happened?"

"Really? I was dancing with strippers?"

"You really don't remember? You were swinging around the pole and everything!"

She smiled. "I was? Was I good?"

I couldn't help but laugh at her. "You were recording the whole night. You better not let that footage get out."

The doorbell rang repeatedly.

Taylor snapped, "Argh! Will you please tell them to stop ringing the doorbell? It's killing me!"

I got up and answered the door. It was Joyce and Denise. I had told them I was going to check on Taylor, and like clockwork, I knew they would be here to see the aftermath of last night's events. They came inside and followed me back to Taylor's room.

"Hey, guess what? Taylor doesn't remember what she did last night," I announced as I walked down the hallway.

Denise shook her head. "Figures."

"Hey, Taylor!" Joyce bellowed once we were inside her room.

"Stop yelling!" Taylor retorted angrily and pulled the covers up over her head.

Joyce flopped down next to her. "You don't remember what you did?" Then she burst into laughter.

Taylor rolled over and partially uncovered her face. "No, I don't."

Joyce continued to laugh. "Oh my God! Girl, you were shaking your ass like a hoefessional!"

Taylor uncovered the rest of her face, sat up, and smiled. "So that's why I woke up with all those dollar bills in my pants!"

We laughed.

"But you all had a good time, right? How 'bout you, Wallflower?" Taylor quizzed.

Denise glared at her. You could almost read the FUCK YOU sign flashing on her forehead. To be honest, Denise and Taylor were "friends" only because of me and Joyce. I didn't think they would ever be friends if it were not for us. I had hoped this would've changed by now, but I guessed that was only wishful thinking.

I picked up a pillow and threw it at Taylor. "Cut it out."

She shrugged. "I was just asking her a question."

"Yeah, it was great. Whoop-whoop," Denise said dryly.

"See, I told you." Taylor belched.

Joyce pushed her. "Ugh! My mouth was open, bitch!"

We spent the rest of the night laughing at Taylor's hung-over ass.

Chapter Two

Sweetest Taboo

RASHIDA

I spent the weekend at home, studying for the test I had on Tuesday. I was really not as focused as I should have been, so I had to cocoon myself from the outside world and social media.

Three days of studying paid off. I got to class early on Tuesday, and Mr. Baker was there waiting for me. He looked handsome in his brown blazer.

"I'm glad you made it," he said.

"I told you I would be here," I replied as I sat down at my desk.

He handed me a piece of paper, and I started to take the quiz. I could feel Robert staring at me as I worked. I had on a little black dress and had just shaved my legs that morning, so they looked extra smooth. For some reason, I felt turned on from having my teacher stare at me the way he was. He was becoming sexier to me by the second. Twenty-five minutes later I was done with the quiz. I got up, walked over to his desk, and handed him my paper.

"Here you go, Mr. Baker."

"Thank you." He looked it over before laying it on his desk.

"I think I'm the one who should be thanking you for letting me make this up."

"It was no problem," he replied. Mr. Baker stared into my eyes, and for a second, there was some real sexual chemistry between us.

Then people started to file into the classroom. Once everyone was seated and class began, I just sat there, fantasizing about Mr. Baker like a little schoolgirl, and I couldn't believe some of the thoughts that ran through my mind. My fantasies really started to turn me on. I felt myself becoming wet as I thought about how he would look naked. It was not like I hadn't had sex in a while. Maybe it was the fact that he was my instructor that turned me on. It was sorta taboo to be with him. I pushed those thoughts aside and focused on the class material. When the class was over, I gathered my books and rushed out of the room, intent on keeping Mr. Baker out of my mind.

But when I was walking to my car, I saw him again.

"Hello, Mr. Baker," I called out.

He turned and looked at me. "Hi. You can call me Robert," he said as he approached me.

"Oh, okay, Robert."

"Here you go, Miss. Haughton." He gave me back my quiz.

I saw an A in red at the top of the page. "Thank you."

"You don't have to thank me. You made the grade."

I smiled. "I guess I did . . . and, um, you can call me Rashida."

"Okay."

We stared at each for a moment and smiled.

"So where are you heading to, Miss Rashida?"

"Well, Robert"—I played with my hair—"I was heading home. And you?"

"I was going to go get a mocha latte. Would you mind joining me?"

"Sure. That sounds good."

There was a Starbucks on Spelman Lane, near Clark Atlanta. We walked inside, ordered our drinks, collected them, and found a seat in the back. The hum of cappuccino machines and light chatter filled the coffee shop as other customers sat around us, enjoying their drinks.

Robert stared at me and said, "You're very different from a lot of young women here in Atlanta."

"Really?" I smiled. "In what way?"

"Well, the way you carry yourself. You're very poised. Confident. Alluring, without being too overt."

I sipped my coffee. "Why, thank you, Robert. I've never heard a man describe me in such a dignified way."

"Even the way you speak, it's almost regal. Your speech pattern is distinctive and clear. A very rare thing here."

"Well, I think I owe that to my parents. My British father and Jamaican mother made sure my brother and I spoke proper English at all times." I smiled, reminiscing about them. "I can get ratchet when I want to, though."

He held up his hand. "Please don't."

I laughed. "I'll spare you."

"Thank you."

"Enough about me. Where are you from originally?"

"I was born and raised in Raleigh, North Carolina. Graduated summa cum laude from North Carolina State University, home of Wolfpack football. I taught at a high school before I eventually got a position teaching at my old university."

"Wow. Seems like you were doing good. What made you move to Atlanta?"

He exhaled and stared into his latte. "Well, after my divorce . . ." He glanced up at me. "I was ready for a complete change, and putting a state between me and my ex felt right. So two years later I'm a single bachelor living in a condo in the city."

I nodded. "How long were you married?"

"Thirteen years."

"Oh."

There was a moment of silence between us; then he continued. "Sometimes I feel the only good that came from it is our son, Quincy."

In that moment it became clear that I was dealing with a man with much more life experience than I had. Normally, finding all this out about a man I was into would be grounds for me to move on, but these experiences were normal for a man his age.

"I hope that doesn't make you wary of spending time with me," Robert confessed.

I shook my head. "No, not at all. Your past is your past. Everybody has one. I'm more interested in the future."

He smiled. "I concur."

For the next couple of weeks that became our routine after class. We would go to Starbucks, drink mocha lattes, and talk about life, music, or anything else that came to mind. Although it was nobody's business what we did outside of class, we were careful never to let anybody from the school see us together. We never did or said anything that wasn't platonic or professional, but there was always this underlying sexual attraction we had for one another. It wasn't until I had passed his class that things changed. We were in Starbucks one evening when it happened.

"This is to you, Rashida." He held up his coffee for a toast.

I held up mine. "Thank you, Robert."

"I guess this is the last night I get to share a hot coffee with you."

"Well, does it have to be?" I looked at him, and he knew what I meant.

He leaned forward in his chair. "I . . . I don't want this to be the last time I see you."

My eyes met his. "Me either."

"Well, you're no longer my student." He grinned, and I returned his smile.

"And you're no longer my professor."

He reached over and touched my hand. It seemed to me that all the bottled-up sexual tension was about to explode; then I felt myself becoming aroused.

"Well, I think I'm ready to go now," I announced.

He glanced at his watch. "Oh, okay."

"Are you coming with me?"

Robert smiled. "Yes, if you wish."

We got to my house at a little after nine. It was awkward as we sat in silence on the sofa. It was like we were tongue-tied and searching for the right words to say. I knew what I wanted, but I didn't want to rush it. The look on his face told me he wanted me too, but I could also see he was a bit taken aback by my house.

As he looked around the room from his spot on the sofa, he said, "This is a very nice place you have here."

"Thanks."

I didn't like telling people about my living situation. It always led to an awkward conversation on how I had acquired this place. I had bought this house two years ago, after I left the dorms over at Clark. I had wanted a place to call home, a place where I could raise a family someday. I decided to change the subject.

"Um, do you want something to drink?" I asked him.

"Uh, no, I'm fine." Once again, his eyes scanned his surroundings. "May I ask you a question? And I hope you won't get offended."

I smiled. "I won't."

"Do you live with your parents?"

I shook my head. "No, this is my house."

"How can a college student afford a place like this?"

That was a question I was asked a lot by people who visited. My house sat on a one-acre lot and had a pool and a private backyard. The main level had an open kitchen, a spacious living room, and a den with a vaulted beamed ceiling and sliding glass doors that opened to a large deck. The house had a fully finished basement with a theater, a bedroom, and a bath. And upstairs there were six bedrooms and four bathrooms. I guessed it was a bit more extravagant than the average home.

"My brother and I inherited some money when my parents died. I was fourteen at the time."

Robert exhaled. "I'm sorry. I shouldn't have asked you."

"It's okay. You didn't know. I know it's a bit unusual for someone my age to have a place like this, but I like having the space."

He looked at me anxiously. "Well, here we are."

"Why is this so awkward now?"

"I don't know. Maybe it's because we're not in the classroom or at Starbucks."

I smiled nervously. "I guess we're both out of our comfort zone."

He reached over and took my hand. "I guess so. Perhaps we should make a new one?" He leaned over slowly and kissed me.

All the butterflies in my stomach started to fly. It was amazing how fast I got aroused from just one kiss. I slid my hand up Robert's leg and felt his stiffening penis.

Soon his hand was up my dress, pulling my panties to the side, touching me. His fingers caressed me, and it felt so good. The more wet kisses we exchanged, the more we fondled each other. My breathing became heavier, and my sexual noises encouraged him to go further. Pretty soon two fingers were sliding inside me.

Before it went any further, I took his hand. "Come with me."

I stood up, and Robert followed me to my bedroom, where he began to undress me. His hands caressed my breasts, and he kissed my nipples. He unbuttoned his pants and found his erection. It wasn't too long, but it was thick. He undressed himself as I lay back on the bed. He took a condom from his wallet, rolled it on, then climbed on top of me. First, he kissed my forehead, kissed my lips, licked my neck, and then pushed inside me. I watched his erection sink inside me and fill me up. Robert took his time, stroked me nice and slow. He was a man of experience, a man who wasn't just trying to get his. He understood the difference between making love and fucking.

Being penetrated made me feel good. Pretty soon his slow stroke tempo turned into rapid thrusts, and I started to buck up and down. I felt his erection hit a spot that made me groan. I could feel my wetness seeping between the cheeks of my ass. We rolled over, and with me on top, I rode his stiffness. My wetness was all over his manhood.

Robert closed his eyes and moaned. He gripped my waist, trying to hold on, trying to prevent his load from exploding, but when I leaned back and danced on his penis, he lost control. He roared like a wounded animal, shivered, then pulled me down on top of him and held me close. Our lips touched, and we held each other, allowing our orgasms to flow simultaneously. I gave him my sexual youth, and he gave me his experience. It was a fair exchange of energy, a release that we both needed.

He caressed my face. "I don't normally do this."

"Do what?"

"Sleep with my former students."

I smiled. "Then I feel special. So what happens now?"

"I would like to see you again, if you don't mind."

"That would be nice."

He frowned. "Are you sure you don't mind being with a man my age?"

"You're not that old, Robert."

"But the gap in years is enough to raise eyebrows."

"I know, and if that bothered me, we wouldn't be here now."

He grinned. "You're like no other woman I've ever met, Rashida."

"And you're certainly one of a kind. The kind of man I want to spend my days and nights with."

We kissed each other again.

After that night we officially began dating. Although ours was not a committed relationship, we agreed to take things slowly and see where it all led.

Although he had his own place, Robert spent the next few weeks at my house, and it felt like he had moved in. I enjoyed his company, but I wasn't in love with him. Maybe that head-over-heels feeling would come in time, so I decided that until then, I would keep all my options open.

Chapter Three

Only For the Night

RASHIDA

Robert and I had been dating for about a month, but I still enjoyed hanging out with my girls. The Gold Room was the spot where we liked to unwind on a Friday night, but as it turned out, tonight I was going solo. Robert was out of town visiting his son for the weekend in North Carolina. I had called my girls, but they were all busy. Joyce had an exam on Monday morning and needed to study. Denise opted to just stay home, and Taylor had a date. So tonight it was just me, and I wanted to dance, drink, and have some fun.

As soon as I entered the Gold Room, I walked up to the bar, took a seat, and ordered a drink. The bartender obliged, and soon I was sipping on a Hpnotiq martini and in a zone. The music was right, and the lights were down low, except for the occasional purple and blue bulbs throughout. The huge chandelier in the center of the club's ceiling was alternating colors, while a fog machine pumped out white clouds, which spread across the floor. The place was half-packed, with groups of ladies on the dance floor, and a few men were looking at them over the railing on the second level. I finished my drink, and the bartender brought me another one.

I stared at him oddly as he placed the glass in front of me. "Who's this from?"

"From the gentleman over there." He pointed toward a man sitting at a booth in the corner.

I could tell right away this was game. When the bartender walked away, the man got up and effortlessly walked over to me. I knew this wasn't the first time he'd done this, but I was impressed nevertheless with his high degree of confidence. As he got closer, I could see he had a medium build and a well-toned body. He was about six-one, maybe six-two, with a mocha complexion and a curly 'fro. Dark jeans, a white button down, matching all-white Nikes, and a gray blazer made him look like his was modeling for *Esquire*.

When he spoke, he sounded quite articulate. "I know this is a bit of a cliché, but when I saw you sitting there, I couldn't resist. I hope you don't mind."

His sexy five o'clock shadow completed the package, and I smiled. "I don't. It's nice to know I still have that kind of effect on men."

"Still? C'mon, I know I'm not the first man to buy you a drink."

"No, but it's still nice when it happens."

"Well, I'm glad I was able to put a smile on your face."

I grinned. "Well, I know I'm not the first woman you ever bought a drink for."

He gave me a sexy grin. "No, but you are the finest I ever did it for."

He was confident without being arrogant. I liked that. I could feel his eyes all over my body. Being able to captivate a man's attention was a turn-on. His stare seemed to penetrate straight into me. Not too many men were able to make me blush, but he did.

"My name is Alonzo."

I couldn't help but think how fine this man was, and his smile was so sexy. By the way he moved, I decided he was a street dude, but he sure knew how to carry himself like a gentleman.

I smiled. "I'm Rashida."

"Nice to meet you, Rashida."

"Nice meeting you too. So what else do you do, other than buy women drinks?" I took a sip of my Hpnotiq.

"You don't know who I am?"

I was a bit dumbfounded by his question. Was his ego about to ruin the good start he was off to? "I'm sorry, should I?"

Alonzo smiled. "I'm Alonzo Hall from WHXZ. *The Quiet Storm* show at midnight?"

"Oh, I'm sorry, but I don't really listen to the radio much at night."

He grinned. "Too busy getting that beauty sleep."

I smiled at his corny line. He was lucky he was sexy. "Something like that."

"So tell me, Rashida, what do you do?"

"I'm a student at Clark for now. Business major."

He nodded. "I like that."

"Really? So if I said I worked at Strokers, would you still be impressed?"

He looked me up and down. "Yes, as long as your long-term goals entailed something beyond swinging on a pole, I would be. But there's something about you that seems way too classy to be there."

"But if I was?"

He smiled. "I think I would become your biggest tipper."

We laughed and stared into each other's eyes. There was energy and chemistry between us. The way he looked and his quick wit stimulated me. "Pretty Wings" by Maxwell began to play, and Alonzo glanced at the dance floor.

"So, would you like to dance?" he asked me.

I nodded and took another sip of my drink. "Sure."

We walked out to the dance floor and started to dance. I turned around and slowly ground my behind on him. I felt him becoming hard. Inhaling his intoxicating cologne, I felt myself relax as he rubbed his big, soft hands over my shoulders and down to my waist. It felt good being in his embrace. I turned around and faced him, bringing my lips inches away from his. I wanted this scenario to play out, but it didn't. After the song ended, he held my hand gently, and we walked back to the bar.

"You're a good dancer," I told him.

"I'm only as good as my partner."

"Do you have a regular partner?" I asked coolly.

"Not in a while."

I nodded. We both knew what was coming next. I was anticipating yet dreading it at the same time. Why did I have to meet him now? Where was he two months ago?

"So since I like to dance and you're not dancing at Strokers"—we both chuckled—"how about I call you sometime?" he asked.

I looked at Alonzo with disappointment in my eyes. My mind drifted to Robert, and I had to admit I felt a little guilty. "I don't want you to think I'm blowing you off, but I've just started seeing somebody."

Alonzo stared at me for a moment, still holding my hand, as if he would give anything to change what he had just heard me say. Just then, I reminded myself that Robert and I weren't in a committed relationship, so why should I let Alonzo just walk away?

I almost wished there was a way to change what I had said or at least take my words back.

He sighed. "Oh, lucky guy. Well, uh, it was nice dancing with you." Alonzo slowly let go of my hand, and I closed my eyes, saddened by this turn of events.

"Thank you for the drink. I'll try to catch your show," I told him.

He nodded. "The mo' listeners, the mo' ratings, the mo' betta." He started to walk away, and I did something that surprised me.

"I wouldn't mind another dance," I called.

Alonzo turned, smiled at me, took my hand, and led me back to the dance floor, where we held each other close. It didn't matter what song was playing; we held on to each other like it was the same slow jam on repeat. Feeling his body next to mine was making me have so many wild notions, and the fleeting thought "What if I had met him first?" crossed my mind. Once again, our lips were inches away. Only this time I gave in to my lust and kissed him. It was wrong for me to cross this line, but I didn't care. I had always been faithful in my relationships, but this time I felt something different and didn't want to let it go. I couldn't. I was tired of always being responsible, always doing the right thing. Tonight I just wanted it to be all about me. I gazed into his eyes, and we both knew what we wanted.

"I'm ready to go if you are," I told him.

He smiled. "Yeah."

I followed him out of the club, we both got in our separate cars, and then I trailed him in mine to a nice two-story house on the south side of Atlanta. The entire drive from the club, I had time to reconsider what I was going to do.

Robert's a good guy, I thought to myself.

What does that have to do with anything? my rational mind retorted. *You're not married.*

I'm trying to make this work, I insisted.

Why? You don't have a commitment to him. It's only been a month.

My mind drifted back to Alonzo and how he had made me feel on the dance floor. *Fuck it*. It was him I wanted. There was no reason for me not to be with him tonight.

I pulled into his driveway and got out just as he was closing his car door. He took my hand, led me to the front door, and we went inside. I noticed a couple of jazz-inspired art pieces on the walls: Duke Ellington in a colorful piece and Miles Davis in another. The black-and-white painting of Aaliyah was beautiful. He had a spacious living room, with oversized plush furniture and a state-of-the-art entertainment system. I liked his style, but I wasn't here for the décor.

"Do you want something to drink?" he asked me.

I smiled. "No."

He smiled too, and his eyes met mine.

I walked over to his staircase and looked up. "You live here alone?"

"My best friend, Sean, lives here too. He's out of town right now."

I raised an eyebrow at him. "You sure about that?"

He chuckled and walked toward me. "Yep, no girlfriend, no kids, just us. I like having room to live."

Normally, I wouldn't believe a guy if he said that, but I did believe him. I felt the same way about having plenty of living space. He pulled me close and kissed me with so much passion, then took me upstairs to his bedroom. What happened next was simply the most intense love-making I had ever experienced. A night I would never forget.

Two months later . . .

My night with Alonzo was special, but afterward I decided not to call him again. If I did, I didn't think

I would ever leave him. As much as I tried to deny it, I still felt guilty because of Robert. He didn't deserve what I had done. After that night I decided it was best to focus on us and really try to make things work.

Tonight we were hosting dinner at my house, and after I got dressed, I began fixing my hair in the mirror.

"You look beautiful." Robert walked up behind me and rubbed my shoulders.

"Thanks. You're not too shabby yourself, Professor."

"So who am I meeting tonight?"

"I told you, my best friend in the whole world. Joyce."

"Okay, so is your friend gonna hate me or what?"

I stopped styling my hair and looked at him in the mirror.

"What? Joyce is gonna like you. So is Denise. Now my other close friend, Taylor, she's the temperamental one."

He sighed. "That's great to hear."

As if on cue, the doorbell rang, and I headed to the front door, with Robert behind me. I glanced back at him. "Don't worry. Everything's gonna be fine."

I opened the door, and my jaw hit the floor. There he was, in front of me again, just as handsome as ever. Alonzo was standing on my doorstep, with Joyce by his side. What the hell was he doing here with her? The smile on his face evaporated. He was just as stunned to see me. I couldn't speak for a second; then I forced out a high-pitched greeting.

"Oh my . . . Hi!"

Joyce smiled. "Hey. Alonzo, this is my best friend in the whole world, Rashida."

Alonzo swallowed hard. "Hello."

"Rashida, this is Alonzo."

We both knew we had no choice but to play along.

He extended his hand, and I shook it. "Nice to meet you."

He played along, saying, "It's nice to meet you too."

This was crazy. How did he end up with Joyce? More importantly, should I tell her what happened between us?

Chapter Four

Seems Like You're Ready

ALONZO

She was the last person I was expecting Joyce to introduce me to. She had always referred to her friend as 'Shida. I had no idea that this was the Rashida I had met two months ago at the Gold Room. I could never forget the love we had made that night or how much I had wanted her to stay.

Here I was standing in her living room, staring at her beautiful face, as she stood next to her boyfriend, Robert. I could tell by the look in her eyes she didn't want Joyce to know the truth, so I played along with it.

This was so damn awkward. After that night I really didn't think I would see her again, and after I met Joyce, Rashida was just a pleasant afterthought. It figured that beautiful women like Joyce and Rashida ran together. Best friends, no less. Just my luck. Over the next few hours, the four of us made small talk, but I avoided eye contact with Rashida.

Joyce and I left finally, and as we drove down the street, Joyce could sense by my quietness that something was off, and decide to talk to me.

"So, what did you think of my friend?"

"Rashida? Oh, she's nice."

Joyce stared at me for a moment. "That's it? Just nice?"

I shrugged. "Yeah, I mean, what are you expecting me to say?"

She sighed. "Nothing, I guess. I was just expecting you to say more than that."

"Sorry. I just got a lot on my mind." I wasn't lying about that. "But Rashida seems like a very nice girl. Her dude seems a bit uptight, though."

Joyce nodded. "Yeah, he does. He's not the type of guy she normally dates."

"Oh really? What's her type?"

"Um, we normally have similar taste in men. So maybe a guy kinda like you," she answered.

I exhaled. "Oh, okay."

"Robert seems okay, but I don't see Rashida being with him for too long. Maybe you could hook her up with one of your boys. How about Sean?"

I shook my head. "Uh, I don't think Sean is the right kinda of guy for her. Don't get me wrong. He's a good dude, but he's a playa. He's like a hawk out hunting women."

Joyce smirked at me. "Hmm. They say birds of a feather flock together, so are you playing games with me?"

I grinned. "Nah, I'm not about that life anymore. There just comes a time when you want something real. Besides, I would never play with your heart."

"That's good to know." She smiled. "But I hope there are other parts of my body you'd like to play with."

She slid her hand up my thigh and rested it on my crotch, where she found something nice and hard. Now, don't get me wrong; despite this awkward situation with Rashida, Joyce was a sexy woman that any man would do anything to get with. I knew because I damn near did too.

We had met each other six weeks ago, while we were in line at Target. I was picking up a few Blu-rays and was standing behind her, admiring the view of her voluptuous behind. She spotted me checking her out. I could tell by the grin on her face that she didn't mind me looking. Her tight red skirt left nothing to the imagination, so I started a little small talk, which we continued as we headed out to the parking lot. We exchanged numbers, and a few days later we went out.

Since then, we'd had nights at the movies, dinner dates at different restaurants, and now dinner at her best friend's. It had been all good, but we hadn't had sex yet. Not that I was in a rush, but she liked to tease me, and that was something I didn't like. We would go so far before she would stop. If I were the same guy I was a few years ago, I would have ended things after the second time she pulled that on me, but I was trying to be a better man these days.

I drove her back to her apartment in Druid Hills and walked her to the door. She took out her keys, opened her front door, then looked at me.

"Would you like to come in?" she asked.

I just stood there, considering her invitation. She could see the hesitation on my face. I wasn't in the mood to be played with tonight.

"Uh, I'm not sure I should," I said at last.

She took my hand and pulled me toward her. "C'mon."

I went inside and had a seat on the sofa. *Here we go again*, I thought. I knew the routine already. I would go inside and get comfortable. She would get us some drinks, such as the Italian Nivuro she loved. Then she would join me on the sofa, we'd make small talk, and then we'd get to kissing and touching. And then she would say, "We can't do this yet." Then I would be left hanging with Nivuro on my lips and a painful erection in my jeans.

If tonight was going to be more of the same, I wasn't going for it. Joyce turned on some Miguel from a playlist on her cell, and it flowed through the wireless speakers on the mantel. She stood in front of me as I sat on the sofa.

"Would you like a drink?" she asked.

I sighed. "Nah, I'm good."

She looked at me and slightly raised her eyebrow without saying a word. I said nothing, and in this uncomfortable silence, I was sure Joyce could sense my frustration.

That was the first time I had turned down her offer for a nightcap. I wasn't trying to repeat the same thing we had done over and over. Truth be told, our dinner with Rashida was still on my mind. Of all the women in the world Joyce could be best friends with, it had to be her.

"I'ma go freshen up a bit. I'll be just a minute." She headed toward her bedroom.

"Yeah. Sure, okay."

The bedroom door closed, and I sat there for a moment thinking about everything. The situation with Rashida was unsettling, and I couldn't deny the attraction I still had to her. Joyce was a good girl, but everything was hitting too close to home. Maybe a relationship wasn't the right thing for us.

"Joyce?" I called out. I had made up my mind it was best to leave. There was no sense in dragging this out any further.

When I got no response, I stood up and headed toward the bedroom door to end things. Just as I reached the door, it opened. There was Joyce, standing before me in a black-lace bra and panty set. My mouth fell open. She looked like she had just stepped off the pages of a *Playboy* editorial spread.

She stepped closer to me. "I know I've given you some mixed signals, and I know you've been frustrated. I just had to be sure this wasn't all a game for you."

"It's not."

"I know that now."

She kissed me. It was the type of kiss that was an invitation to enjoy everything before me. It was an invitation I gladly accepted. My hands rubbed her soft skin. Fingers caressed her back and found her supple ass cheeks to squeeze. She kissed my chin. Her tongue eased out of her mouth and tasted my neck. Her breathing was rapid, almost out of control. A pair of soft breasts pressed against my chest, and in my jeans her hand found my sudden erection, which was dying to be set free. She unbuckled my belt, then unfastened my jeans.

"Slow down," I whispered. "We don't have to rush."

My words fell on deaf ears, because she didn't stop until her hand found the hardness in my boxers. Her hand fondled and stroked my penis, making me growl. She had awakened a beast inside me, a part of me that was dying to be set free. An animal that would show no mercy with the things it would do to her. My jeans fell to mid-thigh, allowing her to pull my boxers down over my ass. My ridged hardness pressed against the lacy material of her panties, damn near pushing inside her.

I whispered, "Are you sure?"

"Yes."

My hands cupped her ass, and I hoisted her up on me. She wrapped her legs around my waist. After kicking off my shoes, I carried her inside her bedroom and laid her on the edge of the queen-size bed. Her long legs dangled over the edge. They say the way a person kept their bedroom was a reflection who they were. It was their most intimate and personal space. I quickly took in my surroundings. This was my first time entering her sanctuary; it was flawless, just like her.

I stared at her long, lean body; her black panties could barely contain her thickness inside. Her golden-brown skin was unblemished and smooth. I finished undressing myself and took a condom out of my wallet. Her full, succulent breasts rising and falling with each anxious breath, Joyce kept her eyes on me as I rolled on the Magnum.

She unclasped her bra and tossed it to the side. I gazed at a pair of beautiful brown breasts with dark areolas and hard nipples. I licked my lips. She smiled. I pulled her moist panties down over her long legs; then she parted her thighs, showing me where she wanted me to be. I climbed on top of her, then kissed her inner thighs as I traveled down into her valley. I drank from the pool between her legs, which quickly became a river. Soft moans left her lips, and her back arched in excitement. I ate her alive like I was a zombie on *The Walking Dead*. Her sweetness drenched my face, and her hands pulled at the sheets. My grip on her legs did not allow her to escape the sweet torture I was giving her.

"Oh, my gawd . . . Alonzo . . . I'm cumming . . . I'm . . . I'm . . . aah . . ."

Another moan escaped her throat, and that victory cry let me know she had arrived at the promised land. Her legs curled back, and uncontrollable spasms made her body shudder. She panted and whined in pleasure. Her breathing was out of control. She was almost done, but I had only just begun. I left her valley on fire, traveled to her mountains, and sucked on erect nipples. My penis rubbed her clit.

"What . . . are you . . . trying to do . . . to me?" she gasped.

"What do you *want* me to do?"

"Anything . . . everything."

"Tell me how much you want it."

"Damn you."

It was my time to tease. "I could stop."

"No! Please! Give it to me!"

"You want it?"

"Yes, please!"

"Okay."

I slowly entered her and watched as her beautiful face made an ugly expression. Joyce was on fire. I felt her wetness surround me. I stroked her deeply and made sure I touched the bottom of her love. More moans and groans from both of us filled the air. Our bodies shifted around the bed as we tried to find the perfect angle. Joyce gave me her all. The classy girl I had met a month ago was now this sex goddess doing things to me I thought about only in my wildest dreams.

After that night it was on and popping on the regular. She wanted it every chance she got, and I was more than happy to give it to her. Our relationship became stronger, but I knew it would be just a matter of time before I saw Rashida again.

And I was right. Rashida invited us to her house for a Memorial Day cookout. The first time we went over there for dinner, I had assumed that the house was Robert's, but then Joyce had clarified that it was, in fact, Rashida's home. She explained that Rashida and her brother had received a large settlement after her parents' death.

We arrived at the cookout fashionably late, and once again it was weird to see Rashida. Robert was at the grill, with a nice crowd of folks talking and drinking around him. Joyce and I mingled after greeting our hosts. After we had strolled around a bit, I wanted a beer and went over to the cooler to retrieve one, but it was empty. Robert told me there was a case of beer in the refrigerator, so I went inside the house to fetch it.

When I entered the kitchen, Rashida was over by the stove, checking on some of the food on the burners. She looked good in the floor-length African-print skirt and the fuchsia-colored bandeau she wore. As I contemplated the style of her skirt, I recognized it as a Nigerian Ankara print. I was feeling her style. She turned just then and saw me standing there. We stared at each other for a second, both of us thinking the same thing. I decided to break the ice.

"So are we going to pretend like it never happened?"

She smiled. "I guess not. Kind of a big elephant in the room, huh?"

"Very big," I agreed. "Looks like we're going to be around each other a lot, and I wanted to clear the air. I just don't want anything to be awkward."

"So things between you and Joyce are good?"

I nodded. "Yes, they are."

"I'm happy for you two." She turned to stir a pot on the stove.

"Rashida, I wasn't expecting ever to see you again."

"I understand," she admitted, her back facing me. "That night was just for us, something we both needed at the time. There's nothing to explain." She turned back toward me and extended her hand. "Friends?"

I shook her hand. "Friends."

Chapter Five

A Girl Like Me

DENISE

I knew I was not the girl every man was tripping over themselves to get with, nor did I want to be that chick. I saw the way men look at Rashida, Joyce, and especially Taylor, and I could do without that kind of attention. Not that I was some kind of ugly duckling, but I just didn't try to put myself out there like that.

I'd been friends with Rashida and Joyce since high school. Taylor was more of a friend by default than by choice. I didn't hate her; I just didn't really have anything in common with her. Our personalities were polar opposites. I'd tried to become closer to her, but she was just too damn ghetto for my liking. She dressed like a video ho and then wanted to call me Wallflower because I chose to dress like a lady. Whatever!

I already knew when Rashida said she was going to have a cookout at her house for Memorial Day that Taylor was going to be underdressed for the occasion. And there she was, forty-five minutes late, as usual, walking up to us, wearing a red miniskirt that barely covered her ass and a matching bikini top, with her breasts bouncing with every step. She had recently dyed her hair blond, which complemented her complexion.

"Seriously? She couldn't put on some clothes?" I muttered.

Rashida chuckled. "You're acting as if this is your first time meeting Taylor. Relax and don't start any drama."

I rolled my eyes. "I never do."

Rashida shook her head. I knew she always tried to stay neutral in our disagreements, but she couldn't just ignore all the ratchet shit Taylor pulled. There was a nice crowd of people here already, and a lot of them were our friends from Clark Atlanta, others were people who worked in the entertainment industry in Atlanta, and some were Rashida's family members. Most of the men were rubbernecking in Taylor's direction, trying to get a glance at her ass as she walked through. Robert was at the grill, while Rashida and I were sat on foldout chairs, with a few others standing by us. A handful of the people here were Robert's coworkers. A few of them were here with their wives, who didn't like the way their husbands were gawking at Taylor.

Rashida got up to greet her. "Hey, sexy gal," she called. "You're gonna get somebody's man in trouble, walking around here with all that ass under that skirt."

"I can't help it if they like what they see," Taylor said nonchalantly and glanced back at a couple of men still ogling her. "Besides, I'm here for the food! Where the ribs at?"

"Robert just took a rack of ribs off the grill." Rashida pointed to a table nearby that had the food on it. "Go help yourself."

"Say less," Taylor said and made her way toward the food.

Joyce was with her new boyfriend, Alonzo, and they were all booed up. He was an attractive man. They looked cute together. He had come to the cookout with a male friend, who was also cute, but I could tell by the way he was dressed—like a wannabe rapper—that he was defi-nitely not my type. As Taylor went over to the table with the food, I could still see a bunch of men staring at her ass and whispering to each other. Disgusting. Even the men here with their significant others were still trying to sneak a peek.

My eyes went back over to where Joyce and Alonzo were standing, and I saw that his boy wasn't staring at Taylor at all. He was staring directly at me. We made eye contact and held it for a good ten seconds. A smile came across his face. I got self-conscious and quickly looked away. He was wearing a black wife beater and skinny jeans. A silver chain was around his neck, with a large crucifix hanging from it. His hair was neatly cornrowed to the back. He looked rough but sexy at the same time. But why was he checking me out like that? He was not the type of guy that paid me any attention. I got up and headed toward Rashida, who was talking to Taylor.

"Wus up, Denise?" Taylor looked me up and down. "On your way to Bible study after this?"

I glared at her. I had on a floral-print dress that stopped just past my knees. I wasn't showing my ass to everyone. I looked appropriate for the occasion. "Hey, Taylor. Nice outfit. Strolling down Bankhead afterward?"

Rashida sighed. "Must you two go at each other's throats as soon as you see each other?"

I looked at Rashida. "I told you she starts it."

Taylor rolled her eyes. "Please! Don't act like you weren't whispering shit about me to Rashida as soon as you saw me. I know I look good. Don't hate."

"I'm not hating on you, but aren't you the slightest bit concerned with how these men are gawking at you?"

Taylor smirked. "Men are gonna look regardless. Besides, I'm comfortable in my own skin." She looked over at Sean. "Speaking of which, you certainly have some fine ones here, 'Shida. Who's that next to Joyce and Alonzo?"

Rashida glanced in that direction. "Oh, that's Alonzo's homeboy, Sean."

Taylor smiled. "Well, isn't he cute? I should welcome him to the party."

I shook my head. Despite all the decent-looking single brothers here, of course, Taylor had zeroed in on the one who looked like he was in G-Unit. I just didn't get her.

For the rest of the cookout, I chilled near the house, sipping on a Heineken, watching some fellas playing spades. Rashida was doing her best to make sure everyone was enjoying themselves. Joyce was sitting on Alonzo's lap, and of course, Taylor had made her way over to Sean and was now flirting with him. He seemed like he was into her. What man wouldn't be feeling a girl who looked like Taylor, especially if she was all touchy-feely with him? I shook my head and went back to enjoying the cookout.

By the time the sun started going down, most of the people had left. Joyce had left with Alonzo, and Taylor was nowhere in sight. I opted to stick around and help Rashida clean up. There were a few people sitting around the grill, and Robert was eating and drinking as he chatted with them. Rashida told me they were some of Robert's coworkers. They were all a bit older than us: I figured they were in their forties or fifties. It didn't seem like Rashida was too interested in what they were talking about. I had never thought Rashida would date an older man, but I guessed you liked what you liked.

I took a bag of trash outside from the kitchen, and as I was walking toward the trash bins, I saw him. He was the last person I expected to still be here.

"Hey. How you doing?" he asked.

"I'm fine."

He noticed the bag in my hand. "Let me help you with that."

I nodded, and he politely took the trash from me and dumped it in a bin.

"Thank you."

"You're welcome. You're Denise, right?"

"Yeah." I was surprised. "How do you know my name?"

"Joyce was telling me about her friends."

"Oh, okay." I stared at his handsome face. He was so sexy up close and personal. "Well, it is nice meeting you."

"My name is Sean."

"I know."

"I saw you earlier by yourself. I was wondering if you came here solo."

"Why?" I quizzed.

"Well, you looked kind of lonely."

What the hell? I thought. *I know this wannabe thug isn't over here taking pity on me like I'm some lost kitten in need of some attention.*

"Listen, Sean, I don't really know you like that, and you definitely don't know me, so it's a bit inappropriate to be having this discussion with you. Excuse me." I turned to leave, and he quickly jogged in front of me.

"Whoa! Hold up, Ma. I didn't mean to offend you. I just wanna get to know you."

I stared at him oddly. "Me? You wanna get to know *me*? Why?"

He grinned. "Because I'm feeling you and would like to take you out sometime."

I was a bit speechless. It was not that I wasn't used to guys asking me out. I did date, but guys like Sean never asked me out. This had to be some kind of joke.

"You want to take me out? Why me? Weren't you flirting with Taylor not too long ago?"

He nodded. "She's cool people, but she's not really my type."

I laughed. "She's not? But I am? Yeah, okay."

"Why is that so hard for you to believe? Listen, Ma, I ain't trying to waste your time, so if you ain't feeling me, I'll leave you alone."

"Wait. You're serious, aren't you?"

"Yes, I am. I just wanna get to know you. Maybe I could call you sometime, and we can get to know each other better. No pressure."

"Okay," I said, blushing. "We can do that."

"Cool."

He pulled out his phone. I gave him my number, and he punched it in. Sean was not at all what I expected from a man who looked like him. And the more I gazed at his fine chocolate self, the more I found myself becoming aroused. Why was he so damn sexy? Pretty brown eyes, perfect white teeth, muscular arms and chest. The smelled of his Versace cologne made me want to get closer.

He gave me a hug as he said goodbye, and Lord knows I wanted to melt in his arms. Part of me still didn't believe this was happening to me. Another part of me couldn't wait for Taylor to see me with Sean. I'd show her that I didn't have be damn near naked to get a man.

Chapter Six

The Way My Bank Account Is Set Up

TAYLOR

It felt like I was waiting in line for some welfare benefits instead of securing a student loan from the business office at Clark Atlanta University. I really hated coming here and waiting in a room filled with students in the same boat as me. It annoyed me the way the admin officer talked like as soon as I got a job, I could pay these loans off in no time. That was a lie. It might be years before I actually got a job in the field I was studying for and could afford to make payments. And that was before factoring in the interest rates, which increased every year. It felt like I was going to become the modern-day equivalent of an indentured servant.

This was my fourth meeting in my effort to get another loan from Sallie Mae's greedy ass, since my Pell Grant no longer covered everything. I'd been drowning in debt for the past three years. For what? To get a degree in a field I was no longer interested in?

I sat in the waiting area for about thirty minutes before I was called back to the financial aid advisor's office. I took a seat across from her at her desk and just sat there watching her tap on her keyboard as she inputted my information into the system. Each annoying click drove me crazy. My eyes scanned the small office, and I noticed the pile of files on her desk from other students. To her, I was just another debtor in the pile.

After a while, my gaze wandered around the office, and I noticed that she had framed affirmations on the walls, including one that read, "I put the *fun* in funding." There wasn't shit fun about this. I was taking four classes this semester, so I knew the loan amount was going to be ridiculous. Even though I wasn't paying the loan back yet, I knew once I graduated, it would be looming over my head like a storm cloud. Once she was done getting the reply from Sallie Mae, she told me my loan amount for this quarter was eighty-five hundred dollars. I just shook my head and signed the paperwork. I was now over forty thousand dollars in debt.

I hated the thought of being this far in the hole. My little waitress job at Pin Up's wasn't gonna help me pay for shit. I just wanted to drop out of this bitch, but if I did that, my mother would look at me like I was crazy. But I was an English major, so what the hell kind of job could I get that would help me pay off this damn loan? A job as a teacher? At an advertising agency? Writing for a blog or newspaper? I would most likely be stuck in some call center job, making minimal payments for the next thirty years! Bullshit!

After leaving the business office, I decided to talk to the one person that I always turned to with my problems. Rashida. I crossed the parking lot, hopped in my car, and raced over to her place.

"So should I just quit?" I asked her as soon as we had made ourselves comfortable on her couch.

Rashida frowned. "Do you really think you should quit?"

"Ugh! I hate it when you do that."

"Do what?"

I glared at her. "Answer a question with a question. That defeats the whole purpose of asking you in the first place!"

She smiled. "I can't tell you what you should do."

"Yes you can! I'm giving you full control over this aspect of my life."

She shook her head. "Absolutely not. I'm solely here as a friend to support whatever decision you make, and I think you know what you should do."

I sighed. "I hate being an adult. I just keep on building up this debt, with no idea how I'm really going to pay it off. I wish I could be more like you."

She laughed. "Girl, I am no role model. I'm still trying to figure everything out."

"But, look, you're getting your degree, plus you're paying for your little brother's tuition, and you bought a house! You don't have to worry about paying back that ho Sallie Mae."

"Yeah, but you know I'm able to do all that only because of what happened."

I could see Rashida's eyes drop with the memory of what had happened to her parents. She wiped her eyes and shifted in her seat, trying to hold it together.

"I'm sorry. I shouldn't have brought that up."

When Rashida was fourteen years old, her parents died in a freak car accident when a Walmart truck lost control and hit them head-on. Nobody else was hurt, but they were killed instantly. Rashida and her little brother, Raheem, were devastated by their loss. The company paid them a twenty-million-dollar settlement, ten million each, and the money stayed in a trust until they turned eighteen. Their grandmother looked after them until they both went to college, and she died a couple of years ago.

"That's okay. It's in the past. You know, Taylor, I can help you with some of those loans."

I'd be lying if I said I had never thought about asking her, but that was not what friends did. "I can't ask you to do that," I told her.

She took my hand. "You're not asking. I'm offering."

I exhaled. "That's a lot of money, 'Shida. I'm not sure I'm comfortable owing you like that."

She shrugged her shoulders. "Then pay me back. Once you graduate and get settled in your career, just make small payments to me interest free. It's better than owing that bitch Sallie Mae, right?" She smiled, and I exhaled.

"You're right. It is better."

"Told ya! So just give me the loan information and who I should call, and we'll take care of it."

I shook my head. "Why are you so good to me?"

"Because you're my friend, silly."

She hugged me, and it felt like the world had been lifted off my shoulders. I'd never met a woman like Rashida before. How could she be so giving? What did I do to deserve a friend like her? I loved this woman. I swear, there was nothing in the world I wouldn't do for her. Our bond was deeper than friendship.

Robert walked in the room as we were hugging. He smirked. "Oh, wow! Now, how can I get in on this?"

I rolled my eyes at his little perverted suggestion. I didn't know what 'Shida saw in this guy. Not only was he old enough to be my daddy, but he was also one of those types of guys who thought they were being funny when they were really just lame. Sure, he was cute, but in a Denzel Washington sort of way. In other words, he was the kind of man my mother would be interested in, not me.

Rashida looked at him. "Really? How inappropriate are you right now?"

He chuckled. "It was just a joke. Everything okay with you, Taylor?"

"Yep, it is now."

"Great." He looked at 'Shida. "I'm going to meet up with Sydney to discuss the new scholarship program we want to establish. I think if we can get the right people involved, we can make this happen."

"That's a good thing." She stood up and kissed him. "Don't worry about me. Go handle your business."

He nodded. "I will, and when I get home tonight, I'll handle you."

'Shida shook her head, and I nearly threw up a little bit in my mouth. This guy was way too corny for my taste. He turned to leave, and as he walked by me, I could see the way he was staring at my legs. I would bet any amount of money that if I gave him an opportunity, he would be eating my ass in a heartbeat. I wondered if 'Shida could see this too.

"So, is everything still good with you two?" I asked after he had left the house.

"Yeah, we're good."

"Great."

Rashida caught my sarcasm and smirked. "I know you don't like him, Taylor. You don't have to pretend."

"I didn't say that."

"You didn't have to. I know you." She got up from the couch and went into the kitchen. There she grabbed a couple of wine coolers from the fridge, brought them back to the living room, and handed one to me. "Robert is really a good man, ya know?" she said as she sat down.

"Hey, you're the one that's got to sleep with him, not me. If you're cool with him, then so am I. But if he fucks up, then he's dead to me."

She took a swig of her drink. "Thanks for the support."

"So what do you wanna get into tonight? The Gold Room?"

"No, I'm cool on that."

"How about the Palace?"

Rashida smirked. "The Pink Palace? You mean the strip club? You wanna go back and watch dem girls?"

"We had fun the last time!" I exclaimed.

She laughed. "You mean *you* had fun! Girl, I ain't trying to watch some chick twerkin' in my face. Besides, Joyce text me earlier and wants us to go out with her to Skate Towne, down in College Park."

"Skate Towne? Seriously?"

"Yeah, Denise is going to be there too."

"So I guess we all gotta go since Denise will be there," I said sarcastically.

"You two really need to stop this mess. C'mon, it's going to be fun!"

About an hour later we were down at Skate Towne. It had been years since I had skated, but I was still nice on them wheels. Even so, I would still rather be at the club than here. But for 'Shida, I sucked it up and decided to have fun. Besides, it would be fun having everybody watch me break it down.

By the time 'Shida and I got there, Joyce and Alonzo had already arrived. But to my surprise, Denise was on the rink, with a man behind her. It looked like he was teaching her to skate. I stared at him closer. It was that fine-ass Sean!

Last time I saw him, which was at 'Shida's cookout, he had been all up on me, spitting game, trying to get in my panties. He was fine as hell with his thuggish ass, so I had given him my number. What was he doing here with Denise? When did they hook up? I wondered.

Chapter Seven

Come Inside

DENISE

I couldn't believe Sean had actually got me in some skates and in the rink, me, of all people. We'd been talking on the phone every day since Rashida's cookout, literally spend hours chatting and getting to know each other. Just the sound of his voice over the phone made me wet, and being with him sent my hormones into overdrive.

Once he'd found out I could barely skate, he had insisted that we go on a double date with Joyce and Alonzo so he could teach me. I was more than willing to be his student. This was our first official date, and he made me feel so sexy by the way he touched and caressed me. Normally, on a first date, I wouldn't let a man get all up on me, but I loved the way Sean felt pressing up next to me. I didn't even mind his hand on my ass as he "helped" me skate. It felt good.

We decided to take a quick break and headed toward the carpeted area on the side of the rink. Rashida and Taylor headed toward us. The surprised look on Taylor's face was priceless. No doubt she was shocked to see Sean with me. The fact that she had damn near thrown herself all up on him at the cookout made this moment even funnier. Sean placed his arm around my waist after we sat down on a bench to catch our breath. I wished Taylor would call me Wallflower now.

Rashida was the first to speak. "Hey, y'all."

"Hey, 'Shida," Sean and I chorused.

Taylor glared at Sean, then muttered, "Hey."

"Wus up?" Sean replied.

"I didn't know you two were a thing. Cute," Taylor said dryly.

"It just kinda happened," Sean admitted.

"I was on my way to Bible study when he stopped me," I added, throwing Taylor's joke back in her face. I smiled and held on to Sean, who had his arm wrapped around me.

Taylor rolled her eyes. I loved seeing her annoyed.

"Well, any guy who can get Denise out here must be a good dude," Rashida said, trying to lighten the mood.

"She just needed the right man behind her." Sean squeezed me, and I could feel his hardness on my butt.

Damn, what did he have in them jeans? All kinds of nasty thoughts ran through my mind.

Rashida smiled. "So I see."

Fifteen minutes later, Sean and I went back out on the rink and enjoyed ourselves. Taylor did her utmost to get Sean's attention, but his focus was on me. I loved that he was actually here to get to know me. During our long talks on the phone, I could tell he always listened to me, and I did the same for him. He told me that he and Alonzo had been best friends since grade school and that he was into music. Sean was an up-and-coming rapper and was working on a mixtape, which explained his street look. I told him I wasn't really into rap music, and he understood. In fact, he said he was glad I wasn't, because he wasn't looking to be with a groupie. Lucky me.

"So what's up with you and Taylor?" he asked. "You two don't like each other much, huh?"

We were sitting on the side of the rink, people watching. The rink had got crowded and fast. People were talking in groups, skating, or just dancing.

"We have our differences, but we're cool."

He chuckled. "So y'all are like frenemies, right?"

"Why is that so funny to you?" I asked, curious.

"It's just the complexities of the relationships y'all women have with each other. Y'all know you don't like each other, but because you got common friends, y'all will put up with each other but low-key hate on each other at the same time. Hilarious!"

"We don't hate on each other."

He looked at me knowingly.

"We don't! Not really. What do you do in that situation?"

"Simple. I don't keep anybody in my circle I don't trust or like. So, outside of Alonzo, there's not many."

"Am I in your circle now?"

He shrugged. "It depends if you want to be there."

"I think I do. You seem totally different from the man I thought you were."

A smirk spread across his face. "And who did you think I was?"

"I thought you were the type of guy who was more into girls like Taylor. Not the ones like me."

"Doing what I do, I see girls like Taylor all the time. Don't get me wrong. She's cool, but a woman like you is a rare breed."

I laughed. "You make me sound like an endangered species."

"In some ways you are. All these girls out here trying to be the next Kim K, Rihanna, or whoever. I just wanna girl who's herself."

He looked into my eyes and kissed me. Our first kiss. Once again, Sean had me breaking all my rules. Kissing on the first date was a no-no for me. There were too many kinds of nasty shit floating around out there to be all kissy face with anyone, but with Sean, it was different. I wanted him. His lips were so soft and nice. How could he make me feel moist just from a kiss? I had almost forgotten we were in a crowded public place, since we had kissed like we were alone.

We got up and did a few more rounds on the rink. Sean never took his hands off me the whole time. We were stuck like glue. I could tell by the look on Taylor's face that she was sick of watching us. I didn't care. Sean was right; we were frenemies.

A few minutes later we left Skate Towne, and Sean took me home. I lived in the same apartment complex as Joyce in Druid Hills. He walked me up to my door, and I had butterflies in my stomach.

I stared into his eyes. "I had a lot of fun tonight."

"Good. I'm glad you were willing to give me a chance."

"Me too."

As I took the keys out of my purse, he leaned in and put his lips on mine. His kisses felt like sex, and I wanted more. His hands cupped my ass, pulling me in. I normally didn't like aggressive men, but strangely, his aggressive-ness turned me on. It took all my willpower to pull away from him. I was captivated by his sexy brown eyes and broke another rule.

"Do you wanna come in for a minute?"

He smiled. "Yeah."

I opened the door, and he followed me inside. What was I doing? I didn't do this sort of thing. This was so out of character for me, but I didn't care. Sean pulled me back into his embrace. His lips were on my neck while his hands unzipped my jeans. I kicked off my shoes, and a soft gasp left my lips as his hand went inside my panties. He played with my clit, and I became a ball of fire. I haven't had sex in two years. I'd dated here and there, but nobody special. Nobody I was willing to give myself to. All the passion that had built up inside me exploded on his fingertips.

Sean led me over to the sofa, and after I lay down on it, he pulled my jeans and panties off. I was naked from the waist down. My legs fell apart, and I felt Sean's lips on my other lips. He licked, kissed, sucked, and then he licked me again. My nostrils flared, I moaned, and my body trembled as he had his way with me. He licked, kissed, and sucked me again. He found a nasty rhythm as he held my legs apart and buried his tongue inside me.

I caught a glimpse of my reflection in my wide-screen TV. It was like watching a flick that starred me. Then I felt it. I came. Hard. I was done. Damn near out of breath. My orgasm had sucker punched me into submission. Any uncertainty I had had once was gone. All my rules had been broken. Sean could have me any which way he wanted.

He stood up and undressed himself. I pulled off my top, unhooked my bra, and dropped them to the side. Sean's eyes lit up when he saw my breasts. I loved the way he looked at me. It made me feel sexy; it made me want him even more. Different tattoos decorated his body. He was like a walking canvass. Wings on his chest, a crucifix on his right shoulder, a young girl's face on his left one. A black panther on his stomach led me down to the other big, lethal black "creature" coming toward me. His erection was amazing. Long, hard, with a swollen tip. He rested the tip on my clit.

He said my name. "Denise?"

"Yes?"

"Do you like it?"

"Yes."

"Do you want it?"

"Yes," I whispered. "I'm so wet right now."

Sean grinned. "Let me find out."

He eased his way inside me. Shallow strokes, then deeper ones. My legs were spread far apart as he penetrated me slowly. Every stroke made me moan and gasp for air. Raw. He was inside me with no protection, and I was too dickmatized to care. All I wanted was him. All cared about was his stroke, his long, deep stroke. His thrusts were hard, aggressive, and wicked, but I matched his intensity with just as much force as he was giving me. We were fucking. No other way to describe what was happening my sofa. I was fucking Sean on our first date, and I didn't care. All the things I had imagined Taylor would do with a man I was doing with Sean tonight.

He turned me around, positioned me on my knees, and pushed back inside me. I groaned, frowned, and looked back as Sean moved in and out of me. I loved each rough stroke he gave me. Being battered and bruised felt so good! My heart raced. This was the best sex I'd ever had, and I could tell Sean was enjoying himself too. His erection had become so ridged, and his groans were almost painful to the ear. He said a few words that sounded like grunts, and then he came. His body collapsed on top of me, and he jerked while he was still deep inside me, enjoying the warmth of the walls surrounding him.

"Are you okay?" he asked after a while.

"I'm perfect."

He withdrew his half-hard erection from me, and I turned toward him. A wide smile was on his face as I nuzzled against him. He kissed me, and his hand caressed my breasts, rubbed my hard nipples.

"Yes, you are," he whispered.

"I didn't mean it like that. I mean it felt good."

"I wasn't too rough?"

"No, I liked it." I paused. "I don't normally do this type of thing."

"What type of thing?"

"Sleep with men on the first date," I said in a shameful tone. The reality of what I had just done started to set in. "Seriously, I feel like I tossed all my values out of the window because I got horny."

"No you didn't. You were living in the moment. Nothing wrong with that."

"I don't know why I did this."

"Do you regret it?"

My eyes met his. "No."

"Do you want me to leave?"

"No, I don't."

He smiled. "Do you want to do it again?"

My hand found his penis and fondled it. It became hard again.

I smiled. "Yes."

Sean eased himself back inside my wetness. This time his stroke was slow and steady. He made love to me. For what seemed like hours, we took turns pleasing each other, switching positions, and making each other moan. I was submissive and fulfilled all his freaky desires. He did things to me that I had never done before. From the living room to the kitchen and the shower, we made love.

I'd never had a lover like Sean before. What had I done to get so lucky?

Chapter Eight

Don't Touch My Hair

RASHIDA

Things between Robert and me had been going good for the past ten months. Not that we hadn't had our issues, but what couple didn't? I thought our major difficulty was our age gap. There was a fourteen-year age difference between us, and that caused Robert at times to treat me like I was his daughter instead of his girlfriend, especially when we argued. I got that he had more life experience than me in some things, but that didn't mean he should dismiss what I had to say. This was something we could work on in time.

Tonight we were going out to dinner with a few of Robert's colleagues. The only one of them I really knew was Sydney Daniels, and he was a bit too arrogant for my taste. No matter what the topic was, he would always make it political in one way or another. He loved to say, "How's *your president* doing these days?" Or if things got really heated, he'd say, "You still haven't answered my question. What has the Democratic Party done for you in the past twenty-five years?"

Sydney was a certified, card-carrying black Republican. I had nothing against anybody personally based on their political views, but I didn't get being black and Republican. Sure, I knew some black Conservatives, but to be a full-blown Tea Party member was a bit ridiculous to me. Most of them discriminated against people who didn't look exactly like them. Considering my financial situation, it would probably make sense for me to be a Republican, but I wouldn't be able to sleep at night. But I digress. If most of his friends were like Sydney, then I was in for one hell of a night.

We arrived at Bacchanalia on Howell Mill Road at about seven thirty that evening. I wore an elegant African Ankara-print one-shoulder dress, matching red bottoms, and silver accessories, and my dreads were up in a bun, with two chopsticks securing it. My makeup was minimal, just the way I liked it. I was the perfect arm candy for Robert in his tailored black Ralph Lauren suit. When we got to the table, Sydney, his wife, Christina, and the two other couples there fell silent. The way they gawked at me made me feel like I had two heads or a third breast. Maybe I didn't look like the traditional housewife they were accustomed to seeing.

Robert pulled out my chair for me. "Everyone," he announced, "this is my better half, Rashida Haughton."

"Hello," I greeted, and they all responded kindly.

Robert introduced them all to me.

Mrs. Katherine Gates was a slightly overweight white woman who looked like she was in her sixties. The way she stared at me made me feel odd, like I didn't belong in their circle.

"Rashida," she sang. "What an exotic name. What does it mean?"

I stared at her for a second, not sure if she was being sarcastic or was really that ignorant. The name Rashida was by no means rare or exotic. She knew she meant *ethnic*, but she didn't have the guts to say that word.

"It's Muslim in origin. It means *conscious*."

She made a funny face. "Oh, that's interesting."

I could tell we were already off to a great start. Everybody's eyes were still on me, and it was clear they were studying and evaluating me. Obviously, I was the youngest one at the table, so I guessed they were thinking I wasn't on their level. Or maybe they wanted to know what Robert saw in me, other than my wide hips, fat ass, and perky breasts. We ordered drinks, and they began to talk about their work at Clark and whatnot. I obviously knew very little about what they did, so I kept quiet and sipped my Chateau d'Yquem.

Before long I caught Sydney looking me up and down. "Well, that's certainly a very . . . festive dress you have on tonight."

I smiled. "I love representing my culture. There's something very liberating about doing it."

He chuckled. "Liberating? I wasn't aware we were still in bondage. You know, land of the free, home of the brave, and all those liberties our founding fathers gave us."

I sipped my wine. "They gave us liberties while they were still slave owners? Interesting. But to your point, I meant more of a mental freedom, because some of us are still afraid to embrace our culture."

Sydney glared at me after that rebuttal. I had anticipated his condescending repartee tonight, but he wasn't ready for me. He was clearly in his feelings now, and I enjoyed seeing the look of frustration on his face. Disdain was prevalent in the eyes of Robert's other colleagues, and I could care less.

One of his counterparts, Phillip, looked at me. "So, Rashida, how did you meet Robert?"

"Funny story. I was—"

"We met in Starbucks," Robert interjected.

I glanced at him and nodded. So he didn't want his friends to know he had hooked up with a former student. I guessed that was a bit uncouth for this crowd.

"Yeah, we just happened to run into each other in Starbucks, and we just clicked," I added.

"I went in for a latte and came out with mocha," Robert joked.

I smiled. "Yeah, that's me . . . mocha." I felt so damn uncomfortable.

"What do you do for a living, Rashida?" Philip asked, continuing with his interrogation.

"I'm a cosmetologist."

Katherine spoke up. "So you're into hair?"

"Yes, I am. I specialize in braiding and natural hair care."

She smirked. "Oh, it must be for your type of hair, right?"

I glared at her. "My type of hair? Black hair? Yes, I do that, along with all kinds of differently textured hair."

She gave me a patronizing smile. "How nice. I just find it so fascinating the way you twist up your hair like that."

"Uh . . . thanks."

"Can I touch it?" She reached for my head.

I pulled back. "No . . . thank you."

"Which establishment do you work at?" Phillip quizzed.

"None. I will be opening my own shop in a few months."

Phillip nodded. "Ah, a small business owner. We can certainly use more people like that. So I take it Robert would be your business partner?"

Robert shook his head. "No, this is all Rashida's enterprise."

"So are you looking for investors?" Philip asked.

I took a sip of my wine. "No, I'm financing this myself."

Katherine had a surprised look on her face. "Yourself? How can a young lady like you afford such a venture?"

I had had just enough of Mrs. Gates's condescending tone. How the hell did she get off asking me about my finances? Did I ask her where she got the god-awful aqua-green dress she was wearing, or why she had all that red blush caked on her pale face? No, I didn't, because I wasn't a fucking bigot.

"I manage just fine, Mrs. Gates. No need to worry yourself about how I do."

Robert glared at me, and I glared right back at him. Then I gave him the *I wish you would* stare. I was annoyed that he wasn't doing anything to check this bitch. That was when Uncle Tom Sydney decided to put my business out there.

"Katherine, Rashida inherited a large sum of money when her parents passed away. She's what they call hood rich."

I glared at his ass. "Sydney, the next time you feel the need to share my personal information with strangers, do me a favor and don't. It's tacky."

He chortled. "You're way too sensitive, Rashida."

"And you're way too much of a jackass," I retorted. "And if anybody else got any questions about me, please do yourself a favor and save your breath. The little ghetto black girl is done for the night."

Robert frowned at me. "Rashida!"

I glared at him. "What!"

Robert knew I was dead serious. He had two options. Option one, try me and I would act a fool up in here in front of his friends, or option two, leave me alone. He wisely chose option two, because I was done answering questions from the peanut gallery. For the rest of the night, no one said anything else to me.

We left the restaurant an hour later. Robert was upset with me, and we drove home in silence. He would barely look at me, which was fine by me, because I didn't want to talk to him, either. But once we got home, it was on. Robert headed straight for the minibar and fixed himself a drink. I went to my bedroom to undress. He followed me and stood in the middle of the bedroom, watching me as I hung up my clothes in the walk-in closet.

"Did you really have to insult my friends like that? It was really immature of you," he snapped.

I glowered at him. "Are you kidding me? Your friends were insulting me from the moment I sat down! Like, wow, look at the little black ghetto girl. Let's find out everything about her because she couldn't possibly be intelligent enough to be here with us."

He shook his head. "You're overreacting."

"And you"—I pointed at him—"should've had my back."

"You were doing just fine until you insulted the entire table!"

"That bitch wanted to touch my hair! What kind of shit is that to ask?"

He walked toward me. "That didn't warrant your rudeness, 'Shida. For god's sake, I got to work with these people!"

I stepped out of the closet. "I know that. That's why I held back. And don't think I have forgotten about the whole 'We met in Starbucks' shit. What's the matter? You're too embarrassed to tell folks you're sleeping with a former student?"

He exhaled. "I don't tell folks about that, because I don't want them to get the wrong idea. It's for your benefit as well."

"Well, thank you for small favors. Excuse me." I stomped by him and got into bed.

"I'm nice to your friends, even the ones who don't like me."

I rolled my eyes and crawled underneath the covers. "Difference being, they don't try to be condescending and insult you in your face."

"Well, it's nice to know they tolerate me, and for the record, I don't care what they think of me. I'm in a relationship with you, not them."

"Well, if I'm your woman, then you need to act like it, and not just introduce me as your better half. Good night!"

Robert had really let me down. I rolled over and pulled the covers up to my chin. I was done arguing about this nonsense and wanted to fall asleep.

In the middle of the night, I felt Robert get into bed with me. As usual, he spooned behind me. Even as annoyed as I was at him, I didn't mind him doing that. I slept better with him next to me. A few minutes later I could feel his erection on my ass, which was typical as well, but when I felt his fingers trying to get inside me, I stopped the party.

"What are you doing?" I barked.

He exhaled. "What do you think?"

"It's not happening tonight."

"Really, babe, c'mon. I'm horny as hell over here."

"That's not my problem." I shrugged him off me.

"Fine!" He rolled over.

I couldn't believe the nerve of his ass. I was not in the mood to get pounded on tonight, after being disrespected by his *friends*. It wasn't my job to cater to his sexual whims whenever he wanted.

Tonight we'd had our first major argument. It made me really think twice about where this relationship was going.

Chapter Nine

Matrimony

JOYCE

"So I had to sit there and get interrogated about my hair, my finances, and anything else that fell out of their mouths," Rashida told me as she braided my hair.

I had asked her to come over and put my hair in box braids. I was bored with my look and wanted to switch it up a bit. I was sure Alonzo wouldn't mind it at all.

"Well, you're a better person than me, because I would've cussed all of them out. You said one of them tried to touch your hair? I woulda dropped that bitch!"

She laughed. "I was ready to, but then that ass Sydney put my business out there, talking about my money like that was the only reason I'm able to open my own business. Like I didn't earn my degree in business. But the part that bugged me the most was the way Robert didn't have my back at all during the entire dinner. He was more upset about *my rudeness* than them coming at me any kind of way. Like, seriously, I'm supposed to be your lady, so you should defend me little."

"Wow. I can't believe he did that. Alonzo would never let anybody disrespect me like that."

"Well, I'm glad he's got your back."

I smirked. "Well, you know, not too long ago, I was asking Alonzo if we should hook you up with his boy Sean."

"What? No! I mean, he's cute and everything, but he's not what I'm looking for. I'm actually shocked to see Denise with him."

"I know! Denise is the last person I ever thought would be with him, but they're certainly booed up. One of the reasons Alonzo said we shouldn't hook y'all up was that Sean, in his words, is a sex-crazed bloodhound with no empathy for human life."

"Damn, and he's with Denise, huh?"

"Yeah . . . she seems so happy with him, so I didn't want to throw salt. I mean, I've never seen her into a guy like this."

"Sean must be turning poor Denise out!"

We laughed.

Then I got serious and changed the subject. "So, uh, I'm thinking I want to introduce Alonzo to my folks."

Rashida was quiet for a moment. Then she said, "Really? You guys are really clicking, huh?"

"'Shida, I really feel like he could be the one."

"Okay."

"*Okay*? That's it? I just told you I think Alonzo could be the one, and all you can say is okay?"

"Joyce . . . I just don't want you to move too fast. Are you sure Alonzo is on the same page? Have you two talked seriously about marriage?"

I thought for a second. "Not seriously like we're making plans, but it's come up a few times."

"Okay."

She was beginning to annoy me. "There's that okay again."

"I'm just saying be careful."

I knew Rashida meant only the best. However, I really wished she was more excited about what I had told her. But maybe she was too caught up in her own drama to be truly happy for me. Alonzo was an amazing man, and Robert was no comparison. Our relationship was moving in a totally different direction than theirs. There was just something different about this relationship, something that I hadn't felt in a long time.

We may not have formally talked about marriage, but I knew that was where we were heading. I mean, what was the point of dating if it was not going to lead to matrimony? I was a twenty-five-year-old college gradu-ate, with a great job as a real estate agent. I was selling luxury homes and making good money. The only thing I needed was a husband to share my life with. I wasn't one of those women who were desperate to get married, but I came from a two-parent home and knew that was what I wanted in life. I was not in a rush, but with a man like Alonzo, it was hard not to envision that future.

That night Alonzo took me to SkyView Atlanta to ride the Ferris wheel. It was my first time on it, and to be honest, I was a little afraid of heights, so I stayed glued to him the whole time. I had to admit, the views of the city at night from atop the Ferris wheel were breathtaking. I wouldn't want to be anywhere at this moment but here with him, I thought.

"Thank you for doing this for me." I rested my head on his shoulder.

He kissed my forehead. "It's what you deserve."

"This should be our thing to do even after we get mar-ried."

After I threw that out there, Alonzo remained quiet. It was an awkward quiet, so thick it was sucking the air out of the gondola we were riding in.

"Alonzo?"

"Yeah?"

"Why does it feel like the mood just got killed in here?"

"No, it didn't."

"So why did you get all quiet after I mentioned marriage?"

"I did? I'm sorry. I didn't realize I did."

I lifted my head off his shoulder and looked at him. "Did I freak you out when I brought up marriage?"

He exhaled. "Maybe just a little. My brain isn't thinking that far ahead yet. Sorry. I didn't mean to upset you."

"You didn't. I was just saying, I like doing this with you."

He looked at me. "Me too. Listen, Joyce, I'm not saying I don't want to get married someday. I'm just saying I haven't given it much thought lately. Marriage is a big, life-changing step."

"I know. I'm not trying to rush you into anything, but that's where I'm hoping we get to."

"I do too. Joyce, you're an incredible woman. I don't plan on letting you out of my life anytime soon."

He kissed me. It was a reassuring kiss. I knew it took men a lot longer to come around to the idea of marriage than it did us women, so I was not going to press the issue. Sometimes it was hard to tell what he was thinking. I wondered if his parents had something to do with why he was not sure about marriage. He rarely spoke about them. Maybe something that happened in the past was clouding his judgment. But I had no doubt that he loved me, and in time, I knew he'd be ready to take the next step.

Chapter Ten

One in a Million

ALONZO

"So what's been going on with you, bruh?" I asked Sean.

We were at the bar at J.R. Crickets, grabbing some lunch. Sean had been spending a lot of time with Denise these past couple of months. Totally out of character for him.

"What you mean?"

"You know what I mean. You and Denise."

He grinned. "Oh, you mean that."

"Yeah, that!"

"It's all good with us. She's special, man."

"I see that! I'm happy for you, man. I don't think I've ever seen you like this with a woman."

"Thanks, man. Denise is one of a kind."

I nodded. "Nice. So she's cool with everything?"

"Yeah."

I stared at him for a second. I was expecting him to give me more of an answer than that. He knew exactly what I was asking about.

"Sean, you did tell her? Right?"

"Zo, everything is good between us right now. I'll tell her when the time is right."

I shook my head. "I can't believe you, man. You shoulda told Denise everything up front. C'mon, bruh. You gotta move better than this."

"Trust me, Zo, Denise will know everything in due time. Just keep it to yourself."

"Now, you know better. When have I ever let it slip?"

He smiled. "I know, I know. I'll handle it."

"Just do it sooner than later, because the longer you wait, the worse it's going to be for you and her."

He nodded. "I hear ya."

I knew he heard me, but was he listening to me? That was two different things. I'd known Sean for most of his life, and I knew him better than he knew himself. I knew Sean would wait until he had no choice before he told Denise everything. My only concern was the fact that Joyce and Denise were such good friends, and I didn't want that crap to hit the fan and blow back in my face. This was typical Sean, never considering how his actions might affect those around him. Regardless, I loved him like a brother, so I hoped he'd do the right thing with Denise.

We hung out for a few more minutes before he had to leave. Once I was alone, I got a table and ordered some wings. As I was waiting for my order to come out, I saw her face come through the doors. *Beautiful.* That was the only word I could use to describe Rashida. She was dressed casually in dark blue jeans, gray Converse, and a gray top that hung off one shoulder, with the words CAKE BY THE POUND printed across it. Her curvy five-foot, four-inch frame demanded the attention of every man in the restaurant.

She spotted me sitting at my table, smiled, and headed my way. We had become good friends over the past few months, both of us respecting the invisible boundaries of that friendship, ignoring the love we had made. It was hard to pretend like it had never happened. Regardless, I didn't think either of us could deny the underlying attraction we both felt for one another.

She stood next to my table. "Hey, Alonzo. What's up?"

"Hey. It's good to see you." I got up and greeted her with a hug. "I'm surprised to see you on this side of town."

"I had some errands to run out here for the salon. I love the wings, so I try to get some whenever I'm out this way."

"Are you meeting someone?"

"Nope."

I gestured to the empty chair in front of her. "Have a seat."

She sat down, and the waitress made her way back to our table and took her order. Twenty honey barbecue wings. It was hard to believe a woman with a figure like that could devour so many wings in one sitting. She was no joke when it came to her food.

"Where do you plan on putting all them wings?" I asked, smiling at her.

She grinned. "In my belly."

"You must be on one hell of a workout plan."

"I need to get back on it. I used to hit the gym every afternoon, but after I get done with all this running around, I'm exhausted. My head hits the pillow, and I'm done."

"Joyce was telling me about that. How's it going?"

"I'm making progress. The renovations are almost done, and 'Shidas Styles should be ready for business by November."

"Shidas Styles? I like that."

"Thank you," she said.

"I got a feeling it's gonna be a very successful business for you."

"I'm glad you feel so."

"Why wouldn't it be? I've seen your work. You got skills!"

She smiled, but I could tell there was a hint of sadness behind that smile.

"What's wrong?" I asked.

"Nothing. Why?"

"There's something else on your mind. Something keeping you from being happy about all this good shit that's about to happen."

She exhaled. "I just wish everybody in my life was as supportive as you."

The waitress returned with both our orders, placed them on the table, then left.

"Who's not supporting you?"

"I shouldn't have said that. It's not that he's not supportive. I just wish he was there for me a little more," she confessed.

"Robert."

She nodded. "I know he's got a lot going on at his job, but it's a little intimidating looking over all these contracts, going to these meetings, and dealing with contractors by myself."

"Hey, you don't have to do it all by yourself. I've dealt with my fair share of contractors over the years, so if you need somebody in your corner, just call me."

She shook her head. "I don't want to inconvenience you with my business."

I reached across the table and took her hand. "Hey, it's not an inconvenience. Just let me know how I can help."

She nodded.

Instantly, I felt an uncontrollable erection in my pants as thoughts of her naked body in my arms flooded my mind. My eyes caught hers, and it felt like electricity between us. There it was again, that damn chemistry. It was hard to ignore it. I slowly let go of her hand. We sat in silence for a minute and ate our wings.

Rashida broke the silence about a minute later. "So how are things between you and Joyce?"

"As if you had to ask. She's your best friend, so you probably know more about my relationship than I do."

She laughed. "We don't talk that much about you. Besides, I'd like to hear things from your point of view."

I wondered how much I should tell her. What did she already know? Talking to the best friend was almost like talking to the enemy. Although I didn't get that vibe from Rashida. In fact, I felt at ease talking to her.

"Everything is good," I said.

She grinned. "Now, why do I feel like there's something else on your mind when you say that?"

I shook my head. "Nothing major, but I do feel like Joyce is ready to take things to the next level."

"The next level, huh?"

"Yeah. I'm not sure I'm ready for that."

"Oh. So what do you think is holding you back?"

"It has nothing to do with Joyce. She's great. It's just my own issue with it."

"Afraid to commit?"

"No . . . I've just seen what marriage can do to people. My mother and father were married twice. Both were miserable. I've seen it all go down. Abuse, infidelity, financial hardship, and more. You put two people together who aren't really in love with each other in the first place and throw a kid in there, and it's a recipe for disaster. I'm not sure I'm ready to walk down that road yet, and I'd hate to put somebody else through it."

Rashida sat for a moment with my words. I wasn't not sure why I had said all that, especially since I hadn't even shared all that with Joyce. I was not sure what Rashida would think of me now.

"I can't say I know exactly how you feel, but I understand your reasons. Maybe in time that will change."

"Yeah, maybe. I hope I didn't just shoot myself in the foot here," I replied.

She looked at me strangely. "What do you mean?"

"You know, Joyce is your girl. I know you talk."

"Alonzo, this right here is between us. I know how hard it was for you to open up to me about this. I wouldn't betray your confidence like that." She looked intently at me, and I believed every word she'd said. She was an amazing woman.

"Thank you."

"No worries. I know how your parents can change your life forever."

"The way your parents changed yours?" I asked.

"Yeah."

"Joyce told me a little bit about what happened to them."

"I still miss them, and I know my brother, Raheem, does too. He was so young when they died. Sometimes I think he was the lucky one."

"You both lost them, and both of you had to mourn. Nothing lucky about that."

"Yeah, but I was fourteen and have more memories. Raheem barely had time with them." I could see the sadness in her eyes. "They've been gone for so long, and I still miss them."

"I understand, and it's okay. You're human."

She smiled.

"And by the way, it wasn't hard," I added.

She squinted her eyes at me. "What wasn't hard?"

"Opening up to you. It was pretty easy."

She smiled once more.

There it was again. Whatever pheromones were in the air had us both feeling some type of way again, forcing us to eat in silence. It wasn't awkward, just a reflection of what could have been if circumstances were different. After we finished our meal, we chatted about unimportant topics and ended our lunch with a hug. We stepped outside, and I watched as she walked to her car. Rashida was definitely one in a million.

Chapter Eleven

Anytime, Anyplace

DENISE

A wall against my face, my skirt around my waist, I felt my fire grow into a raging inferno. I was panting and babbling incoherently as Sean took me from behind. I used my hands to brace myself as I stood with my legs apart, my panties pulled to the side, his hardness pushing deeper inside me. Each thrust he sent into my sex made me feel a sweet sensation of pleasure and pain through my body. I loved it, needed it, and demanded it. I couldn't believe he had got me open like this.

Here we were on a proper dinner date at Tasty China, and all I had done after sitting down was think about fucking him. I'd seen it in his eyes that he wanted me too. So I'd got up from the table and gone to the ladies' room, and he'd followed me. I never would do something like this with any other man, but I couldn't help giving in to anything Sean wanted. I was vulnerable, exposed, out of control, and about to cum. We weren't even in a stall, but in a corner on the far side of the restroom. At any moment the door might open. We would be exposed, but I didn't care. All that mattered was this moment.

I felt his lips on my neck. His breathing was ragged. Sean was working me hard, making sure I felt every long stroke, as if it would be his last before he arrived at the point of no return. But I got there first. I came. My ocean exploded all over his penis. My throbbing clit was on fire. All five of my senses were overstimulated. Moans of gratification left my lips. My legs went weak, but Sean kept me balanced while he stroked me until he lost control and emptied himself. I felt his weight pressing up behind me, and then I felt his seeds trickle down my inner thighs. We stayed in that position, allowing our orgasms to subside, before we broke our connection.

We quickly put ourselves back together, paid the bill, and left the restaurant. A wicked grin was on my face as I sat on the passenger side of his Tahoe, staring at him. The window was down, and a cool summer night's breeze caressed my skin. I could still feel him inside me.

He glanced over at me. "Whatcha looking at?"

"You. I ain't never done anything like that before."

He smiled. "Really?"

"You're making me act so out of character."

"Do you like it?" he asked.

"I shouldn't, but I do. I like everything you do to me. I will definitely be adding this to my book."

He looked at me. "You're writing a book about it?"

"I've been writing a manuscript for a few years now," I revealed.

"Wow. I didn't know you wrote."

"Not too many people do. I just write what inspires me."

He ran his right hand up my bare thigh. "Good, because I plan on inspiring the shit outta you."

Opening my legs farther, I let him touch what was already throbbing. My wetness returned, and I was ready to give in to him again. How could one man make me act like such a freak? I was used to taking my time with men, being guarded and leery of their true intentions, but not with Sean. He had slid right past all my defenses and inside me. He adored me, and I him.

A couple of days later I was with Rashida shopping at Stonecrest Mall. It was the first time we had hung out in a few weeks. Most of my time had been spent working at Emory and being with Sean. She had been busy working on opening her salon. I was so proud of her.

"Hey, let's go in here for a second," I said.

Rashida stared at me. We were standing in front of Victoria's Secret. "When have you ever wanted to go in here?"

"I just wanna look at something."

I walked into the store, and she followed me. I started looking at all the different styles of lingerie. This was a new world for me. I'd never bought lingerie in my life. I'd never seen the point of it . . . until now. Before Sean, having matching bras and panties was the height of sexiness for me. But now I just wanted to give Sean something special to look at.

Out of the corner of my eye, I saw that Rashida was still staring at me like I had grown a second head. I glanced over at her with a smile on my face. "What?"

"Sean has done a number on you. I've known you for over a decade, and I've never seen you trying to be sexy for a guy."

"Well, Sean's different."

"I see that! I'm glad to see you are happy with a man for a change."

"As opposed to what!"

She shot back, "Being moody as hell!"

I laughed. "I wasn't that bad."

"Yes you were. For a second there, I thought you were gonna switch teams."

"Oh, be quiet! You know the type of men I've dealt with in the past. A bunch of jerks and losers." I looked at her. "Have you ever met a man and felt almost instant chemistry with him? I'm sure you felt the same way with Robert."

She smiled. "Something like that."

"Sean is the first man who has ever made me feel this way."

"Well, I'm happy for you."

I ended up buying two outfits: a black teddy and a sheer white bra and panty set. I thought Sean was going to be a very happy man tonight. I knew I would be happy. I was feeling good, happy with myself, but the next thing I knew, I felt light headed. Suddenly I lost my balance, and the floor came rushing toward me. When my eyes open, I saw a few people standing over me. I recognized Rashida but not the two guys in white uniforms.

"Denise! Are you okay?" Rashida asked me, a frantic expression on her face.

"Yeah . . . I think so. What happened?"

"Ma'am, how do you feel?" a uniformed man asked.

"A little woozy."

"Do you need an ambulance?" he asked.

"An ambulance? I don't think so." I glanced around and saw that a small crowd was now gathered around us. "What happened?"

Rashida took my hand. "We were walking, and all of a sudden, you passed out. Did you eat this morning?"

"Yeah," I replied. "I think I'm fine now. Really." But then I felt another wave of dizziness.

Rashida frowned. "No you're not. We're going to the hospital."

A little less than an hour later, we were at Emory University Hospital, where I worked. I had refused an ambulance and had had Rashida drive me there. Honestly, by the time I got there, I was feeling better, but I had to admit I was a little concerned about fainting. That had never happened to me before. As I lay on a bed in the emergency room, the lab tech drew my blood and ran other tests the doctor had ordered. Once the tech was finished, I closed my eyes and waited for the results. About twenty minutes later, my doctor appeared and gave me some news that would change my life.

After I was discharged, I walked out into the waiting area and saw Rashida playing on her phone. As I walked toward her, she spotted me and stood up. A million thoughts were running through my mind.

"So what happened? Are you okay?"

"Yeah, I'm fine."

"Low blood sugar?"

"No, not that." I stared at her in disbelief, then smiled. "I'm pregnant."

Rashida's eyes widened. "Oh my God!"

"I'm going to be a mother."

Rashida hugged me. "Denise! I can't believe it!"

"Me either."

"Are you ready to do this? Are you okay?"

"Yes, I am. I have always wanted kids, but I wasn't planning on it happening anytime soon. But that's okay."

"How do you think Sean is going to take this?"

"I don't know, but he loves me, and I love him. It's not how I envisioned this happening, but I think we'll be okay."

Rashida hugged me again.

I was going to have a baby with the man I loved. What could possibly go wrong with that?

Chapter Twelve

Better You Than Me

TAYLOR

Can I stop by?

Hell no. Delete, I said silently to myself.

Go in the bathroom and take a pic. Let's see if you have on some sexy panties.

Well, of course I do, but you'll never see them, I thought. *Delete.*

Them panties all up in that ass, and that's what excites people.

I bet it does. I bet you got a bottle of lotion and napkins already in hand, ready to release all that excitement. Have fun rubbing one out. Geez.

I had posted one picture on my Instagram, and every guy I had ever given my number to had started blowing me up. Hilarious! Granted, it was me in a bikini for a photo shoot for *50-50 Magazine*. I had got over three thousand "likes" in an hour. Not bad. As I was deleting messages, I got a call from Rashida.

She was calling to tell me to go over to Denise's apartment and informed me that she'd urged Joyce to do the same. When I asked what it was all about, Rashida wouldn't say, but she insisted it was important. In my head, I already knew what it was about. That silly girl had probably got engaged to Sean and wanted to include us in their moment. I knew Denise thought I was jealous of her and Sean, and she probably wanted to rub my nose in it.

Whatever. He was cute and all, but I ain't trying to be with him! I could tell the moment I met him he was a playa. He was all up on me at the cookout, and he was damn sure trying to hook up. He kept on telling me that he was a rapper and was about to blow up. Then he *invited* me back to his studio to listen to some of his music. And, of course, he asked me if I could sing, because I got the look that could go far in the industry. Lines I'd heard a thousand times before. Translation: "Let's go back to my studio, let me sell you the dream, and then you spread your legs for a deal." I ain't one for that type of game, especially if there ain't no money up front. I turned down his offer but told him to hit me up on Instagram.

I didn't always say it, but Denise was a sexy girl. If only she would come out of her shell and dress like she was twenty-four instead of fifty-four, she could have more fun. Sean must've hooked up with Denise because she was an easy target. Poor thing must've gotten dicked down real good by that pimp, but to get engaged just because he got some good dick? That was ridiculous!

Of course, I was in no rush to get over there. I arrived about an hour and a half later than I had said I would. Rashida opened the door after I knocked, and shook her head.

"Nice of you to get here so promptly."

I hugged her. "Traffic."

"Yeah, right."

I went inside and saw Joyce sitting on the couch with Denise. She had the biggest smile on her face. It was weird seeing Denise happy like this. I bet I was right about her and Sean getting engaged.

When she caught sight of me, Denise smiled at me. "Hey, Taylor."

I was a bit apprehensive about her friendliness. "Hey, Denise," I said as I walked into the living room, Rashida on my heels.

"Took you long enough to get here," Joyce snapped.

"Yeah, yeah, yeah, whatever. So what's the big announcement?"

"I don't know, because we've been waiting on you to get here," Joyce replied.

"Well, the wait is over." I flopped down into the recliner. "I'm here now."

Rashida sat down on the other side of Denise.

"Well . . ." Denise cleared her throat. "Um, you all know Sean and I are together."

"Uh-huh," I replied dryly.

"Well, everything just kinda happened so fast," Denise went on.

"Spit it out, girl," Joyce said impatiently.

Denise smiled. "I'm going to be a mother."

My jaw dropped. "What?"

"You're pregnant?" Joyce asked in shock.

Denise shook her head. "Yes, I am."

I stared at her in disbelief. Well, I'll be dipped in shit! Wallflower done gone and got herself knocked up by a playa. I didn't know little Miss Goody Two-shoes had that inner freak in her, ready to pop out. She looked so happy about it. Sadly, she had no idea what kinda baby daddy she done went and got. Soon she would. I felt sorry for her.

I smiled. "Congrats."

"Thank you, Taylor."

I could tell by the look on Joyce's face that she knew more about Sean than Denise did. I guessed Alonzo had already given her a heads-up on the type of playa he was.

"What has Sean said about this?" she asked hesitantly.

"I haven't told him yet, Joyce. I wanted you all to know first."

Joyce nodded. "Oh, okay."

Denise looked intently at Joyce. "Please don't tell Alonzo yet. I wanna be the one to tell Sean."

"No problem."

Denise could sense Joyce's uneasiness. "I know what you're thinking, Joyce, and it's okay. I know Sean and I haven't been together long, but trust me, he's gonna be here for us."

"Okay." Joyce exhaled. "How far along are you?"

"Don't know. I need to make an appointment with my ob-gyn."

Joyce touched Denise's stomach. "I can't believe it."

"Just know that we are all going to be here for you and the baby, Denise," Rashida assured her.

Denise smiled, then looked over at me. I wasn't going to be the one to tell her that her baby daddy to be was a ho.

"Just call me Auntie Taylor," I said. I got up, went over to her, and gave her a hug.

"Thank you!" she exclaimed.

The rest of the night was filled with baby talk. Despite our many differences, I was pretty happy for Denise and was looking forward to meeting the new addition to the crew. It wasn't the baby's fault that his or her daddy was a ho. I kept thinking, *Well, Denise you wanted Sean, and now you got him for the next eighteen years. Better you than me.*

After the three of us left Denise's place, we walked over to Joyce's apartment. The mood was pretty somber; there was no fake excitement among us. We went inside and made ourselves comfortable in the living room. Joyce went to the fridge and got a couple of Cokes for us. I could tell we all had the same thing on our minds.

I cut to the chase once Joyce had passed out the Cokes and taken a seat on the recliner. "So, am I going to be the first one to say it? 'Cause I know all of us are thinking it."

Rashida sighed. "Say what, Taylor?"

"What a major mistake Denise is making having Sean's baby."

"We don't know that for sure," Rashida objected. "Let's give Sean a chance to step up first before we judge him."

I laughed. "Oh, c'mon, 'Shida. We all know Sean's a dog, and only the Lord knows if he makes a hit record, he's gonna have a whole team of hoes across the country! Even Joyce knows it. That's why she's so quiet."

Joyce piped up. "Taylor, Rashida is right. We have to give Sean the benefit of the doubt. We don't know what he'll do."

I took a sip of my Coke. "Shit! The hell we don't! We're supposed to be her friends, right? So shouldn't we tell her what's up?"

"Tell her what? What *might* be? She's happy right now, so there is no need to stress her out this early in her pregnancy." Rashida looked at us. "We're her friends, and it's our job to be there for her as much as we can, and that's what we're going to do."

I shrugged my shoulders. "If you say so."

All I knew was that Denise was lucky to have a friend like Rashida in her corner. If Sean didn't step up and take care of his child, I knew Rashida would make sure that baby wanted for nothing. That was why we all loved her.

Chapter Thirteen

Closer

RASHIDA

"So, I hope you're as focused on class as you are on them Cali girls," I said into the phone.

Raheem laughed. "What are you talking about, sis?"

"Don't play dumb. I see your IG and Twitter page. Lord knows how many DMs you're *sliding* into."

He broke into laughter again. Raheem had called me as I was en route to the shop in Camp Creek. Even though I had no real idea what my brother was getting into, I had a feeling he was running through girls left and right. Raheem was a handsome devil: six feet three, with big brown eyes and a charming smile. I knew girls were all over him.

He laughed. "I promise you it ain't like that."

"Yeah, right." I chuckled. "Nice of you to call me, though."

"I gotta check up on you every now and then. You're all I got."

I knew he meant that. Even though we had lived with our grandmother after our parents died, I was the one he had always relied upon the most.

Raheem was now a sophomore at UCLA and was majoring in theater. I had hoped he would go to school here in Atlanta, but I could understand him wanting to get out of the state and see something different.

"I always got you," I told him.

"I know. Well, I gotta get going, sis. I got rehearsal for this indie film."

"Big part?"

"Supporting. It's a love scene, so you know I gotta go all in!"

We both laughed, and I shook my head. "I bet you will. Bye, Raheem."

"Bye, sis." He ended the call.

It was good hearing from him. It let me know he was on the right track. I wished I could say the same for Denise. I knew she was excited about having Sean's baby, but whether it was the best thing for her was still up for debate. I hadn't wanted to feed into Taylor's negativity, but she did have a point. I just hoped Sean would step up and be a man.

My own relationship with Robert was in a weird space right now. Ever since our fight a month ago, we'd been distant from each other. Of course, we talked, but we hadn't exchanged anything more intimate than a kiss. Robert was spending more time at his condo, and I was focused on getting Shidas Styles off the ground. I did miss him. I missed his sex. I needed to have an orgasm, like, yesterday, and pleasuring myself wasn't cutting it. I was just going to invite him over and get some. Maybe that would help get us back on the right track.

It didn't help that I was spending more time with Alonzo. Even though Joyce knew he was helping me get things ready at the shop, I still wanted him here for my own selfish reasons. Today he was laying down plywood flooring. I walked inside and saw him working; he was on his knees, his back facing me, shirtless. I stood in the doorway watching him. Alonzo wasn't a bodybuilder, but he was certainly cut. Little beads of sweat trickled down the coffee-brown skin of his back. My mind drifted to naughty places, to where I knew it shouldn't be going. Memories I had forbidden myself from reliving forced their way back into my mind, and my body responded. I felt moistness between my legs and swallowed hard, trying to fight the feeling that was starting to consume me. At that very moment, he glanced back, as if sensing I was there. I smiled.

"Hey, Shida." He put his tools down, stood up, and walked toward me with a smile on his face.

"Hi!" Our eyes locked, trapping us in the moment. "I see things are coming along."

"Yeah, like I said, this is easy. I should be done by Friday."

"That's great!" I glanced at his sexy bare chest, and more lustful thoughts penetrated my mind. "I'm so glad you're able to help me."

"I told you it's no problem. Friends help friends, right?"

"Right." I paused. "You look hot." It took all my will-power to walk away from him, but I headed over to his cooler, grabbed a bottle of water, and tossed it to him.

"Thanks."

He unscrewed the top, put the bottle to his lips, and drained it in three big gulps. I grabbed an ice cube for myself from the cooler and rubbed my neck with it, although that was not the spot that was hot. Did he know how he was making me feel? Was he feeling the same way I did? Of course, I was asking questions I already knew the answers to. We both knew how the other felt, but out of respect for Joyce, we pretended like our feelings didn't exist.

He looked me up and down. "You look nice."

I was wearing a formfitting white pantsuit that showed enough cleavage to make a man wonder. It was sexy but professional. "Oh, thanks. I got a meeting I'm heading to in a few minutes."

He nodded. "I see. I thought for a second Olivia Pope had walked in here."

"Ha, ha, ha, very funny. When I saw you half-naked and on your knees, I thought you were auditioning for the next *Magic Mike* movie."

He smiled. "Hmmm. So you think I could make it as a male stripper?"

I exhaled and looked him up and down. "Maybe . . . um, but you would have to work out some more. Tighten up that midsection."

He chuckled. "You lie! You ain't seeing this six-pack I got over here?"

"I must have missed it."

He headed toward me. "Oh, so you gonna play me like I don't go to the gym every day?" He stopped in front of me. "Feel this."

I shooed him away. "Boy, go on with that!"

"That's what I thought." He snickered and pointed his finger at his well-developed abs.

My eyes studied his sexy body, just inches from me. He was in my personal space, daring me to touch him. He knew exactly what he was doing. He was daring me to give in to temptation. If he thought I was going to back down, he didn't know me very well at all. I took my finger and poked his abs.

"Humph. Not bad." I shrugged.

"Oh, please! If you're going to judge me, then you better do it right." He took my hand and laid it flat on his stomach. He held it there, and I felt every ripple on his brawny abdomen. I looked up into his eyes, and he held my stare.

Skin to skin.

This was the first time we'd touched each other like this since *that* night. The first time we had allowed each other to be this close. I inhaled his masculine scent. Sweat and faded deodorant.

Heat.

I could feel the warmth of his body as I slowly caressed his smooth skin. This was more intimate than the first time we danced. This was wrong. We weren't pretending anymore. We were crossing a line.

I was so damn aroused. My hand drifted lower and halted just above his belt buckle. His hand was still on mine, but he wasn't forcing me to touch him, wasn't guiding me. Just allowing me to go farther, to all the places I wanted to go. I was on fire. I was afraid. All my morals were failing me. I was afraid of what I was going to let happen. My heartbeat was out of control. I wanted Alonzo to take me right now. I didn't care if it was wrong. I just wanted him.

Music.

It wasn't in our heads; it was my phone's ringtone interrupting our moment. It was reality barging in, uninvited. I pulled my hand away from his stomach, stepped back, and exhaled. Alonzo let out a sigh.

I pulled my phone out of my bag. It was Robert. His Spidey sense must have been warning him of danger. I answered the call.

"Hey, Robert. I'm at the shop."

Alonzo turned and walked back over to his tools.

"I have a meeting at four, and then I'm free," I told Robert.

We talked for a few more seconds before we ended our conversation. I looked over at Alonzo as he stood by the stack of plywood on the floor. Our moment of weakness had made things awkward. It was hard to go back to acting like nothing had happened.

"I have to get going," I told him.

"Yeah, okay. I'll see you later," he replied, his eyes lower. Then he glanced at me.

"Okay. Bye."

I turned and walked toward the door. I looked back at him, then left. We knew what we had done was wrong. I had been about to fuck my best friend's man, and I was ashamed of myself. What the hell had I been thinking? We both needed to reestablish our boundaries. The problem was I didn't know if I could go back to pretending.

After the meeting I drove over to Robert's place for dinner. We hadn't had a romantic dinner together in a while. As I drove, my mind kept flashing back to what had happened earlier with Alonzo. I had come so close to doing the unthinkable. I'd been so damn weak. Why was I so attracted to a man I knew I couldn't have? A man who was with my best friend, when I was already in a relationship? When I reached the condominium complex, I parked, then walked up to Robert's condo, used my key, and went inside.

He smiled when he saw me. "Hello."

"Hey." I strolled over to him and gave him a little kiss.

When I entered the dining room, I found lit candles on a table set for two. A Conya Doss song played in the background. Something in the air smelled good. It was a familiar scent, but I couldn't put my finger on what it was. Did he hire a cook? Robert had done his best to set the mood.

He escorted me to my chair and pulled it out for me. "I hope you have an appetite."

"You cooked?"

"Of course not," he laughed as he headed toward the kitchen, "but I did get your favorite."

Robert could grill his ass off, but he wasn't much of cook. He could barely boil hot-dog water. Unless he was eating my cooking, he was spending money on restaurant food. He returned with a tray of Chinese food from Gu's Dumplings in Krog Street Market. I smiled. He knew how much I loved the Spicy Crispy Beef and all the dumplings. He put a plate of beef and dumplings in front of me, and I salivated at the thought of devouring it all.

"You sure do know the way to a girl's heart."

He beamed at me. "I'm trying."

He went back to the kitchen and returned with a bottle of wine and poured me a glass. Once he sat down, we ate, but for the most part, we ate in silence. There was still a bit of awkwardness in the air. Not to mention my thoughts of Alonzo didn't make me very talkative. Robert decided to break the silence.

"Rashida, I know things have been a bit uneasy between us since the dinner."

"Yeah, I know." I nodded.

"I know we've put it behind us, but I want to apologize to you again. I should have stood up for you. I realize that now. It was foolish of me not to have intervened and stopped them. Especially Sydney."

I was shocked by his mea culpa. "Really?"

"Yes." He nodded. "I actually had a very serious talk with him, and trust me, you will never have to worry about that happening again."

"Thank you. You didn't have to, but I'm glad you did. I hope this doesn't make working with him difficult."

"Don't concern yourself with that. Business is business." He paused and looked at me. "I'm more concerned with us."

I placed my fork down. "You are?"

"Yes, I am, Rashida. I love you, and I don't want to lose you because I'm an idiot. I know I don't always show it, but I am proud of you and what you're doing."

I smiled. "I think that's the first time I've ever heard you say that to me."

"I told you I was an idiot. I should've said that to you ages ago. I've been so caught up in my own affairs that I've neglected you, and that's unacceptable. I want you to know whatever you need from me, I will be there for you."

I could tell by the look in his eyes that he was sincere. And now I felt so guilty about my feelings for Alonzo. Robert may have been thoughtless at times, but he did love me.

"Thank you, Robert. That means a lot to me."

"I mean it."

I exhaled. "I know. I wanna apologize to you too."

A confused look showed on his face. "What for?"

For being a trifling-ass girlfriend, I thought to myself. But instead, I said, "For being so distant from you. I purposely pushed you away far longer than I should have. I can be a bit vindictive when I wanna be. I . . . love you, Robert, and it's wrong to treat people you love the way I have been treating you."

Robert stood up from his seat, stepped toward me, and took my hand. "There's no need for you to be sorry. This was totally my fault."

I stood up and hugged him. Robert adored me, which made me feel worse. He kissed me with so much passion. It felt nice to be loved. Needless to say, it didn't take much for things to escalate into us making love. Weeks of pent-up sexual energy found a release. I pushed my thoughts of Alonzo to the side and focused on Robert. I decided it was in our best interest that I put some distance between Alonzo and myself. No need to tempt fate by being alone with him anymore.

He was just a fantasy, and there was no place for that in my reality.

Chapter Fourteen

Wish I Wasn't in Love with You

DENISE

It was hard to believe there was a little life growing inside me. I had always wanted to have kids someday; I just hadn't known it would be so soon. I had always figured I would meet someone down the road, fall in love, get married, and then it would happen. You know . . . the norm. I had never, ever seen myself being with a man like Sean, but here I was, pregnant with his child, and I was all right with that. I still hadn't told him about the pregnancy. We were going to see each other at my place tonight, so that would be the perfect time to share the news with him.

My thoughts flashed back to my girls and our little get-together. Taylor had been unusually quiet, but I hadn't expected anything more from her. Joyce's reaction had surprised me. I could tell that she wasn't too pleased with this all, but she didn't understand the bond Sean and I had. Just because things were moving slow with her and Alonzo didn't mean Sean and I were in the same boat. Sean had told me over and over that once his career took off, he wanted to buy a house for us. I knew that was big talk, but I believed he meant every word he'd said to me.

I had just made my first appointment with my doctor. With this being my first trimester, I had to be careful. So I went to CVS to pick up some prenatal vitamins and sundry items. When I returned home, I pulled into the parking space in front of my apartment and noticed a woman two spaces over standing next to a silver car. I didn't recognize her, so she must've been waiting for one of my neighbors. I gathered my things and got out of my car. I was heading to my apartment when I heard her shout.

"Hey you!"

I turned around and looked at her. "Are you talking to me?"

She rolled her eyes and looked me up and down. "Who else would I be talking to? Ain't nobody out here but us."

I folded my arms across my chest and glared at her. "What do you want?"

"You live there?" She pointed to my apartment.

"Yes. Who are you?"

"I'm Christy. I just wanted to make sure you were the chick my man's been cheating on me with!"

My jaw dropped. "What?"

She walked closer to me. "You heard me."

I shook my head. "You must have me confused with someone else. I already have a boyfriend."

"I know. Sean," she said frankly.

As soon as she said Sean's name, it felt as if I had been kicked in my chest. I stared blankly at the woman in front of me. I refused to believe this was happening to me. I shook my head once more. I knew Sean was a hot up-and-coming rapper, so there was bound to be other women trying to get with him who would say anything to break up what we had. Just looking at her, I knew she was that type. I knew I had given Taylor a hard time for some of the things she wore, but she didn't have anything on this chick. She was an attractive bronze-skinned girl but way too *extra*. Pink spandex cutoffs with a matching midriff and high heels. Hair weave all the way down to her ass. She looked like she was auditioning to be somebody's trap queen.

"No . . . no. You don't know Sean," I insisted.

Christy sucked her teeth. "Bitch, please, you the one that don't know Sean!"

I craned my neck and looked at her. "I don't believe you. I've been with Sean for months."

"And I've been with him for *years*! Has he ever invited you back to his place? I bet he tells you he lives in the studio, right?"

I wasn't buying what she was saying. I knew for a fact Sean shared a house with Alonzo. She was just trying to put doubts in my mind. I was not going to let this little stank whore fill my head with lies without my talking to Sean first.

"You don't know nothing about our relationship, and I'm not about to stand here and listen to your lies anymore!" I shouted.

"Damn, he must be really laying that pipe deep up in you, huh?" She chuckled. "I ain't gotta lie. You can ask him. Shit, ask him what bed he was sleeping in last night!"

Just as I was getting ready to cuss this whore out, we heard a car door shut. Christy whipped her head around and glared at the little girl who had closed her car door. She couldn't have been more than four years old.

"Who told you to get out of the car!"

In a tiny voice, the girl said, "I'm hot."

"Then roll down the window and get yo' ass back in the car!"

As I stared at the child, I recognized her face. It was the same as the one tattooed on Sean's arm. The one he had told me was his baby sister, who had passed away years ago. It was a lie. Everything was a lie.

"Oh my God," I gasped.

Christy turned back around to face me. A smirk spread across her face. "You didn't know, did you?"

I shook my head.

"Say hello to Sean's daughter, Draya."

I stared at the girl's little cute face through the car window. He'd been lying to me from the start. He had a child. I felt sick. I touched my stomach and thought about the baby that was growing inside me. I was going to become baby mama number two. I took a step backward. Christy stared at me and shook her head.

"Look, I can see this is all news to you. Don't waste your time fucking with Sean anymore. He's already got a family at home."

I took another step back, then turned and walked toward my apartment. I went inside, closed the door, dropped my bags on the floor, and stood there in a state of shock. Then, without warning, I burst into tears. Uncontrollable sobs consumed me, and tears rolled down my face. Everything I thought I knew about Sean was a lie, a fucking lie, and I had believed every damn word he'd said. I felt sick to my stomach. I ran into the bathroom and threw up in the toilet. I had let him in my life, in my home, and in my vagina like a fool, and now I was carrying his child. How could I have been so blind?

I sat in the dark at my kitchen table for hours, trying to figure out what I was going to do. It would be so easy to go down to the clinic and stop this right now. Why shouldn't I? Wasn't like I had planned to have a baby right now. My life was about to be changed forever. And did I want to be linked to Sean's lying ass for the rest of my life? But would I be able to live with myself if I did it? Even though it was early in my pregnancy, I already felt a bond to the fetus inside me. I'd imagined what he or she would look like, what my days with this baby would be like. Even though my common sense was screaming for me to get an abortion, every fiber of my being was attached to this child.

I heard a knock on my door, and gazed up at the clock on the wall. It read 8:23 p.m. I felt a wave of anger wash over me. I knew it was Sean at the door. I didn't move. I was far from a violent person, but I imagined what it would feel like to stab him over and over again. He knocked again, and it took all my willpower to get up, walk to the door, and open it.

He smiled at me. "Hey, babe, what took you so long?"

I glared at him and didn't answer.

His eyes studied my face. "Dee . . . have you been crying? What's wrong?"

I turned and walked back to the kitchen and had a seat at the table. Sean closed the front door and followed me.

"Denise, what's going on?" he asked as he stood in the kitchen doorway.

I stared at him, then said, "How long were you going to continue to lie to me?"

A confused expression covered his face. "What?"

"Were you just gonna lie forever?"

"Now, hold on. Lie about what?"

"Draya."

That stalled him. Any lie that was about to come out of his mouth was quickly sent the other way. I got confirmation of everything Christy had told me by simply saying one name.

He exhaled. "You saw Christy?" he asked as he sat down in the seat across from me.

"Yeah, I saw Christy," I replied sarcastically. "Let me guess . . . You were just getting ready to tell me."

"Yeah, I was. I know I should have done it sooner, but, uh—"

"But what! You forgot you had a child?" I snapped.

"No, I didn't forget."

"Then what? Why did you lie? What was so hard about telling me the truth?"

"I didn't want you to judge me, like you did the first night we met. I wanted you to get to know the real me." He was calm as he spoke, and that angered me more.

I slammed my hands against the table. "The *real* you? Who is that? The real you is a fucking liar!"

Silence.

He stared at me, then said finally, "I love you, Denise."

"You're a liar."

"I'm not lying about that."

"Oh, so you were just lying about everything else?"

"Just let me explain." He tried to take my hand, but I yanked it away before he could touch me.

I folded my arms across my chest. "Explain it all."

He rubbed his hands over his face and took a deep breath. Whatever lie he was cooking up now was sure to be epic. "I met Christy five years ago, after a show I did. We hooked up, and a few months later she was pregnant with Draya. You gotta understand, Christy is the last woman I ever wanted to have a child with. I was young and dumb when I met her and got with her for all the wrong reasons. She's irresponsible, trifling, and ghetto as hell. The only reason I have contact with her is to see my daughter. She wants us to be together, but I've told her plenty of times there is no way that is ever going to happen." He stopped and looked at the blank expression on my face and could tell I could care less about his story.

"Denise, you're nothing like her, and that's why I love you," he went on. "I didn't tell you about her, because I was embarrassed. You already had it in mind what type of guy I was, and I didn't want to give you more reason to think so, so I left some things out, but I swear I was going to tell you. I just wanted to do it at the right time."

I cut my eyes at him. "The right time was three months ago."

"I know that now, but it was just hard to tell you." He got up, walked around the table, and got on his knees in front of me. "Please, Denise, give me another chance to make this right. I promise I will do anything you say to fix this. I love you. I'm a fool."

I stared at him as he kneeled in front of me, and all I realized was the truth. I had wanted him so much that I had ignored everything I should have seen. I had made it so easy for him to use me. Even now a part of me wanted to forgive him, let him take me in his arms and love me like nothing had happened at all. But I thought I had humiliated myself enough for one day.

"Sean, I broke all my rules for you. You lied to me. I don't think I could ever trust you again."

"Please, baby."

I got up from the table. "I'm pregnant, Sean, and I'm keeping it."

Sean's mouth fell open. "You're what?"

"Now, that's some truth for your ass."

He got up from his knees. "You're having my baby?" He smiled. "Oh my God . . . You're having my baby!"

He was excited. I couldn't believe it. Here I was devastated, and this jackass was happy like he had just hit the lottery. He hugged me.

"Do you know what this means? We're going to be a family," he exclaimed.

I pushed him off me. "You already have one."

"Not like this. Not with the woman I love. This changes everything."

I shook my head. "No it doesn't. I still don't trust you. I'm not going to be petty and spiteful and deny you your baby, but what we had is over."

He shook his head. "Denise, I know you're mad at me, and you have every reason to be, but I promise you I am going to make this up to you. I'm going to be here for you and our baby. You'll see. I know you still love me, and I'm going to prove to you that I want to be only with you."

"Do whatever you want, Sean. I don't care." I turned from his gaze, stormed off to my bedroom, and slammed the door.

I didn't know whether to be happy that he wanted to be a part of our child's life or livid over the fact that he thought he could win me back like I was some trophy. What the hell was I going to do now?

Chapter Fifteen

Tear That Cherry Out

JOYCE

I pulled my hair back into a ponytail the best I could, made sure the laces on my Nikes were tied, and was out the door. As much as I hated running, I knew if I wanted to keep my ass in shape, I had to push myself. I knew it would be so easy for me to give in to my inner fat girl and eat Krispy Kreme donuts every day. If I didn't try to exercise on the regular, I could easily be the next guest on *Extreme Weight Loss*. I had been a bit overweight as a kid and in high school. It wasn't until I got on the volleyball team and started eating right that the pounds had started to fall off and the boys had wanted to get on it.

With my phone playlist on shuffle and my phone strapped to my hip, I started to jog around my apartment complex. I liked to do at least four laps, which was roughly two miles. Beyoncé's album was providing the soundtrack to my morning jog. When I heard the line "I can't wait 'til I get home so you can tear that cherry out," my mind instantly drifted to the last time Alonzo had torn my cherry out. I felt a sweet throbbing between my legs. Memories of his hands clasping my thighs, his face nuzzling and licking my clit sent chills up my spine.

My jogging became more intense, my breathing heavier, and sweat dampened my skin as I became lost in my pornographic encounter with him. Damn that man had a spell on me.

As I rounded the corner of the complex, I spotted Denise taking out her trash.

I jogged toward her. "Hey, Denise. What's going on?" I called.

She had the saddest expression on her face, one that I'd never seen before. I mean, nobody liked taking out trash, but she looked dreadful. The last time I had seen her, she was damn near glowing with excitement over the news of her pregnancy, but not today.

She stared at me, then broke into tears.

"Oh my, Denise. What's wrong?" I hugged her.

She didn't respond, just laid her head on my chest and sobbed. A few minutes later I walked her over to my place. After she pulled herself together, she told me what had made her so upset, and it was just as bad as we'd thought.

I had a seat next to her on the sofa and put my arm around her shoulder. "It's going to be okay, Denise. Even he doesn't want to take responsibility for his child, I'm sure the courts will make him man up!"

She looked at me. "That's not the problem, Joyce. Sean was thrilled when I told him. He wants to prove to me that he wants to be with me and take care of our baby."

"Really?"

"Yeah, but I don't know if I can ever trust him again."

I could see the disappointment in her eyes.

"He's a jackass," I muttered.

"I know, but . . ." She paused and lowered her head. "I still love him. As much as I want to hate his guts, I still love that jerk."

I didn't know how to respond to that. I would never give a man who had lied to me like that another chance, but Denise wasn't me. I had had no idea how deeply in love she had fallen, but I did know that when a baby was thrown into the mix, that took things to another level.

"Do you think you're going to give him another chance?" I asked her.

She looked at me. "How could I? What would y'all think of me?"

"This isn't about *us*. It's about you and this baby." I touched her stomach. "Whatever decision you make, we're going to be here for you."

Denise gave me a slight smile and hugged me. A moment later we heard the front door open, and in walked Alonzo. We had exchanged keys to each other's place a few weeks ago. I got up and walked over to him and gave him a kiss. I wanted to do more, but we had company.

"Hey, babe," he said.

I smirked. "You don't know how happy I am to see you."

He tilted his head and gazed at me. "You are?"

"You'll find out real soon," I assured him.

"I can't wait." Alonzo noticed Denise on the sofa and said, "Hey, Denise. How you doing?"

Denise gave him the evil eye. "You knew the whole time, and you didn't say shit to me."

Alonzo looked like he'd been slapped. "What?"

I looked at her. "Denise, hold on—"

"No! He's Sean's best friend, so I know he knew the whole time he had a child!"

The same thought had run through my head when Denise told me about Sean's child, but I was going to address this later. Not in front of her. I knew best friends covered for each other all the time, but I was Alonzo's girlfriend. He could have told me.

"He told you?" Alonzo asked.

Denise stood up. "No he didn't! His dumbass baby mama came over here and told me!"

Alonzo sighed. "I told him to tell you before something like this happened. I'm sorry, Denise."

"Why didn't you tell me?" Denise barked.

"Denise, he's my best friend, and he assured me he was going to tell you. I found out only recently that he hadn't. I'm sorry, but it wasn't my place to share that with you."

Denise looked like she wanted to attack him. "Fuck you, Alonzo! You're just as guilty as Sean!"

I wasn't going to just stand there and let her go off on my man like that. "Wait a minute, Denise. I know you're upset, but you can't take it out on Alonzo."

"So much for you being here for me!" She stormed toward the front door.

I shook my head. "That's not fair, Denise."

"Neither is life," she retorted. Then she left and slammed the door behind her.

I exhaled. I knew she was still in her feelings, so I didn't take her words personally.

Alonzo looked at me. "I'm sorry, babe."

"I understand why you didn't say anything to Denise, but you should have at least told me."

"And then what would you have done? Gone and told her?"

I folded my arms. "She's my friend. What would you expect me to do?"

"And Sean's my friend. I couldn't betray his trust."

"Well, at least I know where I stand with you." I turned and walked away.

Alonzo followed me into the kitchen. "You see, this is exactly why I didn't want to get involved in their relationship. Because now we're arguing over something that doesn't affect us."

I turned and looked at him. He was right. "I'm sorry. I just feel bad for her."

"So do I. I'ma talk to Sean about it." He stepped closer to me. "Now, enough about them. You said you were really happy to see me? Just how happy are you?"

I leaned my body on his, kissed him, and felt his manhood swell in his jeans. That was what I loved about Alonzo; it didn't take much for his penis to rise to the occasion. His hands caressed my body, and I became a little self-conscious, as I had just run around the complex and wasn't exactly *zestfully* clean. That didn't seem to bother him, as he pulled down my jogging pants. His fingers stroked my clit through my panties. It felt good. I heard him groan, and then he pulled my panties down around my knees. My sex was throbbing, aching to be filled.

"Baby, let's go take a shower," I suggested in a whisper.

Two fingers pushed inside me, and I moaned.

"I want you here and now."

"I know, but—"

Before I could finish my protest, he turned me around, and pushed me up against the kitchen counter. My naked ass pushed out in front of him. His aggressiveness aroused me. It was the first time he'd ever been like this with me. He quickly unzipped his jeans, and I felt him push inside me. I moaned, feeling his girth fill me up. He was in beast mode, as his long, deep strokes were fast and hard. It was like he was trying to crawl inside me. I held on to the kitchen sink for dear life as he had his way with me.

"Does it feel good to you?" he asked.

"Yes, yes," I sang.

Alonzo was fucking me like a man possessed. His skin slapping against mine, he penetrated me over and over again, making me curse and scream his name. He was beating my sex up like a Mexican piñata. We weren't making love. . . . This was fucking. He was fucking me like he was trying to prove a point, and I was determined to keep up. I was throwing it back at him, but he used his body weight to thrust deep up in me. He took control. It was as if he was establishing dominance over me. I gladly submitted and let my man be the man. Once again, hard deep strokes battered my sex, making me moan and groan like a wounded animal. Alonzo enjoyed making me whine in pleasure. He controlled my body with each stroke, making me release uncontrollable grunts.

He withdrew himself from me, turned me back around, hoisted me up on the countertop, and then slid his erection back inside me. He kissed me again. Over and over again, he kissed me, like he couldn't get enough of me. His hips were thrusting his hardness in and out of my wetness. Our sexual energy was in sync as we gave each other what we both wanted. I felt my orgasm come over me, and I shuddered, in bliss. The convulsions were so strong that I slipped off the counter, but Alonzo held me in his arms. I was out of breath.

Damn, I loved this man.

Chapter Sixteen

Love the One You're With

RASHIDA

"How many bottles of champagne do you need for fifty guests?" Joyce asked me.

We were in the middle of Tower Beer, Wine & Spirits on Piedmont Road, buying liquor for Robert's birthday party tonight. Joyce was with me to keep me on point, and that was a good thing, because my mind was anywhere but here. Thoughts of what had almost happened with Alonzo a few days ago were still dancing around in my head. Here I was, fantasizing about my best friend's boyfriend while she was helping me plan a party for my man. Yeah, that was fucked up. Needless to say, I was distracted.

"'Shida!" she said, and the sound of my name snapped me back to the here and now. "Are you listening to me?"

"Yeah. Um, what did you say?"

"What is on your mind?"

Nothing I would dare say to you, I thought to myself. "Girl, I'm sorry. I just got a hundred different things on my mind. I don't know why I decided to throw Robert a party instead of just taking him out for dinner. What the hell was I thinking?"

"Don't worry." Joyce smiled. "That's why I'm here."

"Thank you. You know, the thing I regret more is having to invite Robert's dusty-ass friends."

She chuckled. "Who's that one you say is annoying as fuck?"

"Bitch-ass Sydney, and I swear, if he says anything disrespectful to me tonight, I'ma beat the goofy outta his ass."

Joyce cackled hysterically at my bluntness. "Oh, I would pay money to see you fight him."

"You think I'm playing, but I really want to fight his lame ass." I looked at her. "Anyway, have you heard from Denise?"

"Nah, girl. She ain't answering my calls. She's still in her feelings over the whole Alonzo not telling her about Sean's kid, which is fucked up, by the way, but that was a messy situation for Alonzo to get in the middle of."

"Did Alonzo tell you?"

She sighed. "No. I was a little bothered by that at first, but if he had, I would have told Denise. I understand why he didn't tell me. Sometimes even if you have the best intentions, telling the truth can do more harm than good."

It surprised me that she had come to that conclusion. I wondered if she would say the same about what I had done before they got together.

"I agree," I told her. "Don't worry. I'll reach out to her later."

"Good, because I don't know if it's the stress of the situation with Sean or her pregnancy throwing her hormones off, but Denise has been snapping." She laughed. "We better tell Taylor to lay low."

I laughed. "I know, right?"

We purchased the liquor, then went on to the next store and picked up the remaining things that were needed for the party. Robert was spending the day golfing with bitch-ass Sydney. I refused to let him get to me tonight. After I was done running the streets with Joyce, I went home and called Denise. After the fourth ring, she answered.

"Hey," I said into the phone.

"Hey, Shida," she replied dryly.

"I heard what happened. I'm sorry."

"Don't be sorry. It isn't your fault I got knocked up by a lying-ass dog."

I sighed. "Do you wanna talk about it?"

"No, not now. Listen, I know you're having Robert's party tonight, but I ain't really in the mood to be around anybody right now."

"I understand, but we still need to talk about this."

"I know, and we will," she told me.

"Okay."

"Okay. Talk to you later."

"Bye."

Denise hung up. She was really in a funk. I would be, too, if I had found out about all that while I was pregnant. It was probably the best for her to have some time to herself.

I had a few hours to myself before the party, so I decided to take a nap. When I awoke, I showered and got dressed. Robert got home around seven and got dressed. As I stood in the bathroom, fixing my locks in the mirror, I could barely stand to look at my reflection. Robert had been making a real effort to be good to me, but my feelings for Alonzo continued to get stronger, making me feel even guiltier. Plus, I had been lying by omission to Joyce for months. How the hell did I get myself into this?

I had decided to wear a long-sleeved, dark blue African-print dress with a plunging neckline. I wore my locks up in a bun, fastened by two chopsticks. I normally didn't do a lot of makeup, but tonight I was going to doll it up for Robert. I was pleased with my reflection in the mirror, but on the inside I still felt ugly. Robert wandered into the bathroom, saw me, and his jaw dropped.

"You look amazing."

I smiled. "Thanks."

"I mean it. I don't know what I've done in life to deserve a woman as beautiful as you, but I thank God I found you."

"Stop. You make me sound way better than I really am."

He walked toward me. "That's because you are. I couldn't have a more perfect girlfriend."

I felt sick hearing him praise me like this when I knew I was undeserving of it. I was far from perfect. My cell phone chimed just then, and I glanced at the screen and saw that I had received a text message. It was confirmation for the final surprise arrangement I had made for Robert's birthday party tonight.

I looked at him and said, "I think we should get going."

"As you wish."

About thirty minutes later we arrived at the shop. Taylor had arrived earlier to open it up for our guests. The renovation work had been finished, and I thought it would be great to have a party for Robert there tonight. It was a nice mix of friends and his work colleagues. Everyone was holding a champagne flute in their hand when we walked inside to birthday cheers. Of course, Sydney and his wife, Christina, were front and center. They ambled toward us.

"Happy birthday, old man," Sydney joked.

"I'm not old. I'm vintage, and with this breathtaking woman on my arm, I'm a classic man," Robert retorted.

Sydney looked me up and down. I knew he was making some sarcastic comment about my outfit in his head. "Wow. You certainly look Afrocentric tonight."

I gave him a fake smile. "Well, somebody has to be authentic." I turned my attention toward his wife. "Nice to see you again, Christina."

"You too, Rashida. Your shop is beautiful."

"Thank you."

"Yes, it's quite the shindig you've put together tonight," Sydney said dryly.

"As long as my man likes it, I did my job," I returned.

Robert looked at me. "I love it, babe."

He gave me a kiss, and right after that, I spotted Alonzo with Joyce out of the corner of my eye. Seeing him made my heart skip a beat. The look on his face told me he felt the same thing. More guilt hit me. I saw Taylor on the other side of the room as more people made their way toward Robert.

"Honey, will you excuse me for a minute?" I whispered.

Robert nodded. "Of course, but only for a minute."

I walked over to Taylor, who was recording the party with her phone.

"Make sure you get my good side." I posed for her.

Taylor laughed. "All your sides are good!" She gave me a hug. "So is the birthday boy enjoying himself?"

"Yeah, he is. He's gonna be in heaven when he gets his gift later."

Taylor looked me up and down. "Damn, girl, you gonna bust it wide open on him like that?"

"What? No, not that! That's not a birthday gift! His gift will be here later. You're so nasty."

"So? You better freak him right tonight, while he's still young enough to do it." She looked at me funny and smirked. "You gonna let him put it in your booty hole?"

"Ew! No." I laughed. "You see, this is why I can't talk to you about shit."

A moment later Joyce and Alonzo came over to us. Joyce gave me a hug.

"What are y'all laughing about over here?" Joyce asked.

"About how freaky 'Shida gonna be tonight with Robert," Taylor blurted out.

Just then I looked at Alonzo and felt so awkward.

"Oh my God!" Joyce rolled her eyes. "Anyway, things turned out good, 'Shida."

I nodded. "Yeah, they did."

"The place looks great," Alonzo added.

"Well, thanks to you. You helped make this possible. Thank you," I told him.

He smiled. "No problem."

I felt an even more uncomfortable tension between us. We were standing in the exact place where we had almost crossed that line.

"So, no Denise, huh?" Joyce asked.

"No, I talked to her, and she just needs some more time to herself," I reported.

Taylor scoffed. "What's wrong with her now?"

Taylor didn't know, and I didn't want to talk about it now with Alonzo here.

"She's . . . not feeling well. I'll tell you more later," I said.

"Okay, let's get turnt up in here," she yelled.

I stopped her. "Ah, no, not with Robert's bougie-ass friends here."

"Oh goodness!" Taylor said, rolling her eyes.

Despite Taylor's disappointment, we still managed to enjoy the night. Plenty of rum shots saw to that. When eleven o'clock arrived, I got everybody's attention, grabbed Robert, and walked to the front of the shop.

"Hey, everybody! Tonight we are all here to celebrate, as my Jamaican family would say, another earth-strong day for the man I'm lucky enough to have in my life. I want you to know I really adore you, Robert."

"I love you too," Robert whispered.

"Because you mean so much to me, I wanted to give you something I know you've been wanting for a long time now."

There were a few oh's from the crowd, and Robert looked a little dumbfounded.

The crowd in the room parted like the Red Sea as I led Robert outside. Sitting in the parking lot, with a big red bow on it, was a brand-new black BMW 6 Series Gran Turismo. The look on Robert's face was priceless. It was like he'd seen Jesus. I glanced over at Sydney, who couldn't believe what I had gotten his friend; then his expression morphed into a cynical glare. I smirked at him.

Robert stared at me. "Oh my, you, you . . . I can't believe it! You got me this!"

"I know how much you've wanted it. Every time we see one on the road, you tell me."

He walked around the German automobile in awe, then got inside. He nodded his head. "This is perfect!"

Taylor walked up behind me. "Damn, girl, he gonna get yo' ass pregnant tonight."

"Shut up."

"That's one hell of a birthday gift, 'Shida. Alonzo better not think I'm getting anything like that for him." Joyce laughed.

"I don't think he expects anything like that from you."

"He better not!"

I knew this was a little overgenerous, considering we hadn't been together very long, but my guilty conscience had made me feel like I had to do this. As if this would fix the damage I had done if he found out. I glanced over and saw Alonzo looking at me, and I couldn't help but wish it was he whom I was spoiling on his birthday. That would never happen. I guessed if I couldn't be with him, I might as well love the one I was with.

Chapter Seventeen

I Can't

ALONZO

I loved my job. I knew a lot of people couldn't say that, but I truly did. From ten at night to two in the morning, I provided the soundtrack to most of my grown and sexy listeners' sex lives, with minimal commercial interruptions, on my Quiet Storm radio show. I was not forced to play the top forty of today's R & B music, which was a pale version of the R & B I grew up listening to in the nineties. I got to play Jodeci, Troop, Xscape, R. Kelly, and Sade, songs that made you want to curl up next to someone you loved and do some things.

For the past eight months, Joyce had been that woman for me. She was a great woman, sexy, funny, intelligent, but for some reason, I hadn't been able to connect all the way with her. I enjoyed being with her, and she was the type of woman any man could see himself with for years. I kept on telling myself if I tried a little harder, it would happen, but it hadn't and, more likely, wouldn't. The problem was I'd already made that kind of connection with another woman.

Rashida.

Ever since the first night we met, I'd felt an uncontrollable attraction toward her I couldn't deny. And every time I looked in her eyes, I saw that she had that same desire for me. Discovering that Joyce was her best friend was a cruel twist of fate, one that felt like a kick in my balls. Ever since then we'd been denying how we felt because of Joyce. We had had a moment in her shop not too long ago and had almost given in to our desire. The way it had felt when she touched me was pure magic. In that moment I had wanted her in the worst way. It hadn't mattered that she had a man or that I was with her best friend. It was just us. Our moment was cut short by a phone call from her current lover.

Ever since that day, Rashida had done her best to avoid being alone with me in the same room. Out of respect for Joyce, I hadn't pressed the issue. The problem was that I hadn't been able to get her off my mind. There were even times when I was making love to Joyce and all I saw was Rashida. Fucked up, I knew. I honestly saw no remedy for the situation.

I had just finished my show when the station manager, Mark, called me into his office. Mark was a husky brother in his midforties. He had been in the radio industry for over twenty years and was the one who had given me my first break as an intern years ago, when I was right out of college. He'd always looked out for me. I had a seat in his office. The walls were decorated with framed pictures of Stevie Wonder, Beyoncé, Nas, Gladys Knight, and a host of other musical superstars.

"What's up, Mark?"

He smiled. "Good things, Zo, good things."

"All righty, then." I smiled too. "What's the good word?"

"So you know Kandi Young did that HBO comedy special last month?"

I nodded. "Yeah."

His smile got wider. "And you know she started off working here years ago?"

I leaned forward. "Yeah."

"And you know I was the one who gave her, her first break, right?"

"Mark, c'mon, man! Get to the point! Wus up?"

"Okay, okay. Kandi is getting her own morning show here on WHXZ, and she wants me to recommend a radio personality to help cohost her show. And guess who I got in mind."

A big old smile spread across my face, and I jumped up out of my seat. "Mark, you serious? You ain't playing with me?"

He laughed. "Of course not! I've already told her about you, and she wants to meet you."

I went around his desk and gave him a hug. This was the opportunity of a lifetime! "Mark, you are the man! Thank you!"

"Now, you know I'm always gonna look out for you. The show is going to be nationally syndicated, in all our markets."

I was damn near doing the Running Man. "Aw, man! This is amazing! So when does she want to meet me?"

"Next Wednesday." Mark's facial expression got a bit more serious. "But the thing is she's in Miami, and that's where her show will be based."

I paused in my celebration. "Miami?"

Mark nodded. "Yeah, she's from there, and that's where she wants to do the show. I don't wanna lose you, but it is an opportunity of a lifetime, and you deserve it."

"If I take the job, when will it start?"

"They wanna get the show up and running the third of next month."

I exhaled. "So in three weeks?"

"Yeah." He put his hand on my shoulder. "Take some time and think about it. It's a big decision."

I looked at him. "Thanks, Mark. I'll let you know tomorrow." I shook his hand.

I walked out of his office and took a deep breath. Atlanta was my home, but I had always loved Miami. I would be a fool not to take this job. The only thing I had holding me in ATL was Joyce. How would she take the news? Would she want to come with me? She had a lot of ties here. My mind went to Rashida, since she was here in Atlanta too. My feelings were tied to her, but she was unquestionably unavailable to me. So what was really keeping me here?

I went back to my home in College Park. Regardless of this job offer in Miami, I wasn't going to give up my home. It was paid off. That was something I was especially proud of accomplishing so soon. When the housing market had crashed a few years ago, I had bought this place for a steal. There was no way was I walking away from it. That was an easy situation to deal with, but my relationship with Joyce wasn't. I spent all night thinking about what I was going to do and decided to talk to her about it.

The next day I took Joyce out for lunch at the Cheesecake Factory over at Cumberland Mall. She looked lovely in a baby blue summer dress and a pair of white open-toe, high-heeled sandals. She wore her hair in curls, which looked perfect around her pretty, round face. She was such a beautiful woman. She looked up from her menu and caught me staring at her.

"You got that look in your eyes," she observed.

"What look?"

She gave me a naughty grin. "Like you wanna do something nasty to me."

I reached over and took her hand. "When you look like that, I always want to."

"Nothing like chocolate mousse cheesecake to get me in the mood."

I smiled. "Well, I'm gonna make sure you get a mouthful."

She licked her sexy lips. "I can't wait."

The waitress sauntered over and took our order. After a few minutes of silence, Joyce looked at me again.

"What's on your mind?" she asked me.

I exhaled. "Something happened at work that I gotta talk to you about."

"Oh my God, did you get fired?"

I shook my head. "No, I got offered a cohosting gig on the new *Kandi Young Morning Show*."

She smiled. "Alonzo, that's great! This is a great opportunity for you!"

I nodded. "Yeah, it is."

"Then why aren't you more excited than this?"

"The job is in Miami."

The smile on her face slowly disappeared. "Oh. Miami."

"Yeah."

She interlocked her fingers and asked, "When does it start?"

"Next month."

We sat in silence for a few seconds, letting the moment sink in. We both knew that our relationship had come to a crossroads. A life-changing decision was going to have to be made.

"Would you come with me?" I asked.

She stared at me, then said, "I would, but my family, my friends, and my career are here."

"I know. I know that it's not exactly fair to ask you to change your whole life for me."

She shook her head and smiled. "You're an important part of my life too, and I want to be with you." She reached over and took my hand. "And it's unfair for me to make you choose between this opportunity and me. I would never do that to you, but I just need a minute to think about everything."

"I understand. I'm not rushing you. Just think about it."

She nodded. I could tell her mind was racing. I started thinking about whether it was wise for me to have asked her to come with me, knowing that my feelings for her were not as strong as they should be. It had just felt like the right thing to say, even if I didn't mean it. Dumb! It was so damn stupid of me to have said that to her! What was I thinking? Too late to take it back now.

We ate lunch, and afterward I drove her back to her apartment. We went inside, and I had a seat on the sofa. The mood in the air was awkward. Joyce walked into the kitchen and put her cheesecake from lunch in the fridge, then joined me on the sofa.

She gazed at me and said, "I'll go with you . . . only if we're engaged."

Her words hit me like a ton of bricks. Marriage was definitely not in my immediate future, and she could see the hesitation on my face.

"Alonzo, the only reason I would give up my life here is that I know I'm going with you to make another. Not just moving in with you to play house."

"Joyce, that's not fair. I'm already making one life-changing decision, and now you want me to make another?"

"I'm not asking you to marry me tomorrow, but I need to have some kind of reassurance that this relationship is heading somewhere and I'm not wasting my time."

I rubbed my hand over my face and looked at her. "Well, it feels like you're trying to force me to make a decision I'm not ready to make."

She frowned. "Why not? We've been together for eight months now, and you still don't know if you would want to marry me in the future?"

I shook my head. "Eight months is not a long time, and we're still getting to know each other."

She folded her arms across her chest. "So why should I up and move to Miami with you and change my life just on something that's not guaranteed to work out?"

"So what makes you think that getting engaged is a guarantee for anything? Anything can happen. I'm just saying if you want to be with me, then just be with me."

She stood up. "You're so damn selfish. You want me to give up everything just for you?"

I stood up too. "I'm not asking you to give up anything, but I'm not going to marry you just to keep you in my life."

We searched in each other's eyes for a way to fix this. Both of us were wishing that we could go back in time and redo the past five minutes, but what had been said could not be unsaid. I could see the hurt in her eyes. It was a hurt I hadn't wanted to cause, but there had been no way to avoid it. In the back of my mind, I knew our relationship would end like this, and I hated myself for it.

"So I guess we both have made up our minds," she said.

"Yeah, I guess we have." I took her apartment key out of my pocket and laid it on the coffee table. "I'm sorry, Joyce."

She didn't reply. The damage had been done. I turned and walked out of apartment. As the door closed behind me, I heard her cry. Any way you looked at it, I was the bad guy. I couldn't help but feel a little bit of relief that our relationship had ended now instead of later. Now I had to go tell the woman I loved goodbye.

Chapter Eighteen

Breaking My Heart

RASHIDA

"Go on. Say it. I'm an idiot," Denise sighed as she sat in a chair at my station.

'Shidas Styles was going to open next month. There was still a little construction work left to do in back, but other than that, the salon was ready to go. I had got a call from Denise this morning, and she had sounded dreadful, so I'd told her to meet me here to talk. So far she'd told me everything that happened between her and Sean. I had really wanted Sean to be a stand-up man and be good to her, but instead, he had really disappointed us all. I'd never seen Denise this upset. She was in love with him, in love with the wrong man. I knew the feeling.

"You're not an idiot." I leaned forward in my seat across from her and took her hand. "Just a girl who fell for the wrong guy. It happens to almost everybody at some point."

She shook her head. "I should have seen through his bullshit. You should have heard him, 'Shida. Even after I called him out on his lie, he was still trying to justify lying to me, like he was too scared to be honest with me because I was different. Like I'm stupid."

"Maybe he wasn't lying about that part."

She stared at me strangely. "You can't be serious."

"Listen, I'm not saying he's not a jackass, but you said even after you told him about the baby, he still wanted to be there for you. I bet Sean has never dealt with a woman as classy as you. Trust me, when a man meets a real woman, he knows the difference."

She frowned. "Well, he shoulda known better! I don't care what he wants. I don't trust him."

"And I'm not saying you should, but maybe in his own foolish way, he really does care about you."

Denise was quiet for a moment, thinking about what I had said. I could tell that as pissed off as she was, her heart was still with Sean. But the pain she felt was way too fresh to ignore.

She exhaled. "Well, that's his problem. The only one he needs to care about is this baby."

"That goes without saying."

"And of top of that, Alonzo knew the whole time and didn't say anything to me!"

I was noticeably quiet after she said that. Denise glared at me, as if I should've agreed with her.

"'Shida," she said, aggravation in her voice.

"C'mon, Denise, did you really expect him to throw his best friend under the bus?"

She scowled. "I expected him to be a decent human being and do the right thing. To me, that speaks a lot on his character. I can't believe you and Joyce are defending him."

"You're taking your anger out on the wrong person. If the situation was reversed, I would not betray your trust to Sean. That was something he should have told you."

Denise rolled her eyes, not wanting to hear the truth. "Whatever, I bet Taylor is going to be thrilled to hear all of this. I swear, if she says anything crazy to me, I'ma go off on her."

"Don't stress yourself. I don't think she will take any shots at you over this."

Denise looked at me like I was stupid.

My shoulders sagged. "Okay, I'll have a word with her."

Denise exhaled and ran her fingers through her hair. "I don't know what I'm going to do."

I stood up and pulled Denise up by her hands. "You're going to have a beautiful baby, and I'm going to be there for you the whole way through."

She smiled and gave me a hug. I thought this was probably the first sigh of relief she had had since this all started. Denise was one of my dearest friends; there was no way I was going to let her go through this alone.

A second later, we heard the door open. I turned and saw him. My heart sped up at the sight of his handsome face.

His eyes met mine and then went to Denise. "Hello."

"Hey," I replied.

Denise said nothing. She was still clearly feeling some type of way toward him.

"I hope I didn't interrupt you. I just needed to talk to you, 'Shida," he announced.

"Nope," Denise said sarcastically. "I'll talk to you later, 'Shida."

Denise marched by Alonzo, throwing visual daggers at him the whole way. She exited the shop, and Alonzo walked toward me. Being alone with this man was not good for me.

"I guess she's still pissed at me, huh?" he said, rubbing his forehead.

I nodded. "Yep, but she'll get over it."

He nodded. "How have you been?"

"I'm fine." I took a few steps away from him and picked up my bag off the countertop. "Is there something I can do for you? I got somewhere I got to be in a few minutes," I lied.

He smirked. "You don't have to do that, you know."

I stared at him. "Do what?"

"Make up an excuse so as not to be alone with me. I promise I won't bite."

I smiled. "You know why I do. You and I alone is not a good situation for either of us."

He nodded. "Well, I guess what I got to say will make life a lot easier for both of us, then."

"What is it?"

He exhaled. "I got a job offer in Miami, and I'm taking it."

I stood there for a second in silence. It felt like someone had just slapped me in the face. He was leaving me. I could feel my heart slowly breaking.

I blinked twice. "What?"

"I'm moving to Miami next month."

I felt another slap. "Oh . . . you are."

He took a few steps toward me. "I got a position on the new *Kandi Young Morning Show*. It's a great opportunity for me."

I swallowed my pain. "That's great. What about Joyce?"

He was now standing mere inches away from me. "I asked her to come with me, and she said the only way she would do that is if we were engaged."

My heart broke into a million pieces. He was here to tell me he was leaving and marrying my best friend.

"I couldn't do it," he added.

"Oh . . ."

"We broke up."

I looked into his eyes. I knew that Joyce was probably a mess, but at that moment I couldn't help but think of my own pain. Before I knew it, tears were rolling down my face.

"I'm sorry, 'Shida." He took his index finger and wiped the tears away.

More uncontrollable tears rolled down my face.

"You're leaving me," I whispered.

He hugged me. "I don't mean to hurt you."

I rested my face against his chest, sobbing, while his arms held me. This was crazy. Here I was, crying over a man who didn't belong to me. As selfish as it was, it felt like he was breaking up with *me*. Why was he leaving *me*? There were so many things I wanted to say, but I knew I couldn't. All these emotions that I shouldn't be feeling for him were overwhelming. I slowly pulled away from him and wiped my face.

"I'm sorry. I shouldn't be reacting like this," I told him.

"You don't have to apologize. I've never been in a situation like this. Whenever I look at you, I . . . I just wish things were different."

I nodded my head. "I do too."

"If they were, I wouldn't leave you."

I closed my eyes. Why was this happening to me?

I felt Alonzo's hands cup my face, and I looked up into his eyes.

"Goodbye, 'Shida."

He kissed my forehead, turned, and walked out of the shop. I sat back down in the chair and thought about how much I was going miss him and about everything that could have been. I thought about the first night I met him and the possibilities for us if only I had done things differently.

Two Years Later

Chapter Nineteen

If You Don't Love Me

RASHIDA

A lot had changed for me and my girls in the past two years. Denise had a handsome baby boy named Amir Mickles, who, for better or worse, looked just like his father. Sean had made a little bit of a name for himself in the hip-hop world. His mixtapes and his featured appearances on other artists' songs had put him on the verge of blowing up. He had even moved Denise and Amir into a new house in Decatur. He had been true to his word and had been by Denise's side the whole time, even though they were not officially together. But something told me that on the nights he slept over at her house, he wasn't relegated to the couch, like she said. I believed Sean was the first man Denise had truly been in love with, but that was her business.

Taylor had finally graduated, and over the past couple of years, she'd become a sort of low-key celebrity on YouTube, of all places. She had started a channel, called *Taylor Made*, that chronicled her life as a young college graduate who was trying to make it in the real world. At first, I had thought it was just a joke, but when I'd started watching it, I'd seen she really put some serious work into it. She had invested in a nice camera and had learned how to edit her videos, and now she had a little over seven hundred thousand subscribers to her channel. Most of the blogs she posted were of her going out and basking in the Atlanta night life or giving a makeup and fashion tutorial. She was so successful now that she had been getting sponsorships on her page. The fact that Taylor had the body of a video model had only served to expand her viewing audience.

After her breakup with Alonzo, Joyce had focused on business and had opened a realty company. She hadn't really dated anyone seriously since him. Even though I had had nothing to do with their breakup, I still felt a bit guilty for having feelings for him. To this day she was still pissed off at Alonzo, but I thought, if given the opportunity, she would get back with him if he were still here. I hadn't really spoken to him since he left town; we'd shared only the occasional birthday or Christmas text here and there. I did, however, listen to him every morning on the Kandi Young radio show that he co-hosted, so I guessed in a way it was like I had never lost touch with him. He really had made a name for himself, and so it had been the best move for him.

As for me, I was still with Robert. We have our ups and downs, but we were still together. Both of us had kind of been consumed with our work. 'Shidas Styles had been a success and had become one of the most popular natural hair care salons in Atlanta. It was truly been a dream come true being able to run this business by myself. Robert was now on the college's board of trustees. He was part of the group that appointed the president and managed the institution, including fulfilling the college's mission and purpose, devising institutional policies, and incorporating changes in the academic programs. So, in other words, he was a big deal there.

So, given how busy we both were, our love life had been in a bit of a slump, almost nonexistent over the past few months. I thought we were both partly to blame for this, but tonight I was going to change that. I left the shop at about one o'clock in order to cook a nice romantic meal for us. It had been a while since I had gone all out and made a gourmet meal for him. Most nights it was either takeout or Skillet Sensations coming out of this kitchen. So tonight I was going to fill his belly, ride him to sleep, and catch myself a well-deserved orgasm in the process.

At about 7:20 p.m. that evening, I heard Robert pull into the garage.

"Rashida?" he called out after walking in the house.

"I'm in the den, Robert," I responded from the candlelit room.

"Why the hell are all the lights off?" He flicked on the lights in the living room, then walked into the den and spotted me dressed in a sexy sheer pink dress that hugged my hourglass frame, showing off my thighs. I was sitting at a candlelit table for two, complete with a bottle of wine on ice.

I smiled. "Because it's more romantic this way."

I got up, walked over to Robert, and gave him a kiss. Then I led him to the table and had a seat. Robert sighed as he sat down and looked around, uninterested. Not exactly the reaction I was hoping for.

"What's this all about?" he grumbled.

I ignored his irritated tone. "Do I need a reason to treat my man?"

"No, but you really should have called me and told me about this."

"It wouldn't be a surprise then. Just sit back and relax. I know you had a long day at work, so I made you an exquisite porterhouse steak." I leaned over and rubbed his shoulders. "I even made the macaroni salad of Joyce's that you like."

"'Shida', you should have called me," Robert exclaimed. "I have over a hundred midterms to grade tonight and a board meeting tomorrow morning." He exhaled. "Besides, I got something to eat while I was at school."

"Oh."

"Thanks, anyway, but just put this in the fridge and we'll eat it tomorrow," he told me as he stood up from his seat.

I craned my neck as he walked away. "Really? I went through a lot of trouble to do this for you."

"Sorry, but you should have called me." He stopped and looked back at me. "I'll be late coming to bed, so don't wait up."

After he walked out of the den, I got up from my chair and blew out the candles. I couldn't believe his reaction. What the hell kind of relationship was this? After I cleared the table and put the food away, I went to my bedroom and picked up a book off the nightstand.

So much for romance. This was not how I had envisioned this night going. A little wine, a little dine, some Maxwell, and me in some lingerie were supposed to result in some overdue lovemaking. I couldn't believe our relationship had come down to this: getting off on erotic urban books. When a fictional character was getting more action than you were, you knew shit was bad. I was actually a little jealous. *I gotta stop reading this shit*, I thought.

I didn't know when, but I drifted to sleep while I was reading, and I woke up with hands sliding up my gown. Without a word, Robert climbed on top of me and rubbed the tip of his erection between my thighs, then started to push inside me.

I grimaced. "Robert, hold on . . . I'm not really that wet."

My pleas fell on deaf ears.

Robert growled, "Oh, shit, baby . . . You're so tight!"

That's because I'm drier than the Sahara Desert. So much for foreplay, I told myself silently.

Robert stroked me and was in completely as I lay there with my legs spread. This didn't feel good at all.

"Robert . . . Robert . . ."

"That's it," he yelled. "Baby, say my name!"

I know he can't think this feels good! I'm barely wet, and if he goes any faster, he might start a fire down there, I thought.

Robert continued to thrust himself harder and faster, not paying any attention to my obvious discomfort. Deeper and deeper, Robert rammed himself inside me.

"Oh, God, I'm gonna cum!" Robert screamed ecstatically.

Oh, please hurry the fuck up, then! This shit is killing me!

"Ooh, shit," he sang.

Robert gave me one last big thrust before releasing his semen, and then he went limp and collapsed on top of me, breathing heavily.

"That's just what I needed, baby."

"Yeah, that's what I'm talking about. You really rocked my world. Now, can you get the fuck off me?" I pushed him, and he rolled on his back.

"Good night." He pulled the covers up over him.

I didn't reply. I felt disgusted. Was that all I was here for? I felt as if I was just ridden hard and put up wet. Thank goodness I had started taking birth control a few months ago. I got up, took a shower, then decided to sleep in the other room. I was done with this relationship.

The next day I was with Denise and Joyce, having lunch at La Parrilla Mexican Restaurant. It was one of our favorite spots. Joyce scanned the menu as if she was on a mission.

Joyce looked up at us as we stared at her. "Girl, I'm starving! Do you wanna share a La Parrilla dip?"

"We ain't waiting for Taylor?" I asked.

"We both know Taylor runs on CP time, and I'm too hungry to wait. You better get up on this dip with me."

"CP time? That girl stay late," Denise added.

I nodded. "Yeah, you got a point."

The waiter arrived at our table. "Are you ready to order?"

Joyce spoke up first. "We'll start with the La Parrilla dip."

"Anything to drink?"

"A Malibu," I requested.

"Same thing," Joyce said to him.

Denise handed him her menu. "I'll get a Coke, no ice."

"I'll have that right out for you." He walked away.

I looked at Joyce. "So what did you decide?"

"Yeah, I'm gonna start with the dip, and then I was thinking about the chimichanga or maybe—"

"I meant, are you going to talk to Alonzo?"

Joyce rolled her eyes, as if she knew what I had meant in the first place. "I have nothing to say to him."

Denise looked at her. "Why do you still sound so bitter about it?"

"I'm not bitter!" Joyce snapped.

I stared at her with a raised brow. "Really?"

"Damn it, y'all! I put up with so much crap," she protested.

I shook my head. "No you didn't. Don't lie to yourself. Alonzo was nothing but good to you."

Joyce sighed. "Okay fine. He was. But what he did still hurts."

"It's been two years, Joyce. You can't push a man into a corner and expect him to do what you want him to. He just wasn't ready to make a commitment like that yet." I looked in Joyce's eyes.

"Why not? You would think getting engaged would be the next logical step."

Denise shook her head. "I told you, his character was no good."

Joyce glared at her. "Thank you for always being so damn supportive, and let's not forget who the father of your child is."

Denise shrugged her shoulders. "I'm sorry, Joyce, but I'm your friend, and I'm not going to lie to you."

The waiter returned with our drinks and the appetizer. "Are you ready to order?" he asked after he arranged the glasses on the table.

Out of the blue Taylor flopped down in the seat next to me, dressed in tight hip-hugger jeans and a black belly shirt. "I'll have the Santa Fe Chicken Salad and a margarita," she announced. "What's up, y'all?"

I shook my head. "Hey, Taylor. I'll have the tacos al pastor."

"Chicken burrito," Joyce said irritably.

"Chimichanga," Denise added.

The waiter stopped writing on his notepad. "Okay. I'll be right out with that."

Taylor stared at Joyce once the waiter had left the table. "What's wrong with you?"

Joyce rolled her eyes. "Nothing."

"Alonzo," Denise interjected, clarifying matters for Taylor.

"Oh, you still trippin' over him?" Taylor picked up her menu.

Joyce took a big sip of her Malibu. "I'm not trippin'. I'm venting."

"Oh, that's what you're calling it?" Denise glanced at Taylor. "Damn, Tay, you gotta leave something to the imagination. Do you always have to show everything you got?"

"Sorry, but not everybody buys their clothes at Sears, Wallflower," Taylor remarked, continuing to dig, with a smirk on her face.

Denise gave her an evil glare. "Stop calling me that."

"Calling you what?" Taylor smirked.

Denise's comfortable, laid-back posture turned into a defensive leaning toward Taylor. "I swear, you call me that again, we're gonna have a serious problem up in here."

This argument between them had been going on for years. Although Taylor had never taken Denise too seriously, in recent times, Denise had been less tolerant of Taylor's name-calling. I'd given up on playing referee between them; instead, I just changed the subject.

"Anyway, Joyce is still a bit salty about it," I said now to diffuse the tension.

"I'm not salty. I just think the thought of getting married shouldn't send a man running with his tail between his legs." Joyce stirred her drink with the straw and took another sip.

"Like I said, you weren't on the same page," Denise commented, then sipped her Coke.

I stared at Joyce. "If you tell a man, 'Marry me, or we're over,' what do you expect him to do?"

"She's got a point," Taylor interjected.

"Whatever. He should just grow some balls and be a man. 'Shida, you're supposed to be on my side. You're my friend, remember?"

"I am. That's why I'm being honest with you."

Taylor grabbed a chip and dipped it in the La Parrilla dip. "What's up with you and Robert?"

I took a sip of my drink and sighed. "Robert is finding new ways to piss me off."

"What happened with the dinner you cooked last night?" Joyce asked.

I rolled my eyes. "He said he had work to do, and then he went into his study. Totally skipped dinner."

Joyce shook her head. "Oh, please, he couldn't just put you first for a change? Just for one night?"

I sighed. "I don't know how much more I can take. I don't even know why I'm hanging on to him."

Denise looked over at me. "Maybe he just had a bad day at work. Just don't make any rash decisions."

"At least the sex is good," Taylor quipped.

I frowned. "Sex . . . good sex? What's that?"

They all looked at each other, then back at me. "Details!" they chorused.

I shook my head. "I don't even wanna talk about it."

"Ooh, is it that bad?" Denise asked.

"You better talk." Taylor nudged me with her elbow.

"Okay." I rolled my eyes. "Don't get me wrong. He's a good lover, but lately, it's like he's in a race to get off or something. No romance at all, just humping me like a rabbit."

"Mr. Quickie." Joyce laughed.

I continued. "Yeah, no kissing, no foreplay, not even boo! Just spread 'em and let him dig in!" I pumped my hips forward, as if I was humping the table.

Taylor looked at me painfully. "So you don't even have time to get wet?"

I shook my head. "Just like sandpaper."

Joyce dipped a chip. "So when was the last time it was good?"

I paused, in thought. "Last year sometime."

Taylor stared at me. "Damn! What's going on?"

"I don't know. He doesn't do the little things he used to do when we first got together. The conversations we used to have, the closeness I felt—they are just not there anymore. "

"That's how they all are. They do what they gotta do to get ya, and when they got you, all that good shit goes out the door," Joyce said, with conviction in her voice.

Everybody stared at her.

"Wow. You don't sound bitter at all," Taylor joked.

I laughed. "You need some more than I do!"

Taylor and Denise burst out laughing.

"Whatever. You know it's true," Joyce retorted.

These were my sisters, the only three people I could really call my friends.

Chapter Twenty

Oops (Oh My)

TAYLOR

I pressed RECORD on my camera and had a seat in front of it. I was looking cute in a baby blue summer dress that showed just enough cleavage to please my male viewers. I always tried to give them a little something to fantasize about. My hair was laid, lip gloss popping, and face flawless. I was ready.

"Wus up, peeps! Welcome to another edition of *Taylor Made*. Today's blog is going to be a little different. I usually don't do this, but I kinda felt like I needed to address some of y'all haters out there that be trolling my channel, leaving your little dumbass comments on my videos, then running over to my Instagram page and posting shit on my pictures and whatnot. Let me tell you something. Your lame-ass opinions on my life and what I do don't mean shit to me! I stand by everything I do or say one hundred percent! That's my opinion. You don't gotta like it or agree with it. I live my life for me, not you. Just because you see fifteen minutes of my day doesn't mean you know me. You only see what I want you to. And don't get mad at me if your man keeps liking all my IG pics."

I paused and licked my lips. "If you're having man problems, I feel bad for ya, hon. I got over half a million followers, and your man is one!" I chuckled and brushed a few hairs from my face. "If you don't like me, then you don't gotta watch my videos, because I'm gonna stay doing me! I'ma stay being fly, say what's on my mind, party, look good, and cash checks. So you can stop following me, boo. You can click that UNSUBSCRIBE button and be gone."

I paused and batted my eyes. "But I know most of y'all won't, because even though you're trying your best to hate on me, I know you love me. You just jealous, and jealousy is just love confused with hate at the same time. So keep on watching me with yo' watching ass." I smirked. "Anyway, to all my real supporters, thank you for riding with ya girl! Like I said in my last video, I'm gonna give you all the exclusive coverage at the Rick Ross after-party tonight, so look for that video tomorrow evening. I'm gonna try my best not to be too hung over, so I can edit it, so I can get it up."

I took a deep breath. "If you missed my last makeup tutorial, you can look in my previous post and check it out. That's all I got for you right now. Oh! I'm gonna post another video showing you which dress I'm going to be wearing tonight. So I might post that video before I put up the after-party. Anyway, make sure you hit the LIKE button on this video and subscribe! I'll see y'all tomorrow!" I blew the camera a kiss. "Muah! See ya!"

I stopped the recording. It was time to address some of the morons that had been coming at me. Over the past two years I'd been blogging my life, and it had become a real business. I was working as an intern at Hot 107.9, and whenever a celebrity would come in, I would make sure to get a video of them. The male rappers and R & B artists were especially friendly and didn't mind. My videos led to them inviting me to their shows, after-parties, and, of course, hotel rooms afterward. The hotel invitations I politely declined. Well, there was this one Canadian rapper I did accept a private invite from. I was still getting gifts from him to this day. Him aside, I wasn't trying to be known as the local jump-off.

When I first posted the videos on my channel, I would get over five thousand hits in twenty-four hours. I saw the number of subscribers triple overnight, and this figure went higher with each video I posted. That was when I got serious about the whole blogging thing and started looking at other popular blog channels. Many of the other channels were like full-on TV productions. They had music, graphics, professional-looking editing, and everything, so I decided to do the same with mine.

I used my contacts at the radio station to hook me up with original music and had them school me on how to edit my videos. The response to my videos was crazy! I started doing daily viewing numbers that ranged from fifty to seventy thousand, and I got advertisers from big-name companies to run fifteen-second ads in front of my videos. That was when the checks started rolling in, along with the hate from jealous women. I noticed an increase in my male fans, and the DMs were wild, so I understood why these women thought I was smashing their man. But honestly, there were probably some housewives in Sandy Springs with a wilder sex life than mine. I did date, but I was really picky about whom I let inside my promised land. Too much crazy shit floating around in this world for anybody to be loose with it.

I hadn't been in a serious relationship in years. Maybe because I hadn't met anyone I felt something deep for. Well, I had, but they weren't available, and if they were, I was not sure they would want to be with me, so I'd kept my feelings to myself. No sense in setting myself up for rejection.

Later that night I was indeed at Ross's after-party. It was at his mansion in Fayetteville and was littered with star-studded faces. My homegirl, Chanel Michaels, was with me. She was a blogger whom I had met about a year ago. Real cool chick. We would go together to most industry events like this. Fellas loved seeing two bad chicks walk into the room together. I considered her an industry friend, not like my girls 'Shida, Joyce, and Denise. They were my friends, even lame old Denise, but they weren't up for too many late nights out anymore. Joyce was focused on work, Denise had a two-year-old at home, and 'Shida, who would normally come out with me, was with that asshole Robert. So Chanel and I had become close.

We were seated on a plush white sofa, sipping on champagne, enjoying the vibe. Chanel took a puff of a blunt she had rolled and blew out a cloud of purple haze. She passed the blunt to me, and I took a hit.

"Whoa . . . This is good."

"I smoke only the best!" Chanel boasted.

"I knew there was a reason I hung out with you."

"As long as you don't get this on camera." She laughed.

I shook my head. "I know you, of all people, ain't worried about your public image."

"Nah, but I did promise Chad I wouldn't get too turned up tonight. He doesn't want me to black out and wake up naked in some rapper's bed." She looked around and raised an eyebrow. "What he don't know won't hurt him."

"Yet here you are, puffing away. Glad I don't gotta lie to anybody about what I do." I stared at her. "Isn't he gonna smell it on you, anyway?"

She shrugged her shoulders. "He'll be all right once I come home, crawl in bed, and put it on him."

"The power of the P, huh?"

"Damn right." She took another puff. "So who's gonna feel your power tonight?"

"Not a damn one here. I know that."

Chanel shook her head. "Damn, girl, don't you get tired of being alone?"

I glared at her. The weed must've gone straight to her head, given the way she was talking to me like that. "There's a difference between being alone and being lonely. I'm good."

"If you say so. I need another drink." She got up off the sofa and made her way to the bar.

Her high ass could barely walk straight, but that little comment had got under my skin. I would never admit it to her or anybody else that I did get lonely sometimes. I loved having my freedom, but it would nice to have someone in my life I could share some quality time with. Sometimes I needed more than the occasionally booty call to make me feel good.

I downed the rest of my drink, and the music switched to BMF, and it was like the whole place turned up. I got off the sofa, joined the crowd in the middle of the spacious mansion, and started dancing. A handsome brown-skinned brother stepped to me, and I started dancing with him. Our bodies touched, and I felt a tingling sensation deep inside me. The expression in his deep brown eyes was one of lust. This was a mating dance, the universal language that all men and women knew. Words were not needed to express what he wanted. Sex.

I turned around and pressed my body against his, switched my flow, and he adjusted to my groove. I felt my sexual muscles come alive. This man knew how to dance as he swayed his hips in sync with mine. I felt his hands on me, taking control, making me dance to a new rhythm. I did something I normally didn't do and became submissive. Maybe it was the weed and alcohol in my system making me feel so open. I usually didn't let strange men rub all over me like this, but his energy was intoxicating. He wasn't aggressive, just confident. It felt good being in this man's arms.

Then the DJ killed the mood by switching to another song, one that had a different tempo. I slowly turned around and faced my dance partner. Nice lips surrounded by a neatly edged goatee. Tall, dark, and handsome, dressed in designer clothes. He was just right, just my type. And given my current state of sexual arousal, just the type I could spend a meaningless night of sex with.

"My name is Jacques," he said in a smooth baritone voice.

I grinned. "I'm Taylor."

"Taylor Made," he replied.

"Yes. You watch my channel?"

"I've seen it. You're very good at what you do."

"Thank you." I looked him up and down. "And what is it that you do?"

"Mostly behind the scenes in marketing and promotions." He reached in his pocket and handed me his card.

I took the card and was surprised he hadn't yet invited me back to his place. Given my current mood, I probably would have accepted the invitation. Probably. As I looked him over, I realized he looked kind of out of place in this crowd full of rappers, thugs, and scantily dressed women. His polished speech and his neat appearance seemed more fit for a boardroom than a hip-hop party. I noticed a partial tattoo of wings peeking out the top of his black button-down. I loved men with sexy tattoos. I shifted my body and touched my hair.

"I would love to talk with you more tonight. Maybe at my place?" he said in my ear.

Here was the invitation I was expecting. Parts of my body were screaming, "Yes, let's go," but my heart wasn't in it. He would be a one-night stand. One night of pleasure, then awkwardness in the morning.

I took a deep breath and exhaled. "I'm tempted to, but I can't."

"I understand." He smiled. "I had to ask."

"I hope this doesn't mean we can't discuss business in the future."

"Not at all. Please call me." He leaned in and kissed my cheek. "Have a good night."

I watched as he walked away. Intriguing, to say the least, but not the one I wanted to be with. I glanced at his card again and decided I would definitely follow up with him. I scanned the room for Chanel but didn't see her. I meandered around a bit, but she was nowhere in sight.

I decided to look upstairs and when I got there, I saw different couples talking, smoking, or making out, the typical activities at parties like this. My intuition told me Chanel was somewhere up here. She may have had a man at home, but she was far from loyal to him. She was a playa in every sense of the word. I turned and went down another hallway and encountered more of the same. I walked a little farther and saw a room with the door ajar and peeked in. There Chanel was, leaning back on top of a king-size bed. Her pretty face had an orgasmic expression as a man's face was between her legs, licking, tasting, and slurping her nectar. Her long, beautiful legs were wrapped around his naked body.

After opening the door a little more, I stood there and watched as her male companion ate her out. Chanel's wide-open mouth and the sweetest pleasure painted on her face made the tingling sensation from earlier return. I was not into voyeurism, but I found myself frozen, watching my friend get hers. I quietly stepped inside the massive bedroom. My hand went under my dress, and I touched myself, trying to imagine the sensations she was experiencing. I rubbed my fingers over my panties and felt wetness. My clit became stiff and sensitive to my slightest touch. I felt my own orgasm approaching. Then I saw Chanel's eyes open, and we locked stares. Her lover was unaware of my presence. She didn't say anything, just smiled, then closed her eyes. So I continued to please myself. I wasn't the type to masturbate in public. I could blame it on the weed or alcohol, but the truth was I wanted to cum and didn't care where I was when I did.

Chanel moaned, and a quiet whimper escaped my lips as the feeling became more intense. I shivered and leaned against the wall. Chanel's moans were hypnotic and arousing. It was like our orgasms were linked to each other. Her greedy lover was enjoying his meal, stroking his erection as he savored her flavor. The more he licked, the closer we both got to edge. I closed my eyes. My breathing became heavy, and my legs got weak. Chanel groaned and I gasped as we came at the same time. It was only then that he heard me moaning and enjoying my orgasm. He rose from between Chanel's thighs, turned, and looked at me. He was naked and holding his erection.

"You should join us." He smiled.

I looked at Chanel, who patted the bed. She didn't seem to mind either way. I fixed my gaze on both of them, contemplating his offer. The thought of both of them pleasing me was arousing, but it was only for one night. The same as if I had gone home with Jacques.

"Not tonight." I straightened my dress.

Chanel nodded with understanding, and I exited the room. I needed more than just sex. I needed love, and there was only one person who could give me that. It was about time I did something about it.

Chapter Twenty-one

When I'm With You

ALONZO

Coming home was a good feeling. Being on the Kandi Young show had been such a great experience for me. I had learned so much from Kandi, not to mention the industry networking had been priceless. I'd loved living in Miami, loved the beaches, the night life and, of course, the women. It was all exquisite, but regardless of that, Atlanta had always felt like home. That was why I had decided to move back when Mark called and offered me my own show from 10:00 a.m. to 2:00 p.m. Monday through Friday.

I'd kept my return to Atlanta low key. Only Mark and Sean knew I was moving back. Sean had been living at my house while I'd been in Miami. Of course, with his music career taking off and his son, Amir, he had barely been there half the time. My flight landed at Hartsfield-Jackson Atlanta at noon, and Sean was there to pick me up. I was standing curbside with my luggage when he pulled up in his black Tahoe.

"What's up, Tubbs?" he yelled through the window.

"You know the *Miami Vice* thing wasn't funny the first time you did it. Guess what? It still isn't funny."

He popped the trunk of the Tahoe and got out. "I laughed, so that's all that matters."

We gave each other a man hug and loaded my luggage into the truck. Minutes later we were on I-85 South, heading toward my house.

"I see you upgraded the ride, homie. The music business must be treating you right." Sean's truck was nice and still had that new car smell.

Sean gave me the side-eye. "Bruh, the music business ain't shit. Rapping is a dead art."

"Then how you pushing this?"

"Production. I produced three tracks on T.I.'s last album. Cashed a couple nice checks off that."

"I see!" I nodded. "So you gonna fall back on rapping?"

"Yeah, I can't be out here struggling, trying to sell mixtapes, when I got two mouths to feed. Christy's trifling ass trying to get an increase in child support too." He looked at me. "Please tell me why anyone would need six thousand a month for a six-year-old girl?"

I shook my head. "You know she need that support. So I guess Denise ain't tripping, huh?"

He smiled. "Nah, she barely wants to take what I give her now. I take care of the house note and day-care bills. Whenever I wanna come over and see Amir, it's never an issue. That woman there is special." He paused and nodded his head. "Yeah, special. I regret not telling her the truth sooner, and don't say, 'I told you so!'"

I smirked. "I wasn't going to, but you know I did."

We both laughed.

"Shut up," he told me.

"So are you two trying to work it out?"

"I'm trying. She's not as pissed as she was a while back. We get close every now and then, but then she gets that look in her eye and puts up a wall." He sighed. "She still doesn't trust me."

"Have you given her more reasons not to?"

"Nope. I ain't messing with no other chick. All I'm about is getting this money and taking care of my kids. I know she still loves me, but she's a stubborn woman."

"Yeah, I know she's still probably ain't feeling me, either."

"Nope, she hates yo' ass too," he confirmed, then changed the subject. "So tell me, bruh, how were them South Beach chicks?"

I grinned. "They come in all shapes and sizes. Cuban, Jamaican, Dominican, Haitian, and even the natives. Beautiful women, like a black man's paradise."

Sean glanced over at me. "And?"

"And I took part in all of them."

He reached over and gave me dap. "My man."

"But it's good to be home again."

"So are you gonna holla at ole girl?"

"Joyce? Nah, I can't make the same mistake twice," I replied.

"Now you know I wasn't talking about her, bruh. Rashida."

I exhaled. I knew that was what he meant, and truth be told, Rashida was one of the main reasons why I wanted to come back. She had stayed on my mind over the past two years. I had always asked Sean about her, and he had kept me up to date. The fact that she hadn't married Robert yet told me that just maybe I might have a second chance.

"I'm gonna see what happens. With Joyce being her best friend, it might not work out."

"Well, if she's the one, don't be like me and fuck it up."

Sean exited the highway and headed to my house. Everything was as I remembered it.

I took a few days to get settled again, checked in with Mark at the station, and was ready to start my show in a week. Everything was falling into place, so I decided it was time to see her.

I drove over to Camp Creek and saw that Shidas Styles was open for business, and from the looks of it, business was good. From the outside looking in, I saw eight workstations with hairdressers tending to their clients, but I didn't see Rashida. Feeling defeated, I began walking back to the parking lot. Just then, a gray Maserati parked close to my car, and she got out. There she was, just as beautiful as she had been two years ago. She wore a short, flowing dashiki-style dress and high-heeled shoes. Her legs were long and smooth. Her curves were sculpted like she had been a runner. She wore just enough makeup, as usual. She didn't need it with a gorgeous face like that. Her dreads were intricately styled in an updo. Simply flawless. She didn't see me right away. Her eyes were looking at a small tablet in her hand, so I decided to walk toward her.

When I got pretty close, I called her name. "'Shida."

She glanced up from her tablet. "Alonzo?" A wide smile spread across her face.

I returned her smile. "It's good to see you."

"It's good to see you too!"

I could hear the excitement in her voice, and she hugged me. It felt good holding her in my arms again. Her soft body against mine aroused all my senses. She was physically and mentally stimulating me, causing my manhood to rise. She held on to me like a woman in love, and I did the same like a man in love. Finally, she slowly let me go and gazed up into my eyes.

"I can't believe you're here. Are you just visiting?"

"No, I'm back permanently."

She furrowed her eyebrows. "Really? Uh, what happened with the Kandi Young show?"

"I got offered my own show here in Atlanta."

She nodded. "Congrats! You sounded so natural on that show. I knew it was only a matter of time before you got your own."

"So you've been listening," I noted.

"I caught a few shows. You're good."

"Thanks." I looked back at her shop. "So I see things are going good for you!"

"Yeah, it keeps me busy, but I love it."

"I always knew it would be a success. Your skills are incredible."

She blushed. "You don't have to say that."

"I told you this would happen! I've never seen anybody do the things you do with hair."

"I try my best."

There was so much joy in her eyes, and there were so many things we were saying to each other, without actually saying them. Her feelings for me hadn't changed over the years, and neither had other things.

"How's Joyce these days?" I asked.

There was a slight change in her body language. "She's fine . . . You know how Joyce is."

I smiled. "That's good. I'm glad she's moved on." I paused. "And you?"

She looked away from me. "I'm still with Robert."

I nodded. "Everything okay?"

She looked back at me. "As good as it can be."

I could see it in her eyes when she talked about him—sadness. There was so much I wanted to say, but now wasn't the time, and this wasn't the place, but we both knew the truth. If fate had been different, if she had been with Robert when we met, it would be me who was with her.

"Listen, Rashida . . . I never meant to hurt Joyce. You know that, right? I just couldn't give her what she wanted from me."

"I know," she told me, and her eyes locked with mine. "Sometimes things just happen that are out of our control."

"Yeah, well, I better let you get to work. It was good seeing you again."

"Yeah, you too."

"Give me a call. Maybe we can talk sometime."

She hugged me again. "I will."

I watched as she slowly walked away. Measured, sexy, and breathtaking. When she reached the door to the salon, she turned and looked back at me. She gave me a look that said, *Please don't leave me again*, and I swore to myself I wouldn't let her go this time.

Chapter Twenty-two

Kiss

RASHIDA

I couldn't believe he was back. After all this time, Alonzo was back in my life just like that, and I couldn't stop thinking about him. His time in Miami had done him well. He was still as handsome as I last remembered him. So many emotions rushed back to me at once. When he held me in his arms, I didn't want to let go.

Was it wrong to feel so good in another man's arms? Was it wrong for me to be in love with my best friend's ex-boyfriend? Was it wrong to feel this happy? And even though I knew the answers to these questions in my head, a part of me didn't care. All I knew was he had returned and had come here looking for me. His feelings were just as strong as before, but the same problems still remained.

Joyce's feelings were my main concern. It would ruin our friendship if I were to move forward with him. How could I be so selfish to do that to her? But at the same time, how could I be that selfish to myself to deny my feelings? Humans by nature were selfish creatures, so was it wrong for me to give in to that side? Why should I sacrifice my happiness? I'd already had both of my parents taken away from me, so why should I have to give up on love too? I loved Joyce like a sister, but that kind of love didn't make me feel good at night. It didn't hold me in its arms and make love to me. That kind of love didn't make me feel like a woman, and neither did Robert.

I realized I was still with Robert out of convenience, out of a need not to be alone. I didn't want to be lonely. I wanted to feel loved, and he had done that for a while, but lately we'd been more like roommates than lovers. Roommates who saw each other naked and had passionless sex. An obligational nut that left me unsatisfied. Robert had become just another sex toy in my bed. He was a live-action vibrator that rattled around inside me, trying to make me feel good. Not even someone I could talk to anymore. Regardless of what may happen with Alonzo, I knew that this relationship with Robert had to end.

I arrived home and pulled into the garage, next to Robert's BMW, and exhaled. It was unusual for him to be home before me. I went inside and saw him sitting on the couch, watching TV.

"Hey, you're home early," I acknowledged, then placed my stuff on the counter.

He glanced my way. "The two o'clock meeting got canceled."

"Oh, okay. Let me warm up some dinner." I walked into the kitchen.

"I'm really not in the mood for leftovers," he called out. "How about you cook the salmon?"

I had a puzzled look on my face. "Salmon?" I walked back out into the living room. "Robert, I cooked a steak for you last night, and you made me put it up for tonight."

"I'm not in the mood for steak. I want the fish instead," he replied dryly.

I frowned. "Did you even take it out of the freezer yet?"

"No. Just go ahead and do it now."

I glared at him. "So you've been here for how long? You didn't want fish then?"

Robert stared at me nonchalantly. "Why are you making such a big deal out of it?"

I couldn't believe this man. "I'm making a big deal out of it because I slaved last night to make you a gourmet dinner, which you didn't eat, and now you want me to cook some frozen-ass fish, which you couldn't bother to take out for me!"

Robert got annoyed and sighed loudly. "Well, let's not forget that I didn't ask you to cook the steak in the first place!"

I really wanted to spit in his face at that moment, cuss him out, and act like a really ratchet bitch, but I wasn't going to be that chick. "You know what? I'm not going to argue with you. I'm going over to Taylor's tonight, so if you want salmon, cook it yourself!"

I spun around and headed back to the garage, got in my car, and burned rubber out of there. I was so pissed off! That was it. I was done with him. There was no reason I should feel like this. This had nothing to do with Alonzo being back and everything to do with Robert's trifling ass. A few minutes later I was at Taylor's condo in downtown Atlanta. I called Denise and Joyce, and they came over as well. Taylor took out a bottle of moscato for us, but I needed to dull my senses and calm my nerves with something a little more potent than cheap wine. SZA's "Broken Clocks" was playing on Taylor's phone, and it captured my mood perfectly. Taylor always had the natural herbs I was looking for.

I took a hit of the blunt and passed it to Taylor. I didn't always smoke weed, but when I did, I liked the good stuff. "Why this isn't legal in all fifty states yet is beyond me."

Taylor smiled and took a hit. "Trust me, it will be."

"I can't believe Robert acted like that," Denise said, with a glass of wine in her hand.

"Yep. He actually had the nerve to ask me to cook some fish for him after all that food I cooked for him last night."

Joyce shook her head in disbelief. "What's wrong with him?"

Denise sighed. "That was very rude of him."

"He's a jackass!" Taylor blurted. "I ain't never liked that fool. No offense, 'Shida."

I nodded. "None taken. To tell you the truth, I don't like him much these days, either."

"You probably need to go ahead and cut him loose." Joyce grabbed some pretzels from the bowl in her lap.

"Just like that?" Denise looked at Joyce. "You don't just end a relationship over an argument over some fish."

"And when was the last time you had a relationship?" Taylor asked.

"This isn't about me. This is about Rashida," Denise replied calmly.

Taylor chuckled. "You better pour some water on that thang before it dries up."

Denise stared at Taylor. "I don't have to worry about sex. It's there whenever I want it. And you can ask him . . . It's always good and wet."

Taylor smirked. "Excuse me, then."

Rashida sighed. "Oh, there's a change coming. He just don't know it yet."

Taylor sat up straight and stared at me. "About damn time! When was the last time he told you he loved you? When was the last time he did something special for you?"

I laughed. "I know I should have ended this a long time ago, but despite how much I can't stand him right now, a part of me still cares about him. He wasn't always an asshole."

"He's trash." Taylor took a hit of the blunt and continued. "'Shida, all them emotions you're feeling right now are clouding your judgment. Shit isn't going to change overnight, and I don't wanna be the one to tell ya I told you so." Taylor passed the blunt to Joyce.

"Well, don't then." I looked at Joyce and wondered if I should say this to her or not. But I needed to see how she would react. "By the way, I saw Alonzo today."

Joyce took a puff, then passed the weed to Denise. "Oh really?"

Denise looked at me. "He's back in town?"

"Yeah, I saw him in the Publix over in Camp Creek," I lied. I didn't want to tell her he went to my salon, looking for me. "He's got a new radio show here in Atlanta."

Joyce shrugged her shoulders. "Good for him."

"So you don't care anymore?" I asked her.

"Nope. I realized Alonzo is never going to change, and I never want to put myself in that situation again. You were right. I was being petty about it. I don't wanna be with any man who doesn't want to be with me. I deserve better than that."

I stared at her. "Are you sure about that? If you saw him with another woman, it wouldn't bother you?"

Joyce stared at me. "Not anymore. He's free to be with any woman he wants. It's been two years. I don't have any claim on him."

I nodded. I heard what she was saying, but did she really feel like that inside? Was she just putting up a front because we were here? If she knew Alonzo and I wanted to be together, would she be so nonchalant about it?

"I like this new Joyce," Taylor declared. "She gives zero fucks!"

We all laughed.

"I'm just trying to move on with my life. I don't got time to hold on to the past." Joyce glanced at her watch.

"Damn, it's late. I gotta get up early tomorrow." She got up off the couch and picked up her bag.

Denise also stood up. "I better get going too. Sean has Amir, and I know he hasn't put him down for bed yet." She gave the blunt to Taylor.

"Give Amir a kiss for me," Taylor told Denise. "You know I don't mind babysitting him if Sean isn't available."

Denise smiled at her. "Okay. Sometimes I think he likes you more than me."

"Well, I'm his auntie Tay-Tay."

Denise nodded. "Yes, you are."

Taylor nodded. That was one of the few kind moments between them. When it came to Amir, Taylor showed a soft and loving side we rarely saw from her. Ever since he was born, Taylor, along with me and Joyce, had been there for him. She would always buy outfits she thought he would look cute in and give them to Denise. Amir was the peacemaker they both needed.

I shook my head. "I don't even wanna deal with Robert. I'ma hang out here for a minute."

Joyce and Denise said their goodbyes and left.

Taylor was still next to me, smoking. "'Shida, I didn't mean to sound mean about it, but you could do a lot better than Robert."

"I know. I've just been so frustrated the past couple of months, it's crazy!"

Taylor passed the blunt to me, and I took a puff. Damn, this was some good stuff. I just wanted to get faded and forget about my problems. We talked about her YouTube channel for a few minutes; then the conversation went back to Joyce.

"Do you really think Joyce is over Alonzo?" Taylor asked.

"I hope so. I want to see her happy."

Taylor nodded. "We all deserve to be happy with somebody."

"I agree with that. We just gotta make sure we choose the right one."

Taylor took a hit and blew out a cloud of smoke. "That's not as easy as it sounds. Lately, I've been asking myself if I've been ignoring the right one for me."

I looked at her. "Maybe you have. I know for a fact I made a bad choice being with Robert. I didn't see it at the time, but I know now." I shook my head. "I let the person I should've been with get away, and I regret it. Do yourself a favor, Taylor. If you have feelings for somebody, don't be afraid to let them know. Don't live with regrets."

Taylor nodded. "Thanks for always giving me the best advice, 'Shida."

I smiled at her. "Don't worry. I'll always be here for you."

Taylor hugged me. I closed my eyes. The weed had me feeling faded. She pulled away from me and stared in my eyes. Taylor traced her finger down the side of my face, then leaned in and kissed me.

At first, I was surprised by it, but I kissed her back. Probably out of instinct or curiosity. Maybe both. Taylor was a damn good kisser. Her lips tugged at mine. It felt like I was outside of my body, watching it happen. Before I realized what we were doing, the kiss had escalated into a French kiss. I gently pulled back, a little stunned by what was happening. Before I could say something, Taylor placed her finger on my lips.

"Before you say anything, let me tell you something. I've been holding on to this for a long time now. 'Shida, since the day we met in high school, I've been attracted to you. At first, I thought it was just . . . you know, curiosity, but it never went away."

What? She has? I was a bit confused about where all this was coming from. I had never for a moment thought Taylor liked me like that. "What are you saying, Taylor?"

"I'm saying, I don't wanna have any regrets."

She kissed me again, then gently pushed me back down onto the couch. I felt strange and surprisingly aroused. Taylor kissed my neck, moved down my body, and I closed my eyes, caught up in the moment. I felt something I hadn't felt in months—pleasure. All these months with Robert had left me sexually starved and longing for satisfaction. Taylor's wet kisses went farther down my body. She pushed my dress up around my waist, went between my legs, and kissed my inner thighs. I'd never been with a woman. I had always seen the beauty in other women and had even had a girl crush on a few, but I'd never considered really being with one. Not my thing. But for some reason, this felt good.

I was breathing hard and felt all tingly in my vagina. Taylor was making me wet. This was wrong. This shouldn't be turning me on, but it was. Then she pulled my panties to the side and gently kissed my sex. It felt good. Taylor was one of my best friends in the world and was going down on me. I wasn't not gay, and no matter how good this felt, I had to stop it. I pulled away from her and sat up straight.

"Taylor, I can't do this."

She sat up on her couch, stared at me, and exhaled. I could see the rejection on her face. This was real for her.

"I'm sorry."

She didn't reply. She nodded and looked away from me.

My high was gone, and the moment had become awkward. I got up, straightened my clothes, then walked to the door. Then I left quietly.

When I got home, I noticed that Robert's BMW was gone. He had probably gone back to his condo in the city. *Good.* He was the last person I wanted to see. I went inside and pulled off my clothes. I was naked. Free. I always felt more comfortable that way. I went and took a shower, letting the water beat down on my body. Today had been a very eventful one. Alonzo, the love of my life, had returned to town. Robert had become an even more insufferable mate, and Taylor, one my closest friends, had almost seduced me. What the hell was going on in my life? I needed to make some decisions. It was time I started making choices that were in my best interest.

Chapter Twenty-three

Brown Sugar

JOYCE

I didn't want to show it in front of the others, but hearing that Alonzo was back in town made me feel some type way. It had been two years since we broke up. It had hurt. I had really been falling in love with him, but the feelings hadn't been not mutual. I hated to admit it, but I knew I had pushed him into making a decision I knew he wasn't ready to make. Looking back on our relationship now, even if Alonzo had stayed in Atlanta, I couldn't envision that our relationship would have lasted. I had made it more than it was.

I hadn't been in another relationship since him and didn't want one. In his absence I had dived into my work and had become a very lucrative Realtor by selling high-end estate to some of the wealthiest people in Atlanta. I had become so successful, I'd been able to move out of my apartment in Druid Hills and into a nice five-bedroom, three-bathroom home with high ceilings on Mount Paran Road, near Rashida's house. The house had been empty for five years, and I'd been able to get the place for way below the listed price. Being in the industry had its advantages. I had been here for five months now and had nearly unpacked every box, but there was one box in a corner of my basement that I hadn't opened. It had Alonzo's name written on it.

When I got home from Taylor's place, I went to the basement and retrieved the box. I opened it up and looked at the contents. Three T-shirts, a pair of red and white Jordans, and a few CDs. R. Kelly's *TP-2. com*, Jay-Z's *The Blueprint*, and Maxwell's *blackSUM-MERS'night*. All things he had left behind and that I'd been holding on to for the past two years. Staring at the Maxwell album reminded me of every song we had made love to. I hadn't listened to this album since we were together. He used to say to me that I couldn't have his T-shirts, and I'd purposely wear them with just some panties just to turn him on. I needed to see him and get some things off my chest.

The next day after work, I drove down to his house. Denise told me that Sean had been living there since Alonzo moved to Miami, so I had no doubt he would come right back there. I pulled into his driveway and parked behind his car. My heart was racing. I sat for a second to calm my nerves and reassure myself that I needed to do this. I grabbed the box, got out of my car, and walked to his front door. As I rang the doorbell, my heart was doing triple time. It was too late to run away now. The door opened, and I saw him. Damn him for looking so good. I could see in his eyes that he was shocked to see me.

"Joyce . . . hi."

"Hello, Alonzo."

We stared at each other for a few seconds. I didn't know what I wanted to do more: to kiss him or punch him. Neither would be right.

"How are you?" he asked to break the silence.

"I'm fine."

"Come in." He stepped to the side, and I walked in. He closed the door. "How did you know I was back?"

"'Shida told me she ran into you in Publix."

"Publix? Oh, yeah, right."

"Here." I handed him the box, and he put it on the table in the living room. After opening it, he smiled.

"Oh, wow . . . I was wondering where these were." He held up his Jordans and then placed them back in the box. "Thank you."

"So I heard you have a new show."

He nodded. "Yeah, it starts on Monday."

"Good for you." I exhaled. "Alonzo, I didn't just come here to give you your things. I have something I need to say to you."

"Okay."

I sighed. "It wasn't fair of me to give you an ultimatum. I know that now, and I'm sorry."

Alonzo had a surprised look on his face. I guessed he thought I was going to lay into him like some bitter woman. Lucky for him, I had moved beyond those feelings.

"Wow, thank you. Joyce. I never meant to hurt you. I'm sorry I couldn't give you what you wanted."

"Don't be. Your heart wasn't in it. It only would've ended badly between us."

He sighed. "You're right. I did love you."

"Do you still?" I asked.

He looked at me, emotionless. "I'm in love with another woman."

That was a dagger. I didn't know why I had asked. "I see."

"I'm sorry."

"Don't apologize. You've moved on, and so have I."

He nodded.

I glanced at my watch. "I should go."

"Okay." He walked me to his front door. "It was good seeing you again, Joyce."

I stared at him, and then we hugged. "It was good seeing you too."

It felt good hugging him. Thoughts of the last time I was in his arms flashed in my mind. Explicit thoughts. Our time together had been good, but it was over now. I let him go, stepped outside, got in my car, and left. I felt good about what I had done. It felt like a weight had been lifted off my chest. I wasn't carrying around any resentment anymore. Maybe now I could really move on with my life.

On my way home, I decided to stop by 'Shida's house to tell her what had happened with Alonzo. When I pulled up, I didn't see her car, but I did see a sporty-looking red Audi in the driveway. *Don't tell me she went and bought a new car*, I thought. I knew Robert wouldn't be driving anything as flashy as that. I went to the door, rang the doorbell, then waited. No one answered the door. I got tired of waiting on her slow behind, so I took out the key she had given me, unlocked the front door, and went inside. I walked into the foyer and saw nobody.

I called out her name. "'Shida."

There was no answer, but I heard a noise from upstairs, so I headed in that direction. When I got to the top of the steps, I realized a shower was running. Then I heard it cut off, but the sound didn't come from her bedroom. Maybe it was Robert. *Ugh.* I turned around, started to go back down the stairs, and then I heard him.

"Hello?"

It wasn't Robert's voice. I turned and saw him. He was standing at the top of the staircase, looking down at me. A blue towel was wrapped around his waist, leaving most of his body exposed. He was damn near naked. His body was amazing and in no way average. Water was dripping from his body like rain. He looked like an Olympian swimmer who had just completed the four-hundred-meter freestyle. His face . . . I recognized him.

"Raheem?"

His smile was wide and sexy. "Joyce . . . hey. How you doing?"

My voice cracked when I said, "I'm good. When did you get here?"

"I just got in this morning from L.A."

"Oh, you drove?"

"Yeah, it took about three days, but it felt like I was flying in my little baby out there."

"Oh . . ."

I couldn't keep my eyes off his body: thin waist, broad shoulders, and a strong chest with erect nipples that just begged to be sucked and licked. His arms were so cut and defined by what must have been hours of lifting weights. Droplets of water were still trickling down his brown sugar–colored skin. Nice, sexy lips surrounded by a nicely shaped goatee. Raheem was no longer the skinny little boy I remembered. He was a man. A sexy one at that. I felt a throbbing sensation between my thighs. Two years without sex had left me completely vulnerable to the physique of this gorgeous young man.

His eyes were scanning my body, and then he grinned. I couldn't stand still; I keep shifting my weight, clearing my throat. He rattled my senses and made me feel anxious from looking at him.

"Are you looking for 'Shida?"

I cleared my throat again. "Yes."

"She went to the store. She said she'll be back in a minute."

"Oh." My eyes wandered down to his towel, the only thing on his six-foot-two body that kept him from being nude. In my mind, he already was. All his brown-sugar flesh was exposed to me. The bulge underneath his towel was calling me. Teasing me. Raheem wasn't the only one of us who was wet.

He smiled. "Do you wanna wait?"

What was I doing? This was 'Shida's little brother I was ogling. He was the boy that I used to kick out of her bedroom for being annoying to us when I slept over her place during our teen years.

I snapped back to my senses. "No. I'll call her later."

"You sure you wanna leave?" he asked in a sexy tone.

"No . . . yes!" I spun around and went down the stairs. "Nice seeing you, Raheem!"

I glanced back one last time at his stunning body.

He smiled. "Good seeing you too."

I swallowed hard and quickly went out the door.

Chapter Twenty-four

Count On Me

TAYLOR

I pressed RECORD on my camera and had a seat in front of it. I had recently dyed my hair vibrant hues of auburn, caramel, and honey that flowed down my back. Those colors complimented my cinnamon complexion much more than the blond I had had before. I decided to wear a simple white sweater and faded blue jeans. I wasn't too concerned with being fashionable today. After what had happened with Rashida the other night, I was definitely in my feelings.

I smiled. "Hello, everybody. Welcome to another edition of *Taylor Made*. Uh, today I wanna talk to you about a situation I'm going through. As you all know, I've been single for a while, and I'm not exactly looking for a relationship. If I meet the right person and the situation's right, then I feel like it will happen." I paused and thought about my next few words.

"Yeah, it'll happen. I'm not trying to force it, ya know? Let me ask you guys out there in YouTube land a question. You ever had, like, a friend that you were really close with, and somewhere down the line, you unexpectedly really started feeling them? Like, it wasn't one those things where you always liked them, and you got put in the friend zone. No, you were really just friends, and then, you know, feelings started happening, but then you feel like you can't tell that person how you feel, because you're not sure if they're feeling you like that. Plus, you don't wanna F up the friendship, right?" I paused again.

"Well, if you haven't guessed already, I have a close friend like that. We've been friends for years, and I never told them how I felt until recently." I sat for a moment in silence, shifted my body, and continued. "I wasn't going to, but it just kinda happened, and at first, it felt like the feeling was mutual, until they said it wasn't." I exhaled. "And now I'm not sure if we're still friends. I can't help but think if I hadn't said anything, I would still have my friend." My eyes got watery. I was feeling emotional and didn't like feeling that way. I wiped my eyes. "So my question for you all is, is it better to say how you feel or keep it to yourself? Did I do the right thing? Did I ruin a friendship? You can post your answers in the comments section." I sighed again. "Well, that's all I got today. If you liked this video, make sure you hit the thumbs-up. See you all tomorrow."

I got up and turned off the camera. I was not sure it was a great idea to do a vlog, but I needed to get my feelings out, especially since 'Shida hadn't called or texted me since she left here the other night. I didn't know what I had been thinking, but when she'd told me not to live with any regrets, I'd taken it as a sign to be honest with her. When I kissed her, it had felt so right. I felt something I hadn't felt in years—a real connection—but when she pulled away, I felt like a fool. I was so embarrassed. Obviously, 'Shida had no interest in being with a girl. That must have been some premium weed we were smoking for things to have gone as far as they had.

I sat at my desk in the living room, edited the video, then posted it. I glanced at my phone. No new messages. I sighed. I decided to get out and do some retail therapy down in Atlantic Station. Once I arrived there, I went from the GAP to Old Navy, then spent some time in H&M, trying on some clothes. I vlogged a little bit too. All that and I still couldn't get my mind off what was really bothering me. I wondered if 'Shida had told Denise or Joyce what happened between us. If she had, it might affect my friendship with them as well. I didn't always say it, but I loved them all like sisters. Even when I was fussing with Denise, I still loved her. And ever since she had had Amir, we'd argued less. I really did feel like his auntie. Walking around Atlantic Station wasn't helping, so I went home.

Once I got back to my place, I took refuge in my bedroom. Lying in bed, I was lost in thought. I couldn't believe I was feeling so heartbroken. This was why I hadn't had a serious relationship in years: I hated dealing with emotions like this. Why had I kissed her? Everything would have been fine if I hadn't done that. My cell chimed, and I rolled over and grabbed it off the nightstand. Chanel's picture was on the display. It wasn't who I wanted it to be. With a slight groan, I sent the call to voicemail and put the phone back down. Just as I got comfortable again, my doorbell rang. I wasn't in the mood to see anybody, so I simply lay there. The bell rang repeatedly, so finally I jumped up, pissed off. Whoever was at my goddamned door was going to get their ass kicked. When I reached the entryway, I looked through the peephole and saw her. I froze. I wasn't expecting to see 'Shida.

I opened the door. "Hey."

She smiled. "Hey."

I stepped back, and she walked in and sat down on the couch. I flicked on the lights and sat next to her. Here we were again, in the same spot we had been in two nights ago. I was nervous, and I could tell by the look on her face she was a little nervous as well. She looked cute, as always. Her dreads hung freely. She wore black jeans with a gray-and-black T-shirt and had black-and-white Converse on her feet. She rubbed her hands, and I bounced my leg. We conveyed our nerves in different ways.

"I didn't think you would ever want to come back here and see me," I finally said in a low voice.

She looked at me. "Why would you think that?"

"You haven't called or texted me since."

She smiled. "Raheem drove in from L.A. yesterday, and I got caught up spending time with him."

"Oh? I haven't seen him in years."

"Yeah. Besides, I didn't want to talk to you over the phone." She paused. "I saw your vlog. Why didn't you say anything to me before?"

I exhaled. "How was I supposed to say it? Hey, I've been attracted to you since freshman year? I don't think you would have been so open to that."

"You're probably right. So you're bisexual?"

I nodded. "Yes, but I've never dated women, just hooked up with a few on occasion. But you, you're the first one who really meant something to me."

"Oh my God. All these years I had no idea. You could have told me. It wouldn't have changed anything between us."

"How did I know? I didn't want to take the chance of messing up our friendship."

"Well, I'm glad I know now."

I looked at her, confused. "Are you?"

"Yes." She reached over and took my hand. "It must have been difficult carrying those feelings around for so long. At least now everything is out in the open and we can talk about it."

"What's there to talk about? I know you're not bi, 'Shida."

"You're right. I'm not, but you're my friend, and I love you. In your vlog, you asked if you had ruined a friendship, and the answer is no. It's going take more than a little girl-on-girl action to ruin it."

I smiled.

"Although, you were very good at what you were doing," she admitted, with a raised eyebrow and a smirk.

"So you were curious?"

She chuckled. "Maybe a little . . . It was different. Hell, a few more minutes of that and I would be questioning if I really was bi." We both laughed. "You're a smooth operator."

"Shut up before I finish the job."

She folded her arms over her chest. "Oh, so you gonna take it, huh?"

"Trust me, I wouldn't have to," I responded with confidence.

We laughed, then hugged. It felt good, not sexually but sisterly. No matter what, 'Shida was my friend, and I respected that. There may have been feelings, but now I was thinking it was more infatuation than love. Now that everything was out in the open, I could move beyond it.

After she left, I checked my vlog, and to my surprise, I had over one hundred thousand views and eighty thousand likes in only five hours of it being posted. Most of the comments were positive and supportive of what I did. I guessed showing my emotions for a change was a good thing.

Chapter Twenty-five

Nice For What?

RASHIDA

I was glad I was able to sit down with Taylor and deal with what had happened between us the other night. I'd felt so bad for her after I saw her vlog expressing her feelings for me. I still couldn't believe she felt that way. I guessed you never really knew what was in someone's heart until they told you. I wondered if Joyce could sense that Alonzo and I had feelings for one another when they were together. Probably not. That could be why I felt so guilty about it.

Before I headed home from Taylor's place, I checked my cell and saw I had received a text message from Robert.

I'm sorry. Are you still mad. 7:36 p.m.

Too little too late, I thought. I didn't reply and then deleted his text. I was so over him. The only thing stopping me from breaking up with him was Raheem's unexpected arrival. I was happy to see him, but his arrival couldn't have been at a more awkward time, so I had decided to postpone the inevitable. My mind shifted to thoughts of Alonzo. I wanted to see him again, so I sent him a text.

Hello. Can we have lunch tomorrow? 7:37 p.m.

A few seconds later, he replied.

Sure. How about J.R. Crickets @ Camp Creek at 12? 7:44 p.m.

Sounds good. See you then. 7:44 p.m.

He had remembered that J.R. Crickets was my favorite spot for wings. Thoughts of spending time with him made me smile as I started my car and steered it into traffic. When I pulled into my garage, I saw Raheem's Audi and Robert's BMW. I sighed, knowing I had to deal with Robert tonight. I got out of my car and went inside, and there they were, Robert and Raheem, on the sectional, watching ESPN. I almost laughed at Robert acting like he was really interested in sports. I knew for a fact he hated them.

Raheem looked over at me. "Hey, sis."

"Hey." I put my bag down on a small corner table in the living room.

Robert stood up and walked toward me. "Hey, love." He went in to kiss my lips, but I turned my head and walked away, forcing him to peck the air.

I sat next to my brother and gave him a hug. "It's so good to have you here."

"It's good to be here with you." He hugged me back.

Robert went back to the sofa and sat down. He stared at me, hoping I would talk to him, but I wasn't giving him any attention.

"So what do you plan on getting into while you're here, Raheem?" I asked.

"Well, I have a few auditions coming up. Hopefully, I can get something going out here."

Robert injected himself into the conversation. "Interesting. I thought L.A. would be the ideal place for you to get work."

"You would think so," Raheem replied, "but there are so many actors out there trying to get the same parts.

It's almost impossible to break through unless you know somebody. Atlanta is becoming the new black Hollywood. I got a few contacts out here who have been telling me this is where I need to be. And right now I'm working on an independent film called *The Refill*."

"That's great," Robert said. "And I know Rashida is more than thrilled to have you back here. She's always telling me how much she misses you." Robert smiled at me, but I adverted my eyes from him.

"Well, I hope the auditions go well and you stay out here for a little bit. You know you can stay here as long as you want," I told Raheem.

"Thanks, sis. Oh, Joyce stopped by here earlier, looking for you."

"Oh, okay. I'll call her."

Raheem smiled. "It was really good seeing her again. What's she doing these days?"

"She's a workaholic. I barely see her."

"Oh, so she's not dating anybody?"

I stared at my brother. "No. Why are you so interested?"

"Just asking." He smirked. "She looked good."

I could tell Raheem was more than just curious about her. Not sure how much of a chance he stood. "Yeah, okay. Just remember she's my friend, Rah."

"What's that supposed to mean?"

I pointed my finger at him. "Just be respectful."

A wide smile spread across his handsome face. "I always am."

"Joyce is a good girl. You could do a whole lot worse," Robert chimed in.

I rolled my eyes. "Anyway, I'm gonna head up. I'll see you in the morning." I gave my brother a kiss on his cheek and got up.

"All right, 'Shida. Have a good night."

I walked up the staircase and heard Robert following me. I shook my head, quickly went into my bedroom, and closed the door. A few seconds later the door opened. Robert and I stared at each other for a moment; then I turned and went into my closet.

"Rashida, I know you're still upset with me." He stood in the closet doorway. "I want you to know how sorry I am. I was completely out of line, and I am sorry for speaking to you that way."

I looked at him. "Okay." I continued picking out my clothes for tomorrow.

"Okay? As in we're okay?"

I glanced at him. "Excuse me." I walked by him, sat on the bed, picked up the remote, and turned on the TV.

Robert stared at me. "You're still upset."

"No, I'm not."

"Then what are you? Because clearly you still feel some type of way."

"What I am is over it."

He repeated. "Over it? Over what exactly?"

I stared at him. "Everything."

"What more do you want me to say?" he asked, raising his voice.

"Keep your tone down."

He stood in front of the TV, blocking my view. People didn't say what they meant very often. You had to read between the lines of their behavior and what they said to get to what they truly felt. Energy was the highest form of communication, and I knew exactly what Robert wanted.

"Rashida, I'm trying to make things right here. You have to meet me halfway."

"Meet you halfway?" I snapped. "Robert, I've been trying to meet you halfway for months. Right now, I'm tired and just wanna relax."

"This is so immature of you. Instead of dealing with the situation, you act like a child. If you would just say how you feel, we could be truly over it. I swear, I don't know why I put up with your attitude. I guess I was hoping that being with me would help you mature into a grown woman, but obviously, you still have a long way to go."

I glared at him. "What's immature is a grown man acting like a spoiled child. I'm not your cook. I'm not here to clean up after you and be ignored. And I'm not here for you to roll over on in the middle of the night and poke on whenever you get a hard-on. So don't stand in my bedroom and insult me because I'm not willing to forgive you and kiss your ass. I've been a grown woman taking care of myself long before I met you, so if you can't deal with me, then leave."

Robert stood there with a shocked expression on his face. "Unbelievable. I know I'm not perfect, Rashida, but I do love you, and I'm trying to make this relationship work. I hope you grow up and realize that before it's too late."

He turned and marched out of my bedroom. I got up and locked the door behind him. It was far too late for us. It had taken all my willpower not to explode on him and tell him we were done, but I didn't want to be angry and emotional when I did it. I wanted to have a clear mind and be rational when I did. No screaming and fussing, just a clean break. For now, I just wanted to rest my mind and focus on my lunch with Alonzo tomorrow.

I arrived at J.R. Crickets five minutes before twelve and saw Alonzo sitting at a booth, waiting on me. Seeing his handsome face made me smile. He glanced up, looked at me, and smiled as his eyes took in everything. He stood and greeted me with a deep hug. It felt so good being in his arms and inhaling his scent. I closed my eyes and held on to him a little longer than normal. He didn't mind. Finally, we separated, and I had a seat in the booth with him.

"You look good, Rashida."

"Thank you." I wanted to look sexy today. I wore a trendy African dress that showed a lot more cleavage than I usually did. I could tell by the grin on his face he appreciated my effort.

"I already placed an order for honey barbecue wings."

I chuckled. "You know me too well."

His brown eyes stared deeply into mine. "Not well enough. Not yet."

It was a nice sunny day in Atlanta, and the restaurant was half-full with patrons eating lunch. The ideal day to be out with someone you loved. I should have been nervous about being seen in public with Alonzo. My shop was in the same area, and anybody I knew could run into us, but I didn't care. I was tired of concealing my feelings for him. But there were some matters that needed to be addressed before things could go any further.

"How are things at home?" Alonzo asked.

"Exhausting."

"In what way?"

"In every way. I'm tired of being in a relationship with a man I no longer love. I'm tired of feeling unappreciated. I don't want that." I paused and looked at him. "I'm going to end things with Robert."

"Are you sure about that?"

"I've never been more sure about anything else in my life. It's not because of you," I clarified. "I've held on to this relationship for too long. I thought that if I tried just a little bit harder, I would start to feel a deeper connection to him. I thought that he would learn to love me the way I should be loved. That maybe he could make me feel . . . the way you make me feel."

He took my hand. "I want you."

I smiled. "I want you too. I let you go once, and I don't plan on doing that again. But there is Joyce to consider. I don't know if I can hurt her like this."

"She stopped by."

"She did? When?"

"Yesterday. She had a box of things I'd left at her place and gave them to me."

I leaned forward in my seat. "What did she say?"

"She actually apologized to me for giving me an ultimatum."

I was shocked. "I didn't know she was going to do that."

He nodded. "I told her I was in love with someone else."

"And what did she say?"

"I could tell she felt some type of way, but then she congratulated me and gave me a hug goodbye."

"Wow. I actually asked her about you the other night, and she said she was over you. I wasn't sure I believed her, but now, after you telling me this, she really may be."

He smiled. "Well, that's good, right? She's moved on."

"Yeah, but nonetheless, seeing us together may not be what she imagined would happen next. It might destroy our friendship, and I'm not sure if I can live with that."

"Then can you live without me? That's what it sounds like you're going to have to do in order to spare her feelings."

I shook my head. "I don't want to live without you."

He exhaled a breath of relief. "Then we need to tell her. For better or worse, we have to tell her."

"We have to be gentle. I . . . I should be the one to tell her. I owe her that." I sighed. "I just hope she doesn't hate me."

Chapter Twenty-six

Wild Thoughts

DENISE

Becoming a mother had changed my life. Not that I was some wild party girl before, but having Amir had put a lot into perspective. Everything I did now was for him. I still worked as a medical assistant, but my true passion took an unexpected form. I had always written short stories as a teenager, and in my college years, mostly erotica romance. I guessed I lived vicariously through my characters, and after my relationship with Sean, I had even more material to inspire me. I wrote a manuscript called *Pure Jane*, detailing the escapades of a shy young girl who became sexually liberated after her encounters with a mysterious man. Kinda like *Fifty Shades of Grey* but only good. Joyce had read it, loved it, and given it to a client of hers who happened to be an editor at a major publisher. I was not sure what was going to happen with the manuscript, but I was keeping my fingers crossed.

I hadn't had to raise Amir by myself. Sean had been a big support, even though we were not together. The biggest support had come from Amir's aunties: Rashida, Joyce and, surprisingly enough, Taylor. Over the past two years, Taylor had been here for Amir like he was hers.

I'd seen a side of her I'd never encountered before—a maternal side. I had thought I knew exactly what type of person she was—wild, rude, and a bit promiscuous—but it had turned out I really didn't know her as well as I had thought. Don't get me wrong. We still annoyed each other, but it was not as bad as it used to be.

She dropped by out the blue a few minutes ago to see Amir and drop off a couple of outfits she had bought for him. I had never thought she would be the one to do this, but here she was, standing in Amir's room, dressing him.

"I saw some mini Tims at Kohl's that would go perfect with this. I'm gonna stop by and pick them up before I head home," she told me.

I smiled. "You don't have to."

"Yes, I do," she insisted. "I need my nephew to be looking fly at all times."

"He's not even two yet, Taylor. I don't think he has to worry about being fly yet."

"He's never too young to start."

"Well, it's a good thing he has an auntie like you, because I don't know the slightest thing about that."

She looked me up and down, then smirked. "Oh, I know that."

I shook my head. "Whatever."

Amir had fallen asleep in his toddler bed while we were talking. She gave him a kiss on his cheek as he slept. Then we left his room and headed to the living room, where we had a seat on the sofa. She looked around and nodded in approval.

"You may be fashionably challenged, but you do know how to decorate." She looked at me. "I like what you're doing with the place."

I folded my arms. "Why do you always do that?"

"Do what?"

"Give a backhanded compliment. You can't just say, 'I like what you're doing with the place.' You gotta take a shot at my fashion taste, which is perfectly fine, thank you."

She sighed. "Sorry, force of habit. I just want you to have a little more style with your clothes. You're an attractive woman. I just want you to show it off more."

"Just because my style is not like yours doesn't mean I don't have any." I paused as I registered what she had said. I was shocked. "You think I'm an attractive woman? You've never said that before."

"Denise, you've always been a sexy little thing. You just don't highlight it right . . . although you were able to scoop Sean up with no problem."

"You can have him." I shrugged.

"Nah, I'm good, but don't front like he ain't your dude."

"We're not together. We just co-parent."

"Oh, please, you know every now and then, you let him get some. Don't deny it."

I didn't reply right away. Taylor was right. Even though we weren't together, there were times I did sleep with him. A girl got needs, and that was the one thing Sean was good at doing. It had taken a long time for me to give him any again, but I wasn't about to jump in bed with another man. I had let him know it was just a physical thing and no feelings would be involved. "Just break me off and leave. And only when I want it and only with a condom on," I'd told him. He had begrudgingly agreed to my terms. He wanted us to go back to what we were before, but that wasn't going to happen. I may have forgiven him for lying, but I still didn't trust him all the way.

"It's complicated."

Taylor twisted up her lips. "Ain't nothing complicated about that! You get horny, get some, and then kick him out when you're done. I actually think you're a little bit of a pimp doing him like that. I respect yo' gangsta."

We both laughed.

"You know, Taylor, I never thought I would, but I actually like talking to you like this. Why did it take so long for us to get here?"

Taylor sat back and thought about it for a second. "Maybe because we're very different from one another. I think we both see something in each other we lack, and it annoys the shit out of us."

"So what is it that you see in me that you wish you had?"

She stared at me. "Your humility. I don't know if you've noticed, but I'm not always the most likable person in the world."

"Oh, I know that. Continue."

She glared at me with a smirk on her face. "Like I was saying, I can be a bit abrasive at times. Either you like me or you don't. Sometimes people don't get a chance to know me before they judge me. They just see me and be like, 'I know what type of chick you are,' based on how I look or dress, so I tend to be a little more callous than I need to be at times. Something I'm trying to work on."

I was definitely guilty of that. I had always assumed things about Taylor without getting to know her. It made me wonder what else had I assumed that was wrong.

"What is it that you see in me that you wish you had?" she asked.

"Your confidence. Sometimes I wish I could be as bold as you and say whatever it is I'm thinking or wear any-thing and look good in it. I don't always feel as confident as I want to. I know I'm no ugly duckling, but I ain't you, either."

Taylor leaned forward. "You don't have to be me. Listen, how about we go shopping this weekend and you let me pick out a few things for you? I promise not to go too crazy, but I got a few ideas about what will look great on you."

I smiled. "We've never gone shopping together before, but okay. Let's see what you can do for me."

Taylor jumped up out of her seat. "Yes! Finally!"

I laughed, and she hugged me.

"Trust me," she said with a broad smile on her face, "we're going to have fun!"

"Okay, okay."

We talked for a few more minutes before she left. I was actually looking forward to hanging out with Taylor, something I had thought I would never be.

A couple of hours later I put Amir down for the night, then sat on the sofa with my laptop, working on a sequel to my *Pure Jane* book. I had a glass of zinfandel and a bowl of popcorn next to me. I was on my third glass of zinfandel, to be exact. A lit scented candle had put the aroma of berries in the air. My mind was in a creative space, and this allowed my thoughts to wander into a naughty region of my imagination. I was drafting a steamy scene for my lead character, a scene that had plenty of orgasmic moments, and I managed to arouse myself.

Just then, I heard the doorknob rattle. I jumped, looked up, and saw Sean coming inside. It almost felt like he had walked in on me in the middle of self-pleasuring. His timing was perfect, as usual. Almost like he could detect when my hormones were at their highest. I let out a little laugh and shook my head at my silliness. Even though he didn't live here, he had a key. He did, after all, buy the place for us about a year ago. Sean had lived up to his promise to take care of his son. Anything that Amir needed, Sean would make sure he provided it. He also made sure I was taken care of too.

Sean wore a black tee, black fitted jeans, and Jordans. He had changed his hair from cornrows to a Mohawk fade, which looked good on him. Actually, everything looked good on him.

He looked at me sitting on the sofa and said, "Hey, wus up?"

I saved the document I was working on and folded my laptop. "Hey."

He walked toward me and stared. I had on a pair of pink short shorts and an oversized white V-neck tee that looked like a miniskirt. His eyes were focused on my exposed thighs. I didn't mind the attention he was giving them.

With his eyes still on my thighs, he said, "Is Amir already in bed?"

"Yeah, I put him down about thirty minutes ago."

"Okay."

He went upstairs to Amir's room, and I followed behind him. I stood in the doorway and watched as he stood over Amir's bed. He loved his son. That was one thing I knew without a doubt. I would never do anything to stop him from being with his child. He kissed Amir's forehead and walked out of his room. We stood in the hallway, facing each other. Our backs against the wall in the narrow space.

"Sorry I'm so late. I got caught up in the studio, but I just wanted to see him today."

"That's fine. You know you're welcome here anytime."

His eyes looked me up and down. "How was your day?"

"It was fine." I shifted my body weight from side to side. "A nice slow day at the clinic."

"That's good." He scratched the back of his head.

"Amir is finally getting used to being at the new day care. He's not crying when I leave him now, and he's playing with other kids."

"That's good."

"Yeah, less worry on me. It also helps me stay focused on the new book I'm working on."

"Oh really?"

"Yeah, I just had a few ideas I wanted to get out."

We stared at each other in silence. The obligatory small talk was out of the way; our eyes were saying way more to each other than our words had. The conversation was irrelevant. Sean knew me. I didn't have to tell him what I wanted. Our body language spoke volumes. It had been a couple of months since we had last touched, and I wanted to be touched tonight. I turned and slowly walked to my bedroom and left the door open. I pulled off my tee, dropped it on the floor, and turned around. Just as I knew he would, Sean followed me and closed the door. There I stood in front of him.

Sean walked toward me, embraced me, and planted soft kisses on my lips, neck, and breasts. My hands found the hardness in his jeans, and his hands caressed my backside. I lifted his shirt over his head, exposing half of him, then unbuckled his belt, exposing the part of him I needed most. I pushed him back toward the bed and made him lay flat against the mattress. I stared at his erection standing tall. It was glorious. I reached into my dresser, pulled out a condom, and rolled the latex over his flesh. I removed my shorts and climbed over his erection. It was fun being aggressive. When we first got together, I had allowed Sean to be in control, while I had been submissive. That was then, and this was now. This was sex on my terms, and I loved it. I loved being in control. I was no longer the naïve little girl he'd met. I was a mother. I was his lover, and most of all, I was a woman.

I rode him and allowed his stiffness to move inside me. My hips swayed with rhythm; I danced like I was an island girl. I did a nasty grind on him. I danced in bed like I would never dance in public. I was way too shy to move like this in a club. I didn't like strange men looking at me like a sex object. It made me feel uncomfortable. But this right here made me feel powerful. Making Sean moan made me feel like a woman. I had my way with him until I had an orgasm. After we were both done enjoying each other, he spooned with me.

"You enjoy using me, don't you?" Sean asked me.

"You don't seem to mind."

"But if I did?"

"But you don't."

He chuckled. "We could be so much more than this if you'd let it."

I shifted my body closer to him, and his hands cupped my breasts. It felt good. I needed to feel his touch. I wanted his affection, but not his love. I didn't want to be hurt again.

"I'm fine with the way things are now," I admitted.

"Things can't stay like this forever."

I was silent for a second. "If you don't wanna be here, then you don't have to be."

"But that's the thing. I want to be. I wanna be with you."

I didn't reply. I knew that was what he wanted, and a part of me wanted that, too, but I wasn't gonna look foolish again.

He exhaled. "You're still holding the past against me."

"Obviously, I've forgiven you."

"You say that you have, but I don't think so."

"Then that's your problem, isn't it?" I asked him, not pulling my punch.

Sean got up out of bed and started to dress. I turned and looked at him. I normally had to ask him to leave. Guessed he was in his feelings. He buckled his belt and looked at me.

"I'll be by to see Amir tomorrow."

I nodded. "Okay."

He sighed and walked out of the bedroom. I pulled the sheet up over my body. He had satisfied my physical cravings, and I knew I had pleased him, so why was he so upset? Wasn't this what every man wanted, anyway? I wasn't trying to be mean, but I didn't want to lie to him. I wasn't ready for what he wanted. This was all I could give.

Chapter Twenty-seven

You're Making a Mistake

RASHIDA

I had heard someone say breaking up was hard to do. That was true. It was such a messy process; that was why I had to be in the right frame of mind to go through with it. I felt so annoyed, so much resentment toward him. No man should ever make a woman feel like that. I didn't want to be angry when I spoke to him. I didn't want to argue and resort to name-calling. I wanted my words to be calm and clear. I'd heard of so many people these days breaking up with someone over the phone or by text, which was such a cowardly thing to do to somebody you'd had a relationship with. I needed to see him, look in his eyes, and tell him how I felt. Robert deserved the truth.

I heard the doorknob turn, and I took a deep breath. He walked inside, placed his briefcase down, and saw me sitting at his kitchen table. He was startled to see me in his condo.

"Rashida." He walked toward me. "What are you doing here?"

"I got some things I need to get off my mind." I gestured to the empty chair in front of him.

He stared at me; then his eyes drifted to the key in the center of the table. He looked back at me and knew what this was about. Robert shook his head and sat down. He studied my face, trying to read my emotions.

"What's on your mind, Rashida?"

"Do you love me?"

His eyebrows scrunched together. "Of course I do. How could you even ask me a question like that?"

"You said I don't like to talk about things. Well, I just want to know if you really love me, because I don't feel loved at all. I feel like I'm just an accessory for you. Something for you to put on your arm when we go out. Then when we're done, you put me away and ignore me. You don't even try to make me happy."

He leaned forward and laid his hands flat on the table. "'Shida, I know I haven't been the most attentive man, but I wanna make it up to you. You just have to give me a chance to prove it to you."

"We've been together for nearly three years. You've already proven everything to me."

He sighed. "So you're just going to give up on us? After everything we've meant to each other? You can't sit there and tell me you can't feel the connection we've shared since the first night we made love."

"Robert, the first time we made love was special. I will never deny that, but it hasn't been that way in such a long time."

"So you're telling me the last time we made love, you didn't feel anything at all? Because I felt it." He tapped his finger on the table. "We were connected."

I shook my head. "You honestly thought you were making love to me? Are you kidding me? Robert, all I felt was you pounding me, trying to bust a nut. I didn't enjoy anything about that. There was nothing romantic or passionate about it."

He folded his arms and glared at me. I had hurt his psyche. I wasn't trying to hit him below the belt, but what choice did he give me? This wasn't about sex or the size of his penis. This was about the disconnect I'd felt for months now. Of course, he couldn't see it.

"This is what I get? This!" he snapped. "I try my best to turn you from a spoiled little rich girl to a mature woman, and this is what I get! An ungrateful child who doesn't know what a real man is when he's sitting in front of her! I've bent over backward to show you the better things in life, but you're too immature to appreciate it."

I sat for a second in silence. I had expected this. I knew Robert would go off, insult me to try to draw me into an argument. That was what he did. It was his defense mechanism against the truth. That was why I wanted to be calm for this. In the past I would've gone right back off, but I wasn't going to engage with him on that level today.

I exhaled. "I'm not in love with you anymore, Robert."

He massaged his temples. "How could you do this to me? To us?" He stared at me. "Shida, it's not too late for us."

"I haven't been happy in a long time, and I know you haven't been happy with me, either. We just need to go our separate ways now."

He made a disgusted face and sighed. "A real woman would fight for her man."

"I'm done fighting with you."

"You sure you want to do this?" he asked.

I stood up from the table. "I've already packed up your belongings at my house. You can come by and pick them up when you're ready."

He frowned. "You're making a mistake."

"I need my key back, Robert."

He sat there and glared at me with so much hatred in his eyes. I knew Robert wasn't a violent man, but I thought for a second he might have wanted to slap the shit out of me.

"Please don't make this any more difficult than it already is," I added.

He stood up, fished in his pocket, pulled out his key ring, and removed my key from it. Then he slammed the key down on the table.

I picked it up. "I'm sorry, Robert."

"Get out!"

He shoved the chair he'd sat in underneath the table. Frustration and anger rested on his face. He was done talking.

I walked to the front door and left. Once I closed the door behind me, I exhaled and felt as if a boulder had been lifted from my shoulders, and for the first time in years, I felt free.

Chapter Twenty-eight

I Get So Lonely

JOYCE

"Good morning, Atlanta! Did you miss me?"

Hearing his voice again felt strangely comforting. His voice resonated through the speakers of my CR-V. After we broke up, I had stopped listening to WHXZ because I hadn't wanted to hear Alonzo's voice again. It had been just too painful at times to hear the voice of an ex-lover who rejected me, but now that I'd made peace with that part of my past, it was nice to know he was back again.

I was en route to 'Shida's house. She had texted me this morning and had told me she ended things with Robert last night. I was relieved she finally did. I hated seeing my best friend so unhappy. Over the years I'd made no secret of the fact that I didn't care for him. I had never been disrespectful or rude, but I had tried my best not to be around him. Once she had sent me the text that she broke up with him, I'd told her I would be right over. I didn't like having important conversations like this via text. Occasions like this one required a face-to-face talk.

I pulled into her driveway and saw the red Audi again. After I saw it the first time, I'd looked it up and learned it was a 2017 Audi Quattro, a German sports car with a sleek design, sexy curves, and a powerful engine. I wanted drive it. Raheem had expensive taste in cars and liked them fast. Made me curious as to what else he liked with sexy curves. *Shame on me.* I shouldn't have been thinking of him like that. I got out of my car, used my key to go inside, and my inner fat girl growled at the aroma of pancakes. I headed toward the kitchen and saw 'Shida fixing two plates. I hugged her.

"This is the reason you're my best friend," I told her.

"Hot off the pan for you." She handed me a plate.

I had a seat on a stool at the kitchen island, picked up the bottle of maple syrup that was already out. and poured syrup over my hotcakes.

I took a bite. "Yummm . . . It's like an orgasm in my mouth!"

She smirked. "The one time you don't mind swallowing, huh?"

'Shida had a seat at the island with me. I glared at her. She knew I didn't do that kind of stuff. I had no problem pleasing my man, but I had never seen the point in drinking his semen. That did nothing for me. That was only a power trip for a man to watch.

"I hate you so much now," I told her and took another bite. "So I see that you're in good spirits."

"Yes, I am. For the first time in a long time, I feel happy."

"I'm so glad you ended things with Robert. I don't wish a breakup on anybody, but I was tired of seeing you unhappy. So how did he take it?"

"Exactly the way I thought he would. Bad. It's like he couldn't see how detached we had become. He really thought we were just going through a phase or something. When I told him how I felt, he went off."

"What did he say?"

"He told me that I was a spoiled little rich girl who didn't recognize when she saw a real man in front of her."

I dropped my fork. "What? Are you kidding me? He had the nerve to say that to you! You put yourself through college, opened a business, and run it on a daily basis by yourself. He wasn't saying all that shit about being spoiled when you paid off his condo or when you bought him that BMW for his birthday!"

"I would never throw that in his face. I did those things out of love. I just wanted him to know exactly how I felt. I didn't want to argue with him, so I just ended it."

"Well, you're a better woman than me, because I would have gone off on him."

We continued to eat our food. Five minutes later, 'Shida gazed at me, a reflective look on her face. "We should have never started a relationship at all. We were never equally yoked. I ignored my intuition. Never again."

I nodded. Out of all of us, 'Shida had always been the most levelheaded. I guessed that was why we all always seemed to lean on her for moral support. Losing her parents had forced her to mature faster than the rest of us, but even the best of us still made mistakes.

"Well, I went and saw Alonzo the other day," I revealed.

'Shida looked at me. "You did?"

"Yeah, I still had some things he left behind, and I needed to apologize to him."

"What made you do that?"

"I just had to take an honest look at myself and what I did in our relationship. I knew Alonzo wasn't ready for marriage, but I still pushed him into a corner. I was so angry at him, when I should have been mad at myself. I had to let go of that resentment."

'Shida took my hand. "I'm proud of you."

I smiled. "It wasn't easy, but I'm good now."

"Do you still have feelings for him?"

I thought about it for a second. "Yes, but I'm not in love with him. I care about him. He's moved on, and it's time I did the same."

That was when I saw him walk into the kitchen, shirtless once again. He had on only a pair of red and white basketball shorts. My eyes studied his muscular arms. The last time I saw Raheem, he'd rattled me. I hadn't been ready to see all that bare skin out the blue, but this time I was prepared. I couldn't help molesting him with my eyes.

He gave me a sexy smile. "Hello, Joyce."

I couldn't help but feel like a silly little schoolgirl who had just got noticed by the cute upperclassman. But this wasn't high school, and I was five years his senior. My eyes scanned his body, looking for traces of the skinny kid I'd known years ago. I wanted to find something wrong with him, something to dismiss him as not being man enough for me. I found nothing.

"Hey," I replied.

He gave his sister a kiss on her forehead.

She looked him up and down. "They don't wear shirts in California?"

"It's optional." He grabbed the spatula and flipped a couple of hotcakes onto his plate. He glanced over at me. "'Shida must have made these for you."

"Why do you say that?" I asked.

He grinned. "C'mon, we all know how much you love pancakes."

I was impressed he remembered that. "I guess some things never change."

He nodded, walked toward me, and took the bottle of syrup. He covered his pancakes with syrup, then took a bite. "So what do you do now?"

"I sell luxury homes in and out of the Atlanta area." I watched as he quickly ate his food.

He smiled. "Well, I might have to look you up if I decide to stay here on a permanent basis."

I cleared my throat. "Well, I'm all yours . . . whenever you decide to . . . shop for a house."

"Cool. I'll see you soon." He put his empty plate in the dishwasher, then grabbed a bucket from underneath the sink, and went outside.

I could see 'Shida smirking. I went back to eating my food.

"So, you know he likes you, right?" she said after a minute had passed.

"What? Really, I didn't notice."

"And now I know the feeling is mutual!"

"What? No, no! Raheem is your little brother. He's like family."

"No he's not. He's a single man who's interested in you."

"'Shida, I've known Raheem since he was a skinny little kid running around, annoying us. There's no way I could date him. I'm old enough to be his . . . I'm just too old for him."

'Shida kept on giving me that goofy grin of hers.

I couldn't help but laugh. "Stop looking at me like that!"

"I don't know if you noticed, but Raheem isn't a skinny little kid anymore. He's a grown man. Look, you're both consenting adults. If you want to kick it with him, then don't feel any type of way because he's my brother." She got up and took my plate.

"Well, I don't feel any type of way about it, because nothing is going to happen between us."

After a long breakfast I had to leave Rashida's and head to an 11:30 a.m. meeting with a client in Lithonia. I was so glad Rashida had finally broken up with Robert. I had never personally thought he was a good match for Rashida. As handsome as he may be, they really had no chemistry, in my opinion.

When I walked outside, I saw Raheem again. He was drying his car in the driveway. My eyes took all of him in. He was fine as hell. No matter how sexy he was, I refused to go there with him. He saw me, and a smile spread across his face. He strolled over to me before I got to my car.

"That's a hot ride, Raheem. You're making me wanna trade mine in."

"Yeah, I think it might be time for you to trade up to something better."

I smirked. "Um, yeah, maybe."

"So do wanna take it for a spin around the block? Rev the engine?"

"Ah, that's okay. I don't think that's a good idea."

He stepped into my personal space. "Why not? I think you might like it."

I cleared my throat. "I might, but I really have a meeting I have to get to."

He shrugged. "Okay. Maybe later."

"Rah, I don't think I should." I exhaled.

"You scared?"

"No, I'm not. It's just . . ."

He looked me up and down. "What if you just let me take you for a ride?"

The way he stared at me made me feel some type of way. A tiny voice in my head was screaming for me to ride with him. I ignored it. He could see the hesitation on my face.

"Rah . . ."

"Joyce, how about we just go out and get some lunch later?"

I shook my head. "We can't do that."

"Why not?"

I exhaled again. "You're gonna make me say it, aren't you?"

He smiled again. "I'm not making you do anything. I just wanna take you out."

"Okay, fine. I'm gonna say it. You're my best friend's little brother, and it would be awkward going out with you."

"Not for me, and it shouldn't be for you. We're both grown, and I think you want to."

I let out a chuckle. "Raheem, I don't know what you think is going to happen, but I'm not even dating right now. I'm more focused on my business, and dating you . . . It's just not gonna work out. I'm flattered, really I am, but I don't think I'm the right woman for you, okay?"

He nodded his head. "I hear ya. Well, don't let me keep you from your meeting."

I adjusted my outfit. "Okay, I'll see you later." I walked past him to my car.

"Yes, you will," he called.

I glanced back at him, and he was still wearing that sexy smile on his face, and I couldn't help but blush. That voice in my head was cussing me out now. As curious as I may have been, I felt like it was inappropriate for me to go there with him, but I couldn't help but wonder, *What if*?

Chapter Twenty-nine

Tomorrow Is Not Promised

ALONZO

"Bruh, I'm getting tired of doing this with her."

I could hear the frustration in Sean's voice as he bellowed through the Bluetooth in the truck. He'd been trying to work things out with Denise for a while now. He was a man in love, but she was a woman scorned. It was a messy situation. I wasn't sure how much advice I could give him, especially since I was still trying to figure out my own conundrum with 'Shida. I was driving down I-285, heading home, and was about to merge onto I-85 South. The Atlanta traffic was thick. Four lanes of traffic, with many vehicles jockeying for position at reckless speeds.

"She still doesn't trust you," I told Sean.

"But that doesn't stop her from screwing my brains out when I come over."

I chuckled. "She's using you for sex? So you're the girl in the relationship?"

"You ain't funny."

I switched to the right lane of the highway as I started to merge onto I-85. "I told you, you should've been straight up with her from the start."

"Yeah, yeah, yeah, I know, but damn, it's been nearly three years. How long is she going to hold on to the past? I've done everything I can to be there for Amir, and it's still not good enough for her," Sean vented.

"You've done everything you can for Amir. He's *your* responsibility. You're supposed to do that. But what have you done for Denise to make it up to her? How have you proven to her that she can trust you again?"

He sighed. "Maybe you're right." He changed subjects. "Hey, you gonna pass by Walmart on the way home?"

"Yeah. Why?"

"Can you pick up some Tropicana Fruit Punch? Oh, and a bag of chips! This kitchen is dry."

"What the hell am I? Your wife?"

He laughed. "Bruh, I'm hungry!"

"Then you should've—"

Before I could react, a car in the lane I was merging into rammed into the passenger side of my truck. The impact was sudden. The sound of fiberglass, metal, and rubber colliding at seventy miles per hour was deafening. Unadulterated violence. I felt my body become like a rag doll and fly into the door. My head bashed into the window, and the impact caused me to lose my grip on the steering wheel and sent my truck reeling out of control. My foot smashed the brake pedal as I fought for control over my vehicle. Somehow I coasted to a stop on the grassy area on the side of the highway. My head was throbbing and spinning. Everything in my vision seemed to be swimming. I wanted to close my eyes to stop the constant motion, but I was afraid if I did, I might lose consciousness.

I didn't know how long it took, but the next thing I remembered was being loaded into the back of an ambulance and driven to South Fulton Hospital. Once I got there, the emergency medical team tended to me. After conducting a brief assessment of my condition, they took me to Radiology for X-rays and a CT scan. Despite my swollen head and wrist, the X-rays revealed that I had no broken bones, but I had to wait for the results of the CT scan. I was taken back to my room in the emergency unit, where I was given Extra Strength Tylenol to help with the pain. Just as I was about to dose off, my cell rang. It was Sean. He had been calling since the accident, and I was finally able to answer. I briefly told him what had happened, then got off the phone. I couldn't talk long. I needed quiet.

The CT confirmed that I had a mild concussion, and the doctor recommended I remain under observation at the hospital for the next six hours and that I take it easy for the next few days. A few hours later the pain in my head seemed to have eased. I pushed the call button for assistance to the restroom. Moments later the nurse arrived and then escorted me down the hallway to the restroom, where I relieved myself. She escorted me back when I was done.

"Oh, I see you have a visitor," the nurse announced cheerfully as we approached my room.

"I'll take it from here," Rashida said, walking toward me. I saw the anxiety in her eyes and the worry lines etched in her face.

I leaned on her as she helped me get back into bed.

"Are you okay?" she asked.

I smiled. "I'll live."

Once I was settled, she hugged me and held on to me like she never wanted to let go. I wrapped my arms around her and stroked her hair. Holding her made the pain go away and made me glad to still be alive. The thought of never being able to hold her in my arms again was just as scary as dying.

"So Sean told you what happened?"

She sat in the chair next to the bed. "Yeah, he called me. Why didn't you call?"

"I didn't want to worry you."

Her facial expression was serious. "You were in a car accident and could've gotten killed. The last time someone close to me was in a car accident, they . . . died."

I knew this would affect her, so I wasn't going to tell her yet.

"Hence the reason I didn't want to worry you. I'm fine."

"No you're not."

"I really am. I don't have any broken bones or anything, just a mild concussion."

Rashida gasped.

"Doctor said I should take it easy for a few days and I'll be good."

"And what did they give you for your head?"

"Extra- Strength Tylenol. I'm feeling better. I think I should be able to go to work on Monday."

She frowned. "The hell you are. You're going on bed rest for a few days."

I shifted my body in the bed, making myself more comfortable. "'Shida, I just started my show a week ago. I can't miss days.'"

"You're going to call your manager, tell him what happened, and inform him that you'll be out for a few days," she said firmly. "If you don't do it, I will."

How could I argue with such a beautiful lady like that?

I smiled. "Okay, you win."

She took my hand. "I'm going to take care of you while you recover."

"But what about . . . ?"

"It's over. I ended things with Robert a few days ago." She looked relieved to say that. "I'm going to make some arrangements, then come back here and pick you up, okay?" She squeezed my hand.

I nodded. "Whatever you say."

She rose from the chair and left my room.

Chapter Thirty

I Want You

ALONZO

After Rashida left, I called Mark and told him what had happened, and he told me to take as much time as I needed. Then I made a few calls to my insurance company to make sure everything was set on that end. I wasn't exactly in the right frame of mind after the accident to have that conversation. The driver who had hit me was at fault, so I knew things would go in my favor.

A few hours later I was discharged, and Rashida was right there to pick me up in her Maserati. I could see why she loved this car. She wasn't the type to flaunt her money, but she spared no expense when it came to her ride. This was the definition of a sports car. I sat on the passenger side and watched as she handled the automobile like a professional. The engine hummed as she cruised north on I-75. I noticed that she passed the exits that would take us to her house.

"Are we making a stop somewhere?" I asked.

"No."

I glanced out the window, then back at her. "We passed the exit for your house about two miles back."

She gave me a small smile. "I didn't say I was taking you to my house."

"Okay, so where are you taking me?" I asked and raised an eyebrow.

"You'll see."

"Are you kidnapping me?" I joked. "You plan on tying me up and doing strange things to me?"

She glanced over at me with a wicked grin on her beautiful face. "Are you trying to give me ideas?"

"Well, in my condition, I'm completely at your mercy."

She looked me up and down. "I know."

We continued to drive north, and the landscape changed from urban to forest. Trees and hills for miles on end. We started to drive up a mountain incline, and I soon recognized the area we were driving in—Ellijay, Georgia. We passed a sign that read CUDDLE UP CABIN RENTALS, and Rashida slowed down and turned into long driveway. After stopping the car near the main office, she hopped out, went inside, got the keys to our cabin, and returned. A few moments later we pulled up in front of a cabin on the lake. It looked more like a mansion.

I looked at the two-story wooden cabin, then back at her. "So these were the arrangements you had to make?"

"Yeah, my brother is staying at my house right now, and it would be awkward for us to be there together. So I thought this would be the next best thing. Somewhere quiet, where you can recuperate. Do you approve?"

I smiled. "I do, but other than the clothes on my back, I don't have anything to wear."

She turned off the engine. "I got you covered."

We exited the car; she pressed a button on her key fob and popped the trunk. As she approached the trunk, I took a moment to see what she had on: blue jeans, a white blouse, boots with sensible heels, simple but sexy. In the trunk were two medium-sized suitcases—one pink, the other blue.

"I stopped at Old Navy and picked up a few things," she informed me.

I grabbed the blue suitcase, and 'Shida took the other. We walked up the stairs to a huge wooden deck.

We went inside the cabin, and the interior was amazing. It was a fully furnished home that looked like something out of *Better Homes and Gardens*. Five bedrooms, three bathrooms, and an outdoor fireplace. On the bottom level was a game room equipped with a pool table. This was the type of place I would love to stay at every weekend. With my good hand, I carried my luggage upstairs behind 'Shida.

Once we reached the top of the staircase, she turned and looked at me with a shy smile. "You can choose whatever room you like."

"What room will you be sleeping in?" I asked.

She shifted her weight from one foot to the other, touched her hair, and glanced at me. "I think I'll take the room facing the lake. It has a great view."

I nodded. "Then I will take the one next to it. With it being just us here, we shouldn't be too far apart from each other, right?"

"Right." She paused, and we looked at one another. "Well, you should go lie down and rest. It was a long drive."

I nodded, and we both walked to our respective rooms. She turned and glanced at me one more time before going in her room. I wanted to follow her and not let her out of my sight, but I didn't want to move too fast. Besides, after the long drive, I was a little tired. I wasn't exactly functioning at 100 percent. I went in my room, placed my suitcase on the bed, and opened it. There were two pairs of gray sweatpants, a black pair, and four shirts with various Old Navy designs. One in particular made me laugh. It was a diagram of a pig divided into twenty sections, with numbers in each, and at the bottom each number was labeled as bacon. I found white socks and different-colored boxers as well. All the right size. 'Shida had a good eye.

I glanced at my phone. It was 3:35 p.m. My body was tired from the drive, so I decided to lie down and get some rest, like she had suggested. The queen-size mattress was soft. My mind was on 'Shida. We were only a few feet away from each other and in different beds. That felt wrong. I wanted her next to me. Wanted to touch her and do so many things to her. Blood started to flow in the opposite direction of my brain, and I fell asleep with her on my mind.

When I awoke, I looked at my phone. It was 6:45 p.m. I had slept longer than I wanted to. The aroma of food cooking wafted through the air; it smelled like steak. I decided to change into some of the clothes that 'Shida had bought for me. The lavender-gray sweats and the dark gray pig shirt looked good on me. I went downstairs and then followed the aroma out back.

'Shida was standing by a firepit with a grill fitted over it. She had also made a wardrobe change and was now wearing blue shorts and a black tank top with the word *angel* written in pink letters across her chest. Her long dreads were down and pulled around the right side of her face. She looked angelic indeed. She had a long-handled fork in her hand and was grilling the meat over the open fire. I noticed corn on the cob wrapped in foil on a plate to the side of the grill. She looked up and saw me walking toward her.

"Where did all this come from?" I asked.

"I went to the store while you were sleeping."

I took a seat in front of the firepit. "Smells good."

"Thanks. It should be done in a minute."

I took in the view of the lake. "It's beautiful out here."

She took the steaks off the grill. "I love it out here. It's so . . . peaceful."

"So did you come out here a lot with Robert?"

"No. Being in the woods wasn't his thing." She gave me a napkin with a knife and fork wrapped in it. "It's actually been about four years since I've been here."

She handed me a tray with the steak and corn on a plate, then passed me a beer. She got her tray and sat next to me, and we began to eat our food. The sun was setting, and beautiful colors reflected off the lake. The mountain air was fresh. It was quiet out here. The perfect place to think, the perfect place to connect with someone you loved. I was a city boy, but I could definitely get used to this. The steak was seasoned and perfectly cooked medium well. I enjoyed every bite of it. 'Shida was a hell of a cook. We finished our food and sat next to each other in front of the firepit, sipping on our beers. The sun had gone down, and the crickets serenaded us.

"How do you feel?" she asked me.

"I'm okay. My head feels better. Other than this slight headache, I'm good."

"I almost lost you, again," she whispered.

"After the accident I thought I could be dead right now. We all know life is short, but that really illustrated how real that is." I looked at her. "I thought about you and what if I never got a chance to see you again. That haunted me."

She took my hand. "I don't wanna live my life without you."

Then it happened. I was pulled into her gravity, and we kissed. There was no hesitation or doubt about whether that was the right thing to do. The kiss was soft, moist, and slow. The sensual kiss gradually became more intense. I caressed her shoulders and pulled her to me. Her hands touched my face, and she eased her tongue into my mouth. 'Shida was passionate; years of holding back what we were feeling for each other was spilling out. She got up and straddled my lap. I gave her more deep kisses. My hands traveled to her breasts, caressed her soft flesh. I could feel how stiff her nipples had become through the thin fabric of her tank top. She placed her heat on top of my groin and ground on me. After wanting for so long to hold her in my arms, it was finally happening, and it was better than before. All my senses were aroused by her.

"I've wanted you for so long," I whispered.

"And I've wanted you too."

Her kisses were like an aphrodisiac, intoxicating me and stimulating other parts of me to rise. A sight growl escaped my lips. The beast in me was awake. We stood up and walked back to the cabin, hand in hand. Once inside, we walked upstairs.

She stopped in the hallway and looked at me. "You should go to your room."

"You've changed your mind?"

"No, but I want to freshen up a bit."

I smiled and took her hand. "You don't have to. Trust me, you're good."

"I'll just be a minute. I'm not going anywhere." She kissed me again. "Just wait for me, okay?"

I reluctantly agreed, let her go into her room, and went inside mine. I pulled off my shirt and tossed it. Took off my pants, sat on the edge of my bed, and lob them next to my shirt. I was dressed only in the red boxer briefs 'Shida had bought me.

Each minute that went by felt like some inhumane medieval torture I was forced to endure. I sat patiently, but I was howling on the inside for her to come to me. Another minute went by, and I was living on the edge of madness. Then my door opened, and what I saw was breathtaking. 'Shida had on a black sheer baby doll with nothing underneath.

She walked over to me, and I caressed her gorgeous full breasts. Her areolas were a shade darker than her caramel-brown skin. I caressed her thighs, moved north, and stopped before I touched her vagina. I felt her warmth and inhaled her sweet scent. Her pheromones intoxicated me. Her sex stirred me and brought a new hardness to my penis. I touched her fire. She exhaled, bit her bottom lip, and closed her eyes. She was moist. She was on fire. I eased two fingers inside her wetness and rubbed her clit. Soft moans left her lips. She placed both of her hands on my head and kissed me as my fingers stroked her.

As good as that baby doll looked on her, I wanted to rip it off. I stood up, gripped her hips, took her to the bed, and laid her down. The sheer fabric of her lingerie rose up around her waist and exposed flesh. It showed me her moist lips, which seemed like an exotic, succulent fruit, one I wanted to taste. I pulled off my boxers and exposed my rigid flesh. She smiled and touched it, squeezed and stroked me. Made me growl. She opened her legs, and I crawled over her, placed my hardness on her wetness. She closed her legs, and I ground on her. We kissed, moved around, our bodies sliding against each other, driving each other wild. We changed positions in bed and found a nasty rhythm with each other. 'Shida was flexible and contoured her body in sinful ways around me.

Our grinding caused more wetness, and the sound of liquid sex sloshed between us. So wet, I could feel myself partially entering her. An inch of my erection at first, maybe two, then three inches penetrated her and then slipped out. Her moans became more intense. I cursed, sucked in air. I couldn't take it anymore. She felt so good. I eased inside her. Not all at once. Slowly, inch by inch, I invaded her moist space. Pulled back an inch, then pushed forward. Orgasmic moans filled the air as her face made a sexy frown. I put more of myself inside her, until I couldn't. I wanted to crawl up in her love and exist as one with her. I felt her nails on my back and a soft bite on my neck. 'Shida was insatiable. She moved her body up and down, matching my strokes.

She whispered, "I love you."

"I think I have loved you from the first night we met."

She moaned.

"You feel so damn good."

"Don't stop!" she told me.

I stroked her deeper, made her groan. "I've only just begun."

She grinned. "Show me."

I gave it to her harder. Touched her, loved her, and fucked her. Found a new angle and went deeper. I had to slow down when it felt too good; I didn't want to cum yet. I was on the verge but wasn't ready to quit. I had waited too long for her and was going to make this last. Had to make up for all the time we should have been together. I stared into the light brown eyes of the woman I loved and made her cum. She sang another orgasmic note. I was going to make her cum over and over again.

I withdrew myself from her heat, turned her over, and reentered her from the back. She moved her beautiful brown ass against me. She looked back at me, bit her bottom lip as I pumped into her. Hard and deep. Our movements were pornographic. I had to slow down again; it felt too good. I was going to explode if I kept up this pace. I closed my eyes, tilted my head back, and let her move against me as I held on. 'Shida moved her ass in a wicked rhythm that made me moan. She cursed, quivered, and came again. She may have been an angel in public, but she was a monster in the sheets.

Her legs got weak, and we fell to the side but never broke our connection. I spooned behind her, wrapped my arms around her, and held her close. Two warm bodies out of breath. Our skin was damp with sweat and sex. I gently stroked her wetness.

"You weren't lying," she admitted.

"I'm a man of my word."

"I can't believe I'm here with you like this."

I kissed her shoulder. "This is where I have always wanted to be."

"Even when you were with Joyce?"

I was silent for a moment. Admitting the truth wasn't easy. "Yes."

"Why did you stay with her if you wanted to be with me?"

I exhaled. "I thought I could get over you if I gave myself to her. She's a good woman, but I wasn't in love with her. I know it's fucked up, but it's the truth."

She touched my fingers. "I feel so guilty for loving you, but I can't help it. I tried to forget you, but honestly, I didn't try hard enough."

"Neither did I."

We lay with each other in silence for a moment.

"Do you regret what we did?" I asked.

She turned and faced me. "No."

Caressing my penis, she caused a new hardness to form. She rolled on her back, and I slid my erection back inside her heat. She wrapped her legs around my back. I felt her energy, stroked her with a new sense of urgency. Kissed her lips, her chin, and sucked on her neck like a vampire. I made her moan. I was tired of being unselfish. This was what I wanted, what we both needed, and I gave her my all. She was mine, and I was hers. 'Shida rocked with me, rolled her hips, and made orgasmic noises. It fueled my erection, took me to a new plateau. I didn't want to pull out, but I had to. I was inside her, unprotected, with a loaded weapon.

I grunted, "I'm . . . gonna cum!"

"It's okay . . . I'm on the pill."

That was all I needed to hear. I erupted. My body jerked. I filled her with my seeds and groaned like a beast. 'Shida smiled, locked her legs around me, and kept me deep inside her.

She kissed me and giggled. "I love seeing that look on your face."

I was out of breath. "Get used to it."

She smiled. "I plan to."

Chapter Thirty-one

Back to Life, Back to Reality

RASHIDA

One orgasm after another was the best way to describe the past three days with Alonzo. That man was truly blessed in every sense of the word. I'd never been with a man who made me feel so euphoric both mentally and most certainly physically. The PX90 aerobic workout had nothing on the vigorous workout he'd given me. Alonzo's length, hardness, and size had made me feel like I had experienced a thousand orgasms. Uncontrollable muscle spasms had left my vagina swollen. It felt like his erection had lived inside me for days. It almost felt weird not to feel him inside me now. Alonzo had eaten me like a starving man. His tongue had painted my walls like Michelangelo had painted the Sistine Chapel. A masterpiece. More pleasure than I had thought a woman could experience. Thinking back to my experiences with Robert, I realized how much I had been deprived of and how selfish a lover he was.

Being with a man I truly loved was amazing, but running away with him to a cabin in the woods wasn't real life. It was only a blissful prelude to the drama I knew we had to face when we saw Joyce. I was still at a loss on how to tell her I had fallen in love with her ex, and I was certain there was no easy way to do it. Was I really prepared to lose a lifelong friendship with a woman I considered my sister for a man I truly loved? How did my life become so damn complicated?

We drove back to Atlanta, and Alonzo picked up a rental car from Avis. As we stood in the parking lot next to his rental, I was reluctant to leave his side.

"I don't want to let you go," I whispered to him as he held me in his arms.

"It's only for a couple hours, and I'm coming back to you."

I held him tighter, and he kissed my lips.

"I promise. Nothing will ever keep me from coming back to your arms." he assured me.

"Okay," I sighed. "Just drive safe."

"I will." He smiled. "I'll see you later."

We parted ways, and I knew that I had never felt love like this before. Before we went up to Ellijay, I had told the girls I needed some personal time and would be out of town for the weekend. I checked my phone now and saw that I had a couple of messages from Taylor and Joyce. Nothing important. This thing with Joyce was weighing heavily on my heart, and I needed to talk about it with someone I could trust. Denise. But given her history with Alonzo, I wasn't sure if she was the best person to talk to, but I had to try.

Three hours later, I sat at Denise's kitchen table, watching Amir shove SpaghettiOs in his mouth with a *PAW Patrol* spoon. He looked like such a big boy sitting in the toddler seat, and I couldn't help but notice how much he resembled his father. I wondered if I had a baby with Alonzo, whose features he or she would inherit. But that was just a daydream about happier times to come. Today wasn't that day yet.

It was amazing to see the transformation Denise had undergone from a shy girl to a skillful mother. She was so natural at motherhood, but it wasn't just her motherly instinct with Amir I noticed. Her overall demeanor seemed different. Denise seemed more confident now, and she dressed a little sexier than usual. Today she wore a pair of tight-fitting jean capris and a low-cut tank top that showed more than an eyeful of cleavage.

"So, Denise, what's going on?"

She looked at me, confused. "What do you mean?"

I gestured to her breasts. "You've got some major boobage showing there. Something I ain't never seen going on you." I looked her up and down. "And where did you get that outfit?"

She grinned. "You like it?"

"It looks good on you, but where did that come from?"

"I went shopping with Taylor at Cumberland Mall. We picked out a few things."

My eyes got wide, and I shook my head. "I'm so glad you two are past that pettiness. I was so tired of playing referee between you."

She laughed. "I really like spending time with her."

"My God, the apocalypse is upon us. So when did you two decide to be buddies?"

She down sat at the table with me. "She came over to drop off an outfit for Amir, and we got to talking. We just hashed out our differences and decided to be nice to each other, and you know what? We're good."

I clapped my hands. "About damn time! After all the years of me begging you two to squash it, you two mules finally decided to do it. Miracles never cease. But, anyway, this looks good on you. I know Sean approves."

She shrugged her shoulders. "That's if he's still fucking with me."

"What? What happened?"

She smirked. "Last time he was here, we had a little disagreement. He wants us to be together again."

"Well, you two are still sleeping together, right?"

A wider smile spread across her face. "Occasionally."

"Okay, and as far as I can tell, he's gone above and beyond to be here for you and Amir, right?"

She folded her arms over her chest and sat back in her chair. "Yes, but I still don't know if I can trust him. What he did to me was foul."

I nodded. "I agree, but people mature. Sean is a good father, and I think having Amir and being with you have really settled him down. So if that's the only thing stopping you from being with him, then maybe the issue isn't with him."

Denise sat with my words for a moment. She looked at Amir, then back at me. "Anyway, you said you wanted to talk to me about something important."

It was my turn to exhale. I was still debating if I should tell her or not, but I figured it was either now or never.

"It's difficult. I'm not sure if what I'm doing is right or wrong, but what I do know is what I feel is true."

"Are you getting back with Robert?"

I shook my head. "No, this isn't about him. It's about Joyce."

Denise leaned forward in her chair and interlocked her fingers. "Okay, you're scaring me. What is it?"

"I'm in love with someone."

She smiled. "Well, that's a good thing. Who is he?"

I rubbed my hands and took a deep breath. "Alonzo and I have been in love with each other for years now." I paused and looked at Denise. She was speechless. I continued. "We've never cheated with each other. Not behind Joyce's or Robert's back. I would never hurt Joyce like that. Since he's been back, things have changed."

Denise blinked twice and stared at me without saying a word. My heart was pounding in my chest, and I had no idea how she would react. Would she cuss me out and tell me what a horrible friend I was? Did I just make a mistake? Denise took a breath and looked like she was in deep thought. Then she looked at me.

"How did this happen?" she asked.

"I met Alonzo before he was with Joyce. Robert and I had just started dating, so it never went any further. I never thought I'd see Alonzo again, but Joyce brought him to the cookout I had, you know, the one where you met Sean, and they were together. We decided it would be best not to bring up the past, but over the years our feelings grew for each other."

"Oh my God, 'Shida. Joyce is going to be devastated. You know what this is going to do to her? It's going to change everything."

I closed my eyes. "I know. I never wanted this to happen, but it did."

We sat in silence for a moment.

"Is he worth it?" she asked.

I looked at her. "Yes."

More silence.

"Do you think less of me now?" I asked her.

"I'm not sure. I've known you for most of your life, 'Shida. You're one of the most thoughtful and kindest people I know. If you say you're in love with Alonzo, then I know you mean it."

"But still, I know I'm betraying a friend."

"Look, 'Shida, we're all adults here. I'm not going to lie to you and say this is going to be easy and everything is going to be fine. Joyce is going to be hurt. She may even hate you. We're all friends, we're sisters, and she loves you and you love her. That's real. You have to tell her and accept whatever it is that comes next."

I nodded. Denise had given it to me straight, no chaser. A few tears rolled down my cheeks.

She reached across the table and took my hand. "Whatever happens, I still love you, and I know Taylor will too."

I wiped my tears. "Thanks, Denise."

We stood up and hugged each other. For better or for worse, she was my girl.

Raheem was spending the night in Decatur, catching up with old friends. It was after midnight, and Alonzo was holding me in my bed. Being with him reassured me that what we felt was real. I had told him about my conversation with Denise, and he'd agreed with what she had said. I needed him. If I was going to get through this, I needed his love.

"I know you said you wanted to tell Joyce by yourself, but I think I should be there," he suggested.

"You do?"

"Yes. Joyce needs to know that this was not some random event. She needs to know that what we shared was real, but it didn't work out, because of us. Not you. She needs to know that we didn't do this to hurt her. She deserves to hear that from me."

"I agree. I don't want to sneak around with you and lie to me best friend. Even though I know she might never forgive me."

"We're in this situation now because we decided to hide the truth," he mused as he caressed my face with his fingers. "Had we been honest from the start, maybe we wouldn't be in this situation now."

"I hate this." I rested my head on his chest. "I love Joyce, but I also love you. I don't wanna hurt anybody. All I wanna do is be happy. Am I asking for too much?

Am I really being some kind of selfish bitch for wanting you?"

He caressed my face some more. "No, you're not. We deserve happiness too."

My doorbell chimed repeatedly at that moment, forcing us to sit up.

"Who the hell is at my door at this time of night?" I got up, went to the window, and peeked through the blinds. It was dark outside, but the streetlamps illuminated a black BMW parked in my driveway.

I frowned and looked back at Alonzo. "It's Robert."

A scowl distorted his face. "What the hell does he want?"

"I'm not answering it."

I stood in the middle of my bedroom, arms folded, fists balled, ready to kill him. Alonzo had parked his rental car inside the garage, so Robert thought I was home alone. The doorbell continued to ring franticly.

"I'll answer it," Alonzo announced.

"No. I don't want him knowing my business. The less he knows, the better. He's just trying to piss me off."

He folded his arms. "It's working."

I growled. "Wait here, please."

Alonzo sighed and nodded. I left my bedroom and stormed down the stairs. I was going to cuss his ass out. Before I opened the door, I thought to myself that this was what he wanted, so I exhaled, counted backward from five, and found my composure. When I opened the door, he was dressed in a gray sweat suit, with white-and-black Nikes on his feet and a smug smile on his face.

"What do you want?" I asked coldly.

"I came for my things."

"At this time of night? You couldn't come in the morning?"

He shrugged his shoulders. "It's my stuff, and I want it now."

"You're being petty, Robert."

"And you're not? You're the one who quit on us."

"I'm not going to argue with you. We're done."

"Fine. Then give me my stuff." He attempted to push the door open, but I held it firmly.

"No! Go home. I will drop it off to you later."

He stared at me and smiled. His eyes went up and down my body. I had forgot that all I had on was my negligee. It was sheer, revealing my nakedness underneath. I folded my arms and covered my chest.

"Nice outfit. That must be new, because I have never seen it before."

"Whatever. Bye."

I attempted to close the door, but he blocked it with his foot and probed, "Who do you got up in there?" He paused, but I didn't reply. "We've been separated less than a month, and you're already sucking somebody's dick?"

"Get the hell off my property. Now!"

He shrugged and smiled smugly. "Soon as I get my stuff."

"Do you really want to do this?" I glared at him. "You really want me to call the police on you? You do know how well black men fair in these situations, right?"

The smug smile on his face evaporated. He stepped back, and I slammed the door in his face. I turned and saw Alonzo standing behind me, fists clenched, ready to go to war. My man was ready to fight for me. That was what a man was supposed to do, and I loved that about him

Chapter Thirty-two

Not Like This

JOYCE

I was on my way to meet a client who was interested in buying a home located on Paces Ferry Road. It was a twenty-five-thousand-square-foot, six-bedroom, nine-bathroom property that I had been trying to sell for seven months now. The asking price was just under three million. I arrived ready to sell the shit out of it. The best word to describe what my commission was going to be was *redonkulous*!

Shortly after I got to the property, my phone vibrated. It was a text from 'Shida.

Hey, Joyce. Can you come by tomorrow after work? 12:52 p.m.

I replied right away. Yeah. Is everything okay? 12:53 p.m.

Yeah. Just need to talk. 12:54 p.m.

Okay. 1:01 p.m.

I hoped whatever it was had nothing to do with Robert. That man had been the source of too much drama in her life. At any rate, we would deal with it together. I walked around the house, making sure everything was in order. It was impressive as ever. The doorbell rang, and I put a big smile on my face. I walked to the door, ran my hands down the curves of my hips, and quickly tugged at my little black "seal the deal" dress. When I opened the door, he was the last person I was expecting to see.

"Raheem, what are you doing here?"

This was the first time I'd seen him with this many clothes on. Dark blue jeans, a burgundy button-down, and Adidas in matching colors. He looked good.

"I'm here to see the house."

"What? No. I was on the phone with Mr. Peterson."

He smiled. "Mr. Peterson, as in Ron Peterson? He was just a middleman I had contact you to set this up." He stepped past me. "I'm very interested in seeing this." He looked around.

I wanted to be pissed, but looking at his sexy face, I wasn't able to maintain my annoyance. In all honesty, if he wanted to, he could afford the house. I closed the front door.

"All right, Mr. Haughton. Let's begin the tour."

As we walked around, I showed him the lavish open-floor kitchen, the master bedrooms, the lower-level game room, and the infinity pool in the backyard. Raheem followed behind me, and I caught him staring at my ass. Truth be told, I enjoyed the attention, but I remained professional.

We ended the tour in the living room. I smiled and faced him. "Mr. Haughton, that completes our tour, so when can we move you into your new home?"

"You're good, you know that?"

"Yes, I know."

"The house is nice." He nodded and glanced around again. "Definitely on my list of possibilities."

I folded my arms. "Possibilities?"

"Yeah. Of course, you know I can't buy the first house I see."

"Why do I have the feeling you aren't really interested in this house in the first place?"

A sly grin spread across his face. "I admit, I did have an ulterior motive in meeting you here today. I wanted to spend some time alone with you."

I smiled. "Look, Raheem, I'm flattered that you went through so much trouble to see me, but I don't think us being together like that would work."

He stepped closer to me. "So are you saying that you're not feeling me?"

I looked him up and down. He was so damn fine. It was impossible for me to deny that.

"I didn't say that." I exhaled. "Raheem, I've known you since you were a little boy. It just feels weird looking at you like you are . . ."

He finished my thought. "A grown man? Joyce, I'm not a kid anymore."

"Yes, I know that, but I'm five years older than you."

"That's okay. I like older women."

I shook my head. "That's not my point. Why do you want to be with me?"

He stared at me. "You're a very attractive woman, but I can't help but wonder why you're still single."

"I made some mistakes in my last relationship, so I've just been focused on my work." I shook my head. "Why am I telling you this?"

"Because you're trying to think of a reason why you shouldn't date me."

He touched my hand. First contact. His touch sent electricity through me, and I felt a sweet throbbing between my legs. No one had made me feel like this in a while. I should have moved my hand away, but I didn't. I was infatuated. Shit, I was turned on. I guessed Raheem decided while my defenses were down, he should shoot his shot. He leaned in and gently kissed me. He was good.

His kiss made me wet. Then he pulled away, and our eyes met. In that moment, I forgot that I had known him since childhood. I forgot that I was five years his senior, and it didn't matter that he was my best friend's little brother. All he was to me in that moment was a sexy man. I kissed him back.

We went back to my place to talk and drink. We sat on the sofa, talking about old times, and I was surprised by how funny and intelligent Raheem was as our conversation went from film to politics and then back to us. He maintained eye contact with me, gently touched my hand, and even touched my thigh. As our comfort level grew, more touching occurred. He aroused me; then he surprised me.

"You know, I've seen you naked before."

"What?" That confession disarmed me. "No you haven't. When?"

"Senior year. You were spending the night at our house. I got up and went to the bathroom. You remember the bathroom upstairs had two doors? I opened one of the doors, and you were getting out of the shower. You didn't see me. You had a towel wrapped around your head. I saw your reflection in the mirror and saw enough to give me wet dreams for a month!"

My mouth fell open. "You little perv!" I gently slapped his arm.

He chuckled. "Hey, I was thirteen. What was I supposed to do?"

I smiled. "So you liked what you saw?"

"That moment is still engrained in my brain." He looked down at my breasts and smiled. Raheem could see how hard my nipples had become as they poked through my dress. He was turning me on, and I felt flirtatious.

"Are they the same as you remember?"

Raheem gazed in my eyes, then took his hand and pulled the strap of my dress over my right shoulder. I wasn't wearing a bra. My breast was exposed; nipple was rock hard. He stared at it, licked his sexy lips, then looked at me. There was no protest from me to stop, so he took his hand and did the same to my left dress strap. My dress was down, and my breasts were exposed. He took my right breast in his mouth, made circles with his tongue, and pinched the left nipple with his fingers. It felt good, and I moaned. My hand touched his groin, and I felt his hardness. He moved to my left breast and gave it the same attention he had given the right.

I wanted to touch him. I unzipped his jeans, stuck my hand inside, and found his erection. Damn, he was certainly blessed. He kissed me, I fondled him, and his hand went under my dress. I parted my thighs and let him touch it. I moaned again. He unbuttoned his jeans, and I fished his penis out. He was only semi-hard, but he was long. It had been over two years since I had touched one of those. Two years since I had felt a man's girth in my hands. With both hands, I stroked him slowly and felt his erection grow while he groaned. He had a beautiful brown dick. We were on my sofa, making out like two horny teenagers after school. It felt so damn good, but I knew if I let this continue where it would go.

"Raheem, we . . . gotta stop. We can't have sex."

"That's too bad. So many things I was going to do." He gave me another kiss. "But if you want me to stop . . ." His voice trailed off, and he continued to kiss my neck, then went down and licked my left nipple. I didn't stop him. He touched my clit through my panties. Damn, it felt so good.

"Ah . . . shit . . . I mean it. We gotta stop."

I said the words but didn't stop playing with his erection. I couldn't stop rubbing my fingers over his rigidness.

I didn't want to stop feeling him. His breathing had become choppy, and his caress on my wetness became more intense.

"Take off your panties."

"Nooo . . . I can't do that," I sang.

"I want to eat your pussy."

"Why?" I whimpered. "Why would you say that to me? Oh gawd, why you gonna do this to me?"

"I wanna taste you. Would you like that, Joyce?"

I hummed, "Yes."

He slid down my panties and pulled them all the way off. I lay back on the sofa and felt his hands between my thighs as I stared at the ceiling. My opened legs gave him a clear path. Then I felt his tongue on my skin. I shivered. He licked. I moaned. He sucked my clit, and I sang an orgasmic tune. It felt like he was writing his name in cursive with his tongue on my walls. Then he just started scribbling everywhere, driving me crazy. I was squirming on the sofa, riding the waves of the orgasm that took over my body. Raheem stirred me like coffee, then drank my nectar like it was honey. I was on fire. An inferno that had been smoldering for two years was now out of control. My orgasm consumed me. At that moment I was like, *Fuck it*. Why was I pretending like I didn't want him? Why was I denying myself pleasure? I wanted penetration and needed to feel him inside me. I pushed up on my elbows and looked at him, my breathing ragged.

"Do you have a condom?"

He smiled. "Yeah."

I returned his smile. I got up off the sofa and let my dress fall. I was naked. Raheem stared at my body with amazement, like a man who had just seen his childhood fantasy come to life. He started unbuttoning his shirt, kicked off his shoes, and pulled down his jeans. Now he was naked, too, with a body that looked like he lived in the gym. His erection was at full sail, pointing right at me. He fished into the back pocket of his jeans and pulled out a condom. A part of me wanted to laugh because he had it so accessible, like he knew what was going to happen, and another part of me was glad he had come prepared. I glanced back at his erection, bit my bottom lip, then turned and walked to the stairs. Raheem followed me up to my bedroom. He ripped open the wrapper, then rolled the latex over his hard-on. I crawled over the top of my bed, put an arch in my back, and pushed my ass up in the air.

Raheem whispered, "Goddamn."

Then I felt him behind me, felt his erection pushing inside me. I was so wet. I felt him stretching my walls, filling me up with his stiffness. I gasped. He had so much, almost too much, for me to handle and was so damn hard. It had been so long since I had felt a man inside me. For a moment, I thought I had waited too long and my vagina had shrunken. I shifted and adjusted myself. Raheem eased back, then pushed forward. Each time a little deeper; and each time it felt better. We found a sensual tempo. His strokes were so fluid and deep, I was in heaven. I called God's name over and over again. He had me speaking in tongues.

Then he flipped me over and took me in the missionary position. I turned my head to the side. I felt self-conscious looking at his face while he fucked me. I didn't want to see him as the little boy I knew and ruin this moment. Raheem touched my face, turned my head, and our eyes locked. That little boy was nowhere to be found. All I saw was a man, a grown one at that, handling his business. I smiled, and we kissed. This was the beginning of something special.

We fell asleep after taking each other to the moon and back. Later I got up, went to the bathroom, peed, then walked back into the bedroom. Raheem was sound asleep. I usually didn't take men to my bed so quickly, but I guessed he was an exception to the rule, since I'd known him for over thirteen years. I heard my phone chiming from downstairs and went to get it. There was a text message from a number I didn't recognize.

Rashida is not your friend. 9:23 p.m.

I frowned at message. *Who the hell sent this to me?* I wondered.

Who are you? 9:24 p.m.

A moment later a new message appeared.

She has betrayed you. 9:25 p.m.

Who the fuck are you? 9:26 p.m.

Now I was pissed.

A picture text came through next. I opened it and saw Rashida and Alonzo. It seemed like the photo was taken from a distance, but I could tell who they were. They were face-to-face, talking in her driveway. Another picture text came in, and it was of them kissing. That made me pause. I stared at the image. His hands were on her ass, and her arms were around his neck. It was a passionate kiss. I felt like I had been shot in the chest. I didn't understand what was happening. I was naked in my living room, staring at an image I couldn't comprehend. My best friend and my ex-boyfriend were together. I felt hurt more than anger. There was another text message.

They are together right now. 9:27 p.m.

I glared at the message from my unknown informant and wanted to scream. I looked at the floor and saw my dress. I quickly put it on, slipped on my shoes, and grabbed my keys. I thought about waking Raheem up and asking him to leave but decided to just go. I jumped in my car and sped to 'Shida's house, which was ten minutes away, still trying to make sense of the two pictures I had seen. There had to be a logical explanation for this, but I couldn't think of any.

I pulled into her driveway, parked, got out, and used my key to open the front door. The house was bathed in darkness. My breathing was rapid. What was I doing? This was wrong. I was going to leave, but then I heard a sound that came from upstairs. It was more of a passionate whine. The same sound I had been singing a few hours ago. It was 'Shida. I went up the stairs, stopped at her bedroom door, and listened. I heard more passionate moans, and my heart began racing. The images from my phone flashed through my head, and I felt anger. I swung open the bedroom door and saw nothing. Then my eyes saw light glowing from the master bathroom, so I walked toward it. The door was ajar, so I pushed it open, and then I wished I didn't see what I saw.

My best friend was lying in the bathtub, in the arms of my ex-lover, with ecstasy written all over her face. Another gunshot to my chest as I watched Alonzo make her orgasm. Her eyes opened, out of focus, then focused on me. His eyes saw me too. Shock was on their faces. They weren't expecting company. 'Shida sat up and covered her breasts.

My voice cracked, "Oh my God . . . Rashida!"

"Joyce . . ."

"How could you do this to me? Why would you do this?"

She shook her head. "I can explain."

Alonzo spoke. "We both can."

I didn't want to hear it. My best friend had betrayed me. I turned and quickly left her house. What more could she say?

Chapter Thirty-three

No One to Blame but Myself

RASHIDA

This was probably one of the most horrible moments in my life. The absolute worst way for Joyce to find out. Why had she come here? How did she know? Those questions had racked my brain as I cried in Alonzo's arms last night. I had tried to call her to explain, but all my calls had been sent to voicemail and my text messages ignored. I had felt like I could've died when she saw me, and a part of me had wanted to. I was an emotional wreck. Later that morning, I had called Denise and told her what happened. She was mortified and said she would try to contact Joyce.

I was alone in my bed now, trying to figure out how to fix this, but I had no clue where to begin. Joyce had seen her ex-boyfriend giving me an orgasm. That was pretty high up on the list of unforgivable betrayals.

I could smell the breakfast that Alonzo was making in the kitchen, but I had no appetite. I didn't feel like getting dressed or putting on makeup. But I got dressed, anyway, put on all black, like I was mourning a death in the family, the death of a lifelong friendship. I saw my reflection in a mirror on the wall. My eyes were red and puffy from crying. I felt miserable and looked like a mess. A few minutes later I went downstairs. Alonzo stared at me, and I could see the regret in his face as well.

"How are you holding up?" he asked.

I shrugged my shoulders and sat down at the kitchen island.

"I made some eggs if you're hungry."

I shook my head. Alonzo had a seat at the island with me. I looked at him.

"Alonzo . . ." I searched his face for answers. "What are we going to do?"

"I don't know."

"Did you see the look on her face? The pain in her eyes? She was heartbroken. I did that to her. I hurt my best friend."

"You didn't do it on purpose."

"Doesn't matter. I did it." I sighed. "She's never going to forgive me."

"She's hurt. It's gonna take a while for her to deal with it, but you're her best friend, and eventually, she's going to come around."

"There are some things you can never forgive."

Alonzo exhaled. He knew that was the truth. As far as Joyce was concerned, I was probably sleeping with Alonzo the whole time they were together. The doorbell chimed just then, and I got up to answer it. I looked through the peephole and saw Denise, with Amir in her arms, and Taylor. I exhaled and opened the door and saw disappointment on their faces. They followed me into the living room; then Alonzo emerged from the kitchen and stood to the side. Both Denise and Taylor glared at him.

"So it's true?" Taylor asked.

I nodded. "Yes."

Taylor shook her head. "I thought Denise was lying. Why didn't you tell me?"

I stared at her. "I was going to when the time was right."

She sighed. "Well, how about now!"

Alonzo interjected, "Whoa, calm down. That's not helping."

Taylor shot daggers his way. "Don't you say anything! This is your fault! I was always cool with you, but this was some low-down shit."

"It's not his fault, Taylor," I interjected. "If you're going to blame anyone, blame me. I love him. We love each other. I've kept this from all of you. There was no way I could tell you and make you understand any of it. I'm sorry."

Taylor exhaled, shook her head, and sat down. Not too long ago she had revealed a secret crush on me that she had had for years. She understood how I felt. I looked at Denise, who gave me a reassuring nod. She was preparing for it all.

"Did you see Joyce?" I asked.

Denise shook her head. "No. She wouldn't even open up her door."

I sat down on the adjacent sofa. "This wasn't supposed to happen."

Alonzo sat down next to me. The front door opened, and in walked Raheem, with an agitated look on his face. He made a beeline to me and stopped in front of us.

"So you must be Alonzo, huh?" He glared at him.

I quickly rose and stood between the two most important men in my life.

Alonzo stood up. "I am. Who are you?"

"Alonzo, this is my brother, Raheem." I looked at my brother and saw anger in his eyes. He must have known what happened. "Raheem, why are you so upset?"

"Are you sleeping with Joyce's ex?" he asked, not mincing words.

I felt ashamed of myself. "Yes."

"What the hell, 'Shida! Why would you do this to her?"

"Wait a minute. How did you find out?" Taylor asked Raheem.

He looked at her. "Joyce told me while she was crying her eyes out. I could barely console her. I finally got her to come back to bed and sleep for a bit."

"*Bed*? What were you doing over at Joyce's house?" I asked.

There was a pregnant pause.

"I spent the night."

Taylor's eyes got wide like saucers. "You two are hooking up? Why am I just now hearing about this?" She looked at Denise.

"Don't look at me. This is new to me too. I'ma go lay Amir down."

She headed toward the guest room down the hallway. Raheem looked back at Alonzo.

"Bruh, I don't know you, but you're messing with two very important ladies to me. So if you're just running game here, then we gonna have a problem."

"I'm not," Alonzo assured him. "I'm in love with your sister and have been for a while now. What Joyce and I had ended a long time ago, for reasons that had nothing to do with 'Shida. We knew you all would have some issues with us being together, and our plan was to talk to each of you about it. Obviously, we didn't have a chance to do that." He kept his gaze on Raheem. "I understand you're upset, but I meant no disrespect to Joyce, and I damn sure mean none to 'Shida. We've waited a very long time to be together. That's the truth."

Denise returned to the living room and had a seat next to Taylor. Raheem glared at Alonzo, then looked at me.

"Everything he said is true," I declared. "You know I love Joyce like a sister. I never wanted to do this to her. I realized being with Alonzo could end our friendship, and

I don't want that. I would fight tooth and nail to avoid it, but I can't deny how I feel about him."

Raheem exhaled. "Damn, 'Shida. This is a mess."

"I know."

"What I wanna know is how Joyce found out, because I didn't tell her," Denise demanded.

"I know I didn't," Taylor added. "I didn't know shit until now."

Denise looked back at me. "So who else knew?"

I shook my head, and then it hit me. There was only person who had a reason to hurt me. Why hadn't I realized it from the start? "Robert."

Alonzo frowned. "What?"

"How did that asshole find out?" Taylor snapped.

"He came here the other night," I told them. "He got suspicious when I wouldn't let him in. That son of a bitch."

Taylor growled, "I never liked him. We need to go kick his ass!"

Alonzo glared. "Oh, he'll be dealt with. Believe that."

"None of that will fix this situation with Joyce," I told both of them.

It had been a week since Joyce had seen us together. A week since I had ruined our friendship. That night continued to play in my mind like it was on an endless loop. She had cut off all contact with us. The only person who had contact with her was Raheem, and he wasn't telling me much. I decided to give her space to deal with it, but what I really wanted to do was go to her and beg for her forgiveness. I wanted to explain that this wasn't a premeditated betrayal of her trust. I should have told her the truth from the start. That was my mistake. An error in judgment she may not forgive, but I still had to try.

I went to her house early that morning and parked across the street. I hoped to catch her as she was heading out to work and tried to prepare myself for whatever she might say. I saw her come outside, dressed business casual for work: black slacks, a black two-button blazer over a green blouse, a black bag over her shoulder. Her face was serious; she was focused.

I got out of my car and headed toward her. As she was about to open her car door, I called her name. "Joyce."

She saw me, froze, and glared at me. I knew that look. It was the look that she gave before she would cuss somebody out. A look that said she could kill me if she wanted and feel no type of way about it. Up until today I'd never been on the receiving end of that rage.

"Joyce, can I talk to you? I just wanna explain to you what happened. I know you must hate me right now, and I don't blame you, but we didn't do this to hurt you. We . . . love each other. I know it's crazy, but it's the truth. I was never with him when you two were together." I paused and looked at her. "Robert is the one who sent you over to my house that night. He set this up to get back at me. We were going to tell you. That's why I wanted to talk to you. And you gotta believe me when I say we didn't plan on this happening. It just did. I'm so sorry."

She didn't say anything to me, just stared at me like I was an idiot.

"Joyce?"

"Alonzo told me he was in love with another woman. I just didn't know *you* were that woman. You could have told me then, but instead, you kept it from me. You were my best friend, 'Shida. I loved you. I never thought you would be that self-serving bitch, but it's cool. You want him, he's yours. Hope you both have a great fucking life together. Just do me a favor and stay the hell away from me. Excuse me, but I have more important things to do than listen to you."

Angrily, she got into her car, started it, and peeled off. Her words had cut like a knife, and tears rolled down my face. I would have rather she run up on me and whup my ass than hear those words from her. I hadn't felt pain like this since my parents died, and I deserved every bit of it.

Chapter Thirty-four

Can't Stay Like This Forever

DENISE

Dear Denise Varner,

The editorial team at Dolphin Books is pleased to inform you that your manuscript *Pure Jane* has been accepted for publication! An email will follow this one with a contract attached for your review.

Welcome to Dolphin Books, and congratulations on what promises to be an exciting time ahead!

Sincerely,
Chelsea Phillips
Acquisitions Editor

I read the email on my phone again and couldn't believe my eyes. I screamed and startled Taylor, who was playing with Amir.

"What the hell!" She looked at me like I was crazy. "What happened?"

"They accepted my manuscript!"

Taylor smiled. "They're going to publish your book?"

I rocked from side to side. "Yes!"

"You're going to be a published author!"

I beamed with joy. "Yes!"

Taylor squealed, got up from the floor, and hugged me. This was incredible. I was expecting a rejection letter when I saw the envelope, considering it had been only two months since I had submitted *Pure Jane* to Dolphin Books. I thought getting a response this soon was a sure sign of a rejection. Only in my wildest dreams did I think a major publisher would accept my work.

"I'm so happy for you, Denise!"

"Thank you. This so unbelievable . . . My book is going to be read across the country."

"We need to celebrate! We need to call 'Shida, Joyce, and . . ." She paused. "Never mind. I forgot."

It had been two weeks since we'd heard from Joyce. Ever since she'd found out about 'Shida and Alonzo, she had been incognito and hadn't accepted any of our calls. Frankly, I was tired of it.

"You know what? You're right, Taylor. We should all celebrate."

"Oh really?" Taylor grinned.

"Yeah, this bullshit between Joyce and 'Shida has gone on long enough. Grab Amir, and come on."

A few minutes later we were at Joyce's. Taylor knocked on the door as I rang her bell. We weren't going to leave until we spoke to her. Finally, we heard the lock click. The door swung open, and there stood Joyce, annoyed as hell.

"About damn time you opened up," Taylor barked.

"You thought you were going to get rid of us that easy?" I added and shifted Amir in my arms as he waved innocently.

Joyce shook her head and gave a slight smile. "Hi."

We joined for a group hug and went inside. Once we were in the living room, Amir took off running, and Joyce turned and looked at us.

"Are you okay?" I quizzed.

"Yeah, I'm fine. I'm sorry I've been so antisocial lately, but I shouldn't have taken it out on you guys."

Amir came back, and Joyce bent down to give him a hug and a kiss. "Hey, little man! I missed you."

He took off running again.

"You damn right," Taylor snapped with an attitude, "you shouldn't have. We're your girls, and we're here for you."

Joyce folded her arms and glared at Taylor when she flopped down on the sofa. I could tell this was going to be an epic showdown. The aggravation on Joyce's face was visible, and Taylor was never known for being the voice of reason.

"And for 'Shida, right?" Joyce said sarcastically.

"Yep, we're not taking sides," Taylor replied with equal sarcasm in her tone.

Joyce glared at her. "You know what she did to me, and you're cool with that?"

"No, but there are reasons behind it," Taylor insisted. "If you would just—"

"I don't give a damn about the reasons!" Joyce snapped. "Listen, I really don't wanna talk about it, so if that's why you're here, then it was a waste of a trip."

I decided to intervene. "No, that's not the only reason we stopped by." I showed her the email I had received from Dolphin Books. "Guess who's gonna be a published author!"

Joyce grinned. "Oh my God! Congratulations!" She hugged me.

"Thank you! If you hadn't hooked me up with Chelsea, this never would have happened."

"Your talent made it happen. I just made a connection! I'm so happy for you! We need to celebrate!"

"Just us, huh?" Taylor asked.

Joyce twisted her lips. "Yep, just us."

"Taylor!" I called out in an attempt to stop what she was going to say next.

She sighed and dropped the matter.

The pain Joyce felt was still very fresh, and it was going to be a while before she was ready to talk about it. I hated that two of my best friends were at odds now and there was no way I could fix it. I guessed we just had to give it time. We went out to TGIF for drinks, and afterward Amir and I went home. As I was putting him down for the night, I heard the front door open. A few seconds later Sean was standing behind me.

"How's my little man?"

I turned and smiled at him. "Wide awake and waiting for you."

Sean went over and kissed his son. I watched as he played with him. Sean had just come from the studio. As usual, he looked fine as hell, and given the good news I had got today, I was more than ready to have some celebratory sex with him. I stepped out into the hallway to give him some alone time with his son. After he put Amir down, he went out into the hallway and found me waiting for him there.

"Why are you smiling like that?" he asked.

"Because I heard from Dolphin Books today, and guess who's going to be their new author?"

He smiled. "Congrats! That's awesome!"

I wrapped my arms around his neck, and we hugged.

"I knew you could do it!"

I smiled. "You did?"

"Yeah, you're a dope writer."

"Thanks. I have plenty of inspiration to draw from."

I kissed him. Feeling his body next to mine aroused me. His hands caressed my ass, and I sucked his bottom lip. Touching him like this made me moist. Freak mode was on. I was going to do so many nasty things to him tonight.

"C'mon. Let's go to my room."

I stepped away and headed toward my bedroom, but Sean didn't move. I turned and looked at him. He exhaled and shook his head.

"Aren't you coming?"

He scratched the back of his head. "I told you things can't stay like this forever, Denise."

"What are you talking about?"

"I'm talking about this. Us. I don't wanna keep doing this with you."

I chuckled. "You're saying you don't wanna have sex with me?"

He made an exasperated expression. "Of course I wanna have sex with you! I wanna have sex with you all over this house every day of the week, but I wanna be more than your gigolo. I wanna be your man. I love you."

His words stalled me. I wasn't expecting him to say that. I'd never heard him be so direct and passionate toward me. I could see how much he meant what he said. A part of me had been longing for him to say these words, but another part still remembered the past. I still remembered his lies, and I still had my doubts.

"You say that, but how can I be sure you won't lie to me again?"

He shook his head. "Denise, I've learned my lesson, okay? You wanted to punish me, make me see the errors of my ways. Well, you have. Trust me, you have, and if I could take it all back, I would, but I can't. I've tried so hard to prove to you that I've changed. I want you and only you. I love you. I love my son, but if you can't trust me now, after all this time, then maybe you never will."

He turned and went down the stairs, then looked back at me one last time and left. For the first time, I felt like he meant it. I didn't want him to leave. Was he right? Was I just being stubborn? What he did to me was wrong, but did I take pushing him away too far? He had tried his best to make it up to me, and I'd been using him. Maybe I needed to get over my insecurities.

A few days later I decided to swallow my pride and go see him. I asked Taylor to babysit Amir, and she was thrilled to. I drove over to Sean's studio in College Park. It was in an office space over on Old National Highway. I went inside and saw him behind the control board, working on some music with his engineer. Making the transition from artist to producer was the best career move he'd ever made. His engineer saw me standing outside the door, looking in through the glass panel, and tapped Sean's shoulder. He got up and opened the door for me.

"Is everything okay? Is something wrong with Amir?"

"No. Everything is fine. I just wanted to talk to you."

"Oh, okay." He looked back at his engineer. "Hey, Jamal, can you give us a minute?"

He nodded and got up and left the room.

"I hope I didn't catch you at a bad time," I said.

He shook his head. "Nah, you good. We just mixing this record."

We had a seat on the green sofa in the back.

"What's going on?" he asked.

"I wanted to talk to you about what you said to me the other night."

"Okay."

I took a deep breath. "Sean, when I first met you, I was completely shocked that a guy like you would want to be with me. I wasn't exactly the most outgoing type of girl, but being with you changed me. I fell so hard for you, so fast. I did things with you I've never done with anybody before." I smiled and shook my head. "I don't regret any of it. I knew my friends doubted you, but here I was, defending you like you were the Prince of Zumunda and you could do no wrong. So when I found out you lied to me, I was humiliated."

He lowered his head. "I'm so sorry, Denise. I was an idiot. I should've told you the truth from the beginning."

I touched his hand. "You've already apologized. I just never truly forgave you. You've been an incredible father to Amir, and despite my bitterness and me using you as a gigolo, as you say, I just became so guarded and jaded that I couldn't truly forgive you. But, Sean . . ." I paused. "I do love you."

He smiled. "I love you too, Denise."

"So, if you're still willing to be my gigolo, I would love to be your girlfriend again."

He caressed my face. "I'm not your gigolo. I'm your man, although gigolo services are included in the package."

"That's good to hear." I paused for a moment. "There's one more thing we need to discuss."

"What is it?"

"You should bring Draya to the house. She's your daughter and Amir's big sister. She should be around him and me more often. My differences with her mother shouldn't be taken out on her. She's a part of this family."

"I'm glad you said that." He smiled. "And don't worry. I will make Christy understand that too."

He kissed me with so much passion, so much commitment, that I let go of my doubts. I was his, and he was mine. I could tell. With a love like this in my life, my next *Pure Jane* book was going to be a national bestseller.

Three Months Later

Chapter Thirty-five

Gorilla in the Room

JOYCE

He looked bigger than life on the theater screen, and the high-definition resolution made his face crystal clear. I sat next to Raheem in the Landmark Theatre's Midtown Art Cinema, watching him in an independent film called *The Refill*. Raheem played the part of a cop who had become addicted to prescription drugs. He was good, damn good. His character was charming and, at the drop of a hat, a menacing killer. Watching him play this part made me almost forget that I had been dating him for the past few months. We'd taken our time to get to know each other, and any thoughts I had about him being too young for me had long been put to bed.

After the movie was over, there was a red-carpet event in the lobby, and Raheem had his picture taken with the cast. There was a line of people taking pictures with professional cameras, cell phones, and tablets. Even Taylor was in the front, videotaping it all for her daily vlog. Raheem looked like a Hollywood A-lister as he posed for the pics. I was so proud of him. He even walked into the crowd, grabbed my hand, and had me pose with him on the red carpet. Good thing I had decided to wear this black Prada dress and matching high-heeled shoes. I felt like a celebrity for a while.

As we were posing for pictures, I saw her in the crowd, taking our picture. We made eye contact. 'Shida was dressed in a short off-white dress. It was the first time in a few months that we'd seen each other. I could see a remorseful expression on her face, and then she turned and went to the back of the lobby. Honestly, a part of me missed her. My anger over the situation had faded somewhat. What she did hurt me, and I hadn't wanted to talk to her at the time, but now that some time had passed, I wanted to understand why she would do this to me. How did things between her and Alonzo start? I knew she had tried to explain it to me, but I hadn't been in the mood to listen to her. I had just wanted to hurt her as bad as she had hurt me. But I needed to get past my anger; I was at a point now where I wanted to hear her side. It was just awkward talking to her.

I walked off the red carpet and saw Taylor and Denise. They must have come with 'Shida. When everything went down, I had kept my distance from them for a while, but we had started talking again. At the end of the day, they were my friends and had nothing to do with what was going on. I'd just told them I didn't want to discuss the situation. They both had reluctantly agreed to my conditions, although I could tell it was a struggle for Taylor to hold her tongue.

They trotted toward me as I lingered by the concession stand, and we greeted each other with hugs.

"Oh my God, Raheem was incredible! He's gonna win a freaking Academy Award. I know it!" Taylor exclaimed.

I smiled. "I don't think they give Oscars for independent films, Taylor."

"Well, they should, because he was fabulous!"

"I couldn't believe that was Raheem on the screen," Denise chimed in. "You must be proud of him."

"I am. He's an incredible man. Are you all coming out with us for drinks?"

Taylor replied, "I'm going."

"Uh, I came with 'Shida," Denise reminded us, "so . . . I'm not sure if she's going."

"Oh, okay. Well, she should go. He's her brother," I stated matter-of-factly.

A stunned expression shadowed their faces. It was the first time I had agreed to be in the same place she was going to be.

"Really?" Denise was shocked. "Okay, we'll just go ask her real quick."

Both Denise and Taylor turned and went to find 'Shida. I watched as they went over to her and told her the news. I could tell by the look on her face that she was just as surprised as they were. I guessed this was my way of extending the olive branch.

After the red carpet we drove over to Local Three Kitchen and Bar on Northside Parkway. Raheem and I arrived first. We had reserved a dinner table, a round table that could seat eight. Soon after Taylor, Denise, and 'Shida arrived. 'Shida had a seat directly across from me. We made eye contact and exchanged a friendly head nod, but we didn't speak. My heart was racing. It was the first time in my life it felt awkward being in the same room with her, and I imagined she felt the same way.

I held up my champagne flute. "I would like to say a word or two about the man of the hour. Raheem, I never thought I would be with you like this. You used to get on my nerves so much, but I guess things have changed a little since then."

Everybody laughed.

I went on. "I am so proud of you. You're so talented, and I know this is just the beginning for you." He smiled. "And on a personal note, I just wanna thank you for being by my side and keeping me sane these past few months. You're very special to me. Thank you."

Raheem leaned over and gave me a passionate kiss. It was the first time we'd kissed in front of the girls.

"You go, boy! Get it, get it!" Taylor urged.

Denise surprisingly chimed in and clapped her hands. "Raheem, you the real MVP."

I looked at them clowns and said, "Shut it!"

Raheem laughed. "Y'all stupid."

"Do you mind if I say something?" 'Shida asked me.

I shook my head. "No, not at all."

'Shida held up her glass of champagne. "I just wanna say how proud I am of you, Raheem. Not only of the incredible performance you gave tonight, and not just because you're my brother. I'm proud of the man you have become. We lost so much at such a young age. It wasn't fair." She paused. "But we made it. And I'm sure Mom and Dad would be so proud of you right now. I love you."

Raheem replied, "I love you too, sis."

I looked at 'Shida and could see tears in her eyes. I knew the emotional connection they shared was a little bit deeper than that of brother and sister. She was like a second mother to him. I held up my glass once again and said, "Cheers."

Everybody at the table did the same. The rest of the night was filled with small talk about Raheem's performance and his future projects. It felt like everybody was tiptoeing around the awkwardness between 'Shida and me. She wasn't very talkative and barely looked at me. Taylor and Denise were doing their best to talk about anything other but the eight-hundred-pound gorilla that was sitting at our table with us. Ignoring the situation became unbearable, so I decide to break the ice. I looked across the table at 'Shida.

"So how have you been, 'Shida?"

It was like everybody froze and you could hear a pin drop. She had a shocked expression on her face.

"I've been okay. Everything at the shop is going fine."

I nodded. "That's good. Are you trying to grow your dreads longer?"

She smiled. "Yeah, I wanna try some new things."

"I like it. You said you wanted to do that a while ago."

She nodded. "Yeah, Robert was the only thing stopping me from doing it. He didn't want me to look too Afrocentric. It might have scared his colleagues on the board."

We shared a knowing chuckle.

"So, Alonzo couldn't make it tonight?"

Dead silence enveloped the table. That gorilla was now dancing on the tabletop. 'Shida stared at me for a few seconds, and Raheem took my hand underneath the table. The looks on Taylor's and Denise's faces ran from panic to dread.

"He decided he didn't want to make the night awkward, so he didn't come."

I respected the honest answer. "I understand. Guess this is awkward enough, right?"

She nodded "Yeah."

"I know it's been difficult between us lately, but I would like to talk about it later." I gave her a slight smile, and she returned the gesture.

'Shida replied, "That would be good."

An expression of relief appeared on everybody's faces. I hadn't planned on doing this tonight, but it had needed to be done, and I needed to understand what had happened. No matter how mad I was at 'Shida, I couldn't deny that I still loved her, and if there was chance to fix what went wrong, I was willing to try.

Chapter Thirty-six

Sorry, Not Sorry

RASHIDA

I was completely taken off guard by Joyce. I knew we would see each other at Raheem's movie premiere, but I had no idea she was going to invite me for drinks afterward, much less make conversation. It felt so weird being around her after three months with no communication at all. At the end of the night, we all stood in the parking lot, and Joyce headed toward me.

"'Shida, I would like for all of us to get together and talk if you still want to," she announced.

"Yes, I do." Then I asked, "All of us?"

"Yeah, you, me, and Alonzo. I would really like to get everything out in the open."

Her tone was even and controlled. I couldn't see any emotions on her face. I didn't know if she wanted to have this meeting to cuss us out or to work things out. Maybe our conversation at the dinner table had just been a front for everybody else and she wanted to really go in on me in private. Either way, I had to accept it.

"Okay. Your place or mine?"

"Your house."

I nodded. "Is tomorrow evening, about five, okay?"

"That'll be fine."

We stared at each other for a moment, and then she turned and walked back to Raheem's car and got in. I hated that things had become so awkward between us, but then, what else did I expect? I got in my car, and Denise was already on the passenger's side.

"What did she say?"

"She wants to talk to me and Alonzo," I answered.

An uneasy expression was on Denise's face. "Both of you? Wow. What do you think she's going to say?"

"I don't know, but I just hope we can work things out."

Denise took my hand. "I think she's ready. She still loves you. Just let her get her feelings out."

I forced a smile. "I hope so."

I was anxious all day. I left work early and got home about 2:15 p.m. Alonzo followed me home in the new truck he'd purchased to replace the one that was side-swiped a few months ago. Before we met up, he bought some Jamaican food from Jamaica Mi Krazy on Spring Road. He got me a plate of curry goat, rice and peas, and fried plantains. As soon as we got home, we sat down at the kitchen table and enjoyed the food. Dishes like these reminded me of my mother's cooking. This was comfort food for me. Alonzo knew exactly how to settle my nerves.

The past few months with him had been wonderful. I'd never been happier in a relationship in my life. But this happiness had come at the expense of my friendship with Joyce. It was a bitter transaction. After I ate, I curled up on the sofa and watched Taylor's latest YouTube vlog on TV through Chromecast. It featured Raheem's movie premiere last night. Taylor's editing skills were fantastic, and her vlogs looked so professional. It almost felt like I was watching *Entertainment Tonight*. I saw Joyce and

Raheem together on the red carpet, and they looked so happy together. I was glad that at least she had him to lean on during this time.

Alonzo joined me on the sofa and put his arm around me. I leaned back on him, glanced at my cell, and saw that it was nearly five o'clock.

"Are you okay?" he quizzed.

I shook my head. "Not really. I have no idea what she's going to say."

"You said that things went good with her last night, right?"

"Yeah, but we were in public. I've really missed her."

He kissed my forehead. "I know."

The doorbell rang, and I exhaled. She was here. I was anxious. I rubbed my hands together, took another deep breath, stood up, and went to the front door. I opened it and saw her. Joyce looked casual in black jeans, a plain gray tee, and Converse. Her hair was pulled back in a ponytail.

"Hey," I said.

"Hey."

I stepped aside, invited her in, and followed behind her. She stopped in her tracks when she saw Alonzo seated on the sofa. He stood up.

"Hello, Joyce."

"Hello," she replied.

Alonzo and I sat on the sofa, and Joyce sat on the adjacent love seat. There was an uncomfortable silence.

"Do you want some water or anything?" I asked.

"No, I'm fine." She exhaled. "Listen, I know this is awkward, so let me just ask you both, how did this happen? When did you two fall in love?"

I looked at Alonzo, and he nodded.

I stared at Joyce. "I think we should start at the beginning. I met Alonzo a few months before you started dating at the Gold Room. We just connected . . . in a way that I never have with any man before. It was only one night."

Joyce nodded. "So that first night Alonzo and I came over for dinner, you already knew each other."

I nodded. "Yes. I . . . didn't know what to do." I exhaled. "Looking back on it now, I should have told you, but I didn't. It's my fault."

Alonzo spoke up. "No, it's not just on you. I could've said something, too, but it was just easier for us to pretend like it didn't happen. That was a mistake."

Joyce stared at us. "So knowing how you felt about 'Shida, why did you stay with me?"

"I never thought I'd see her again after that night. I was attracted to you, and when I saw her again, I figured there was no chance of things working out with her, so I tried to work things out with you," Alonzo explained.

Joyce frowned. "So, I was the second option?"

"No. I cared about you. You know that."

"But you were still in love with 'Shida, right?" Joyce asked, pressing.

He exhaled and nodded. "Yeah."

Joyce looked at me. "And you were in love with him?"

"I was attracted to him, but I was with Robert, and he was with you. We agreed to just be friends, but the more we were around each other, the more our feelings grew. We made the decision not to be together no matter how much we wanted to be."

Alonzo added, "We both know why things ended with us. It had nothing to do with 'Shida."

Joyce sat there for a moment like she was reliving the events of the past. We weren't making excuses for our actions, just telling the bitter truth.

"So, when you came back to Atlanta, you came back with the intent to be with 'Shida?" she asked.

He stared at her. "Yes. I knew that she was still with Robert, but I was tired of denying how I felt."

"Joyce, you knew how bad things were with me and Robert, and even you were telling me to leave him," I said. "I knew I wanted to be with Alonzo. I know that probably makes me the worst type of friend, but I couldn't deny it anymore. I'm sorry . . . If you hate me, I . . . understand, but I love you, Joyce. Our mistake was not telling you the truth from the beginning, and I regret that every day."

Joyce opened and closed her hands, then took a deep breath, like she was processing the logic or irrationality of our words. I sat awaiting her judgment like a hooker in court.

"I should hate you both," she said at last. "But I don't. Not anymore at least. And believe me, I tried really hard, but the truth is I'm not in love with you anymore, Alonzo. Being with Raheem has made me see how it feels to have someone one hundred percent invested in a relationship. I was just hurt that my best friend would sleep with you behind my back. You're like my sister, 'Shida, I just never saw that coming, but now I understand the reasons."

Tears poured from my eyes. "I know no matter what I say or how unintentional my actions were, at the end of the day, I hurt you."

Alonzo said, "We both did."

"I guess the question is, can you forgive me?" I said.

Joyce smiled. "I already did."

Tears fell from my eyes like a waterfall. We both stood up and hugged each other. I cried tears of joy as she embraced me. It was an ugly cry, but I didn't care. I had my friend back. I had my sister again. I looked at her face, and she was crying too. She wiped my tears away.

She said, "I missed you."

"I've missed you too."

We hugged again.

"Joyce, I'm not expecting everything to go back to the way things were, but I promise to be a better friend to you."

"'Shida, we all make mistakes. We just have to learn to communicate with each other no matter what. We've known each other since we were little girls. I know you didn't have malice in your heart. We can't help who we fall in love with." She looked at Alonzo. "As for you . . . you're a very lucky man. Whatever hang-ups you have you better get over them. She deserves the best."

He smiled. "Yes, ma'am."

She gave him a hug.

"Not to dredge up the past, but why did you come over here that night?" I asked.

Joyce pulled her cell out of her bag, went into her messages, and showed them to me. Alonzo looked at them as well. I read them, and it confirmed what I had suspected. "I received these from an unknown number. I tried calling it back, but it says the number is no longer in service."

"Doesn't matter. We all know who sent them," Alonzo said.

Joyce frowned. "So what are we going to do?"

"Fuck him," I said. "He doesn't matter. All that matters is that we're good. Just let him be miserable."

That was exactly what we did. I didn't feel the need to have some juvenile revenge on Robert. Well, he might have woken up one morning and found that the BMW I had bought him was missing. And in his parking space, he might have found a box of the stuff he had left behind at my house, with a note attached to it that read:

Here's your stuff back..
P.S. I decided to take back my stuff too. Sorry . . . not sorry.

That BMW was, after all, still in my name, and I had a set of keys. I wasn't a spiteful person, but don't mess with me.

That evening I invited Joyce, Denise, and Taylor over to my house, and Denise and Taylor were happy to see Joyce and me together again. It was nice to have my girls back. Joyce showed up first, and Taylor and Denise arrived together a little later.

"So, we're all good now?" Taylor asked, looking at Joyce and me sitting on the sofa together.

Joyce chuckled. "Yes, Taylor, we're good."

"Great, because I was so tired of you two bitches acting up."

"Oh, shut up." I rolled my eyes. "If anything is a miracle, it's you two being best buddies now. Your spirit animals are probably Tom and Jerry. "

Denise looked at Taylor. "Us not getting along? Do you have any idea what she's talking about?"

Taylor shrugged. "No, not at all."

Joyce waved them off. "Yeah, right."

They both joined us on the sofa.

"So what are we watching tonight?" Taylor asked. "And I don't wanna watch *The Color Purple* again."

"It's my favorite movie," I retorted.

"We know," they all replied in unison.

"Whatever. It doesn't matter what we watch," I told them. "What's important is we're here together again. I know that a lot of the turmoil has been my fault, and I wanna apologize to all of you."

"You don't have to apologize. We all have, at one point or another, messed up. What's important is that we don't let anything come between us," Denise declared.

Joyce took my hand. "She's right. We have to communicate with each other no matter how painful it might be. We're not just friends. We're sisters."

"Yeah, so let's make a vow that no penis will ever come between us." Taylor paused. "Unless it's a really big penis. Then you just gotta take one for the team. Anyway, you all know what I mean."

We all broke into laughter.

I looked at my sisters. "I love you all."